Sargeant Nadine Shell stunned him.

Her golden, luxuriously thick ponytail and careless bangs covering her forehead gave her appearance a certain girlishness. But there was nothing girlish about the command in her voice or about the large, dark eyes now staring into his. She reminded him of a cat perched on a windowsill, assured that the birds would come. Infinite patience, ultimate cool, as compelling as she was unnerving.

Ever since the first official had arrived, cops had been jumping down Ben's throat questioning him about the murder. He'd been frisked, questioned and had his hands sprayed with stinking icy-cold liquid to check prints. He'd kept his head. Better, he'd kept his mouth shut.

So far.

As guilty as he felt, as off kilter as she'd thrown him, he wondered how long he could keep his head around Nadine Shell.

ABOUT THE AUTHOR

Sheryl Lynn says, "If you ever get a chance to go on the radio, do it. Airwaves carry their own brand of magic. Besides, all the deejays I've met are just as funny and charming in person as they are on the air." Along with writing Intrigue novels and enjoying her family, Sheryl prepares for her future career as a radio entertainer. She plays the radio real loud, and in between songs, she dazzles the cat and dog with her repertoire of animal jokes and political commentary.

Books by Sheryl Lynn

HARLEQUIN INTRIGUE
190—DOUBLE VISION
223—DEADLY DEVOTION
258—SIMON SAYS

Ladykiller
Sheryl Lynn

Harlequin Books

TORONTO • NEW YORK • LONDON
AMSTERDAM • PARIS • SYDNEY • HAMBURG
STOCKHOLM • ATHENS • TOKYO • MILAN
MADRID • WARSAW • BUDAPEST • AUCKLAND

To Mickee Campbell, Roberta Smith and
Abby Manus—three ladies well worth writing for.
And to Tom, my hero, for saving me, again. And with
special thanks to my favorite deejays, Mark Goldberg
and Mark Stevens.

ISBN 0-373-22306-4

LADYKILLER

Copyright © 1995 by Jaye W. Manus

This edition published by arrangement with Harlequin Enterprises B.V.

Printed in U.S.A.

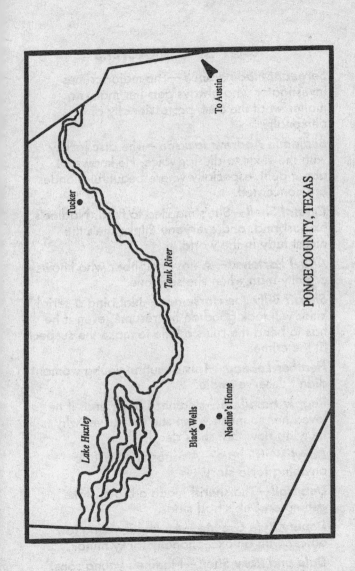

PONCE COUNTY, TEXAS

To Austin

Tucker

Tank River

Lake Huxley

Black Wells

Nadine's Home

CAST OF CHARACTERS

Sergeant Nadine Shell—The major crimes investigator who always gets her man, no matter what the cost, professionally or personally.

Benjamin Andrew Jackson—The disc jockey with the sexy, to-die-for voice. He knows all about guilt, especially where beautiful blondes are concerned.

Crystal Shell—She's married to Fred, Nadine's ex-husband, and everyone thinks she's the nicest lady in the world.

Angel Parteneu—A nosy neighbor who knows a guilty man when she sees one.

Sheriff Billy Joe Horseman—Nabbing a serial killer will look good on his résumé, even if he has to bend the rules a little to make the suspect fit the crime.

Heather Labeau—This beautiful young woman didn't deserve to die.

Reggie Hamilton—Heather's boyfriend. If he loved her so much when she was alive, why is he lying now that she's dead?

Daryl Wafflegate—A reporter who'll do anything for a story.

Deb Hall—The sheriff made a big mistake getting on Deb's bad side.

Deputy Kyle Greene—An eager young law officer with an exceptionally tricky mind.

Dale and Rory Shell—Nadine's young sons.

Chapter One

Not again. No, this can't be happening.

Denials skittered like billiard balls in Ben's brain. He backed one step, then another, his gaze fixated by the small, still woman on the ground. The pink-yellow glow from the streetlamp carved her into a still life— no, a still death. His bones ached, every muscle quivered, and his eyes grew scratchy and strained. Screams welled in his throat, catching under his tongue until he felt certain he'd choke. Get up, stand up, move... *breathe!*

Not again. Let me wake up, let this be a dream...not again...

NADINE SHELL considered insomnia's good points. She finally had the time to give her father's house a decent cleaning. Funny how grimy old men living alone could be, no matter how neat and organized they seemed on the surface. Her mother had been the clean freak, sticking to rigorous schedules as naturally as a bird answers the urge to migrate: wash the windows on the first Monday of the month, turn the mattresses every fourth Saturday, laundry on Saturday, vacuum Monday, Wednesday and Friday, the day's dishes washed, dried and put away no later than seven o'clock. Despair loudly on a daily basis over a husband and daughter who failed to acquire her habits.

Her father hadn't been a slob, exactly, but as Nadine studied the linoleum on the kitchen floor, now stripped of wax buildup and polished, the smells of cleanser and wax seemed rather alien. Even the color seemed strange. She'd forgotten the linoleum had that blue speckling.

The telephone rang. She hurried to answer before the noise awakened her sons.

Sheriff Billy Joe Horseman boomed, "We got a murder in Black Wells!"

Nadine winced away from the earpiece. "What did you say?"

"Hate to roust you at this hour, but it's murder. We got a murder!"

She let the word *murder* sink in. Not we have a body or an accident or even a homicide. He'd said *murder*, flat out.

As the major crimes investigator for the Ponce County Sheriff's Department, Nadine had handled plenty of deaths: automobile accidents, hunting accidents, drownings, suicides, Saturday night fights gotten out of hand, and a few drug overdoses. Outright murder was rare, especially in Black Wells, Texas. In eight years, she had investigated only seventeen murders. Only one had occurred in Black Wells.

"Are you sure?" she asked the sheriff.

"Got a dead girl with a bullet hole," he said crudely. "Sure I'm sure. I'm headed to the Algernon Hotel right now. How soon can you get there?"

"The Algernon? Doesn't your daughter work there?"

"Yeah, and I about died where I stood when I got the call. First thing I thought was, it's my Meggie, but it's another girl."

"I have the boys, so I'll have to take them home. Be there quick as I can. But, Billy Joe, don't touch anything on the scene. Understand? *Nothing.* Cordon off the area, get hold of the coroner and Bob Underhill, but do not touch anything."

"Okay, okay," he said, sounding distracted and in a hurry to end the conversation. His car phone crackled, fading. "I know the procedure."

Sure he did—whatever he might have read in a manual. Sheriff Billy Joe Horseman was a politician, not a cop. Running unopposed in the last election, he'd made a lot of noise about the county needing a civilian's perspective to keep a firm hand on law enforcement. Trouble was, his civilian's perspective meant a television-cop-show view of police procedure.

She said, "I'm counting on you not to let anyone contaminate the scene." Unsure whether he'd heard or paid attention before he hung up, she lowered the handset onto the cradle. Murder. What a lousy way to start a Sunday.

She went to the boys' bedroom and tapped on the door. Dale and Rory awakened instantly. Like puppies, they were either fast asleep or wide-awake, with no in-between grogginess.

Unlike their father, she thought with an inner grimace. It took a stick of dynamite to get Fred out of bed, and a pot of coffee to make him human. She tapped the door again and said, "Mama's got to go to work, fellas. Up and at 'em."

Dale groaned. "Aw, Mama... You said we could clean out the barn today. You said—"

"It's work, bud. Sorry. We'll have to do it next weekend. Let's go." She clapped her hands. "Get a move on."

She exchanged her grubby sweats for a pair of jeans and a flannel shirt topped by a sweater. By the time she'd dragged her long blond hair into a ponytail, the boys were dressed and waiting for her.

Dale shot his younger brother a glare. "Rory snores. *Loud.* Next weekend can we clean out Granddaddy's bedroom? I want my own room. I don't wanna sleep with a baby. A *snoring* baby."

A finger of pure sorrow tightened against Nadine's voice box. She hadn't entered her father's bedroom since the day he died. Behind that closed door lay too many reminders of her failure to save his life.

"I don't snore," Rory said, standing on tiptoe to bring himself closer to his brother's height. "Take it back."

The thrust of his jaw and the twist of his mouth reminded her so much of her father, she had to turn away. She called her ex-husband's home.

When his wife answered, Nadine said, "Sorry to wake you, Crystal, but I have a call. I need to drop the boys off."

"No problem. I'll unlock the door," Crystal said. Nadine heard Fred grumbling in the background. "Stop being a booger, honey. Go back to sleep."

Booger? Nadine grinned. She had a lot of names for her ex; none of them were as cute as *booger.*

She hustled the boys to the car and put a quick stop to the automatic squabble over who got to sit in front.

As soon as she shut the driver's door she looked in the rearview mirror. "Dale, fasten your seat belt."

"Aw, Mama—"

"Don't 'Aw, Mama' me, young man. I shouldn't have to tell you every time." She eyed the ten-year-old sternly until he complied.

Rory touched her side with a finger. "You forgot your gun again, Mama."

She patted her ribs, then shrugged as she started the engine. "Guess so."

Rory protested. "But what if the bad guys shoot at you?"

"Honey, I'm an investigator, not a street cop. By the time I get where I'm going, the bad guys are usually long gone."

"But what if they're not?"

Dale piped up. "Daddy says guns don't kill people. People kill people. The bad guys will just conk her on the head with a bat or something."

"Oh, thank you very much, Mr. Morbid," she said.

Both boys had powerful personalities, and their days of accepting easy answers were growing fewer— a fact that alternately caused her despair and pride. She told Rory, "Don't you worry about bad guys. If worse comes to worst, I'll just tell them I'm Rory's mama. Everyone knows better than to mess with you."

He gave her a narrow-eyed look filled with a skepticism beyond his eight short years. Like Dale, he was getting too big to be her baby boy.

She drove into town and turned down the tree-lined street where Fred had built a two-story antebellum-style home for his new wife. Nadine couldn't look at the house without thinking that at least part of the marital problems leading to her divorce had been caused by housing. She needed to live in the country. Even Black Wells was too big and busy for her. Fred longed for neighbors and a lawn to mow. He was fresh paint and interior decorating; she was old wood and root cellars.

Crystal was waiting for them at the door. Under the fanlight, framed by the white enameled molding, she wore a blue silk robe and looked like part of the decor.

Rory ran to greet her, shouting, "Hey, Mama Crystal, guess what? Mama taught me how to do percents! I can do it all by myself now!"

Crystal smiled broadly and threw up her hands. "Well, goodness! Then you can do all my percents from now on. They're too much a puzzle for me." She shared a mom-to-mom smile with Nadine.

Handing over the boys' overnight case, Nadine said, "Sorry about screwing up your weekend."

Crystal waved away the apology. "Don't fret. Me and Freddie didn't have any plans, anyway. He just—"

Fred's growl interrupted her. He stuck his tousled head out the doorway. "Sun isn't even up. Why do you promise to take the kids, then jerk them around like this, Nadine? They'll end up in therapy because of you."

She and Fred had a rule: no fighting in front of the boys. At times like this, though, laying into him full bore tempted her more than a person should be expected to resist. "I'll call the boys later."

"When? Midnight? You're just like your father. You have no concept of time, and no respect for other people's schedules, and—"

Crystal struck Fred's chest with a light, admonishing slap. "Oh, quit carrying on, sugar. Get on back to bed. I'll keep the boys quiet. Go on, shoo."

Still grumbling, Fred withdrew. Crystal flashed an apologetic smile. "He's such an old grumpy bear in the morning. Don't pay him no mind."

The boys looked at each other, then looked to Crystal. All three of them snickered. Seeing her sons and their stepmother acting as if Fred's grouchiness were an inside family joke made Nadine feel left out. She squashed the rise of jealousy as unbecoming and petty.

She kissed her sons, and promised them that next weekend for sure they'd go to work on sorting through the treasures in the old barn. They gave her cheerful smiles and assured her everything was cool. They understood solving crimes was important.

Did they truly understand? At times like this, when her precious hours with the boys were cut short, Nadine felt uncertain whether *she* understood. Being a top cop was poor consolation for being a rotten mom.

"Love you guys," she said, needing to leave, but hating to. She backed down the sidewalk.

"Love you, too," the boys called, already bouncing inside.

Mild resentment nagged her as she slid behind the steering wheel. Men separated their family lives from their professional lives so easily. Must be nice.

NEAR THE MAIN ENTRANCE of the Algernon Hotel, Ben Jackson sat in the back seat of a patrol car. The door was open, so he kept his hands tucked between his thighs as protection from the cold wind. He wondered whether the month of February in central Texas was always as bleak and harsh as this one had been.

A pair of handcuffs hung icy against his wrists, an uncomfortable reminder of what happened when a person called the Black Wells police about a murder. No matter how hard he tried to push it away, the eerie sense of déjà vu clung to him. He should have followed his instincts and run.

The rumble of a downshifting engine caught his attention. A light-colored Chevelle pulled into the parking lot. For a moment he admired the 1968 SS 396 with its sleek design and purring-tiger engine. Ben associated Chevelles with moonshiners and brainless young drag racers. The woman who emerged from the muscle car surprised him.

Her posture said authority, and the police officers and fire fighters who guarded the scene made way for her. Dressed in civilian clothing, with her thick ponytail catching golden sparks from the parking-lot lights, she approached the sheriff. A bulky man, both tall and wide, the sheriff dwarfed the woman, and she had to look up at his face. Even so, Ben sensed it was her, not the sheriff, who assumed control of the scene. An impressive woman.

Ben caught the attention of the young police officer standing outside the car. He asked, "Who's the blond lady?"

"That's Sergeant Shell, sheriff's department." He cut a wary glance at Ben. "She'll want to talk to you."

Of course. Don't they all? Ben thought. Would she be the first to ask straight out if he was a killer? "Got a cigarette, uh—" he peeked at the man's name tag "—Officer Trews?"

The officer patted the pockets of his blue nylon jacket. He brought out a crumpled pack of generic menthols, handed it over and told Ben to keep the pack.

Ben withdrew one and straightened it between his fingers. His mouth watered in anticipation so sharp it disheartened him. "I quit a year ago," he said. "Can't imagine why."

"I ought to quit, too," Officer Trews said, giving Ben a considering look. Perhaps a hostile look. "Stress. You know."

Ben strained his wrists against the handcuffs. Stress... Or had the officer actually meant guilt? *Want me to confess?* he thought, looking at the police officer. Fat chance. He intended to keep his big mouth clamped tight.

He turned his attention back to Sergeant Shell as she directed fire fighters positioning spotlights on tripods. She was definitely the lady in charge—the lady who'd hang him if she could.

NADINE BREATHED DEEPLY, smelling exhaust and the faint sweaty odor of working men. A sullen northerly breeze pushed air heavy with moisture. She shivered inside her coat. While men moved around her, she absorbed the overall scene, taking note of the few nonofficial vehicles in the parking lot and the lights blazing from inside the hotel. Cars on the street slowed to watch the commotion, but none stopped, and she saw no pedestrians.

The sheriff, resplendent in full uniform, with a wool coat straining over his big belly, beckoned excitedly to her. He pointed toward the front of a Dodge van, insisting she look at the body now.

Talking loudly enough for everyone on the scene to hear him, Billy Joe explained in detail the call-in to the Black Wells Police Department and how they had recognized the murder as outside their expertise so they had called him and he had contacted his people on his car telephone. Tuning him out, Nadine looked at the victim. She thought her heart might break.

The woman was young, little more than a girl. She was slim, blond . . . and very pretty.

The sheriff said, "Her name is Heather Labeau, age twenty-one. She's a student. Works part-time at the radio station." He jerked a thumb toward the hotel penthouse, which housed radio station KWBK.

"I know her. She used to work at the steak house over on Main Street. Nice girl." Grief shoved at the bottom of her diaphragm, making each breath painful. Violent death was never easy to accept—especially violent death of the young and the vibrant. Grit scratched her eyes; she rubbed them hard with the pads of her fingers.

"We've got the boy who allegedly found the body and allegedly called it in." While the sheriff spoke, he looked longingly toward Janice Murphy, a reporter for the local newspaper. "Took him right straight into custody, read him his rights, patted him down. Everything by the book."

Nadine grasped Billy Joe by the arm and firmly led him to a safe, noncontaminating distance from the body. Quietly she asked, "Are you saying you have the man who killed her?"

"I don't know if he killed her. That's your job."

Confused, she looked at the patrol car parked near the hotel. All she could see was a shadow of a man inside. "Then— Who is he?" She figured in a short while she'd have an irate citizen to whom she'd be apologizing profusely. Life with Billy Joe was always a ton of fun.

"Benjamin Andrew Jackson. He's the—"

"Disc jockey." Sunrise made a fiery show, promising rain or—judging by the temperature—sleet later on today. The light still wasn't good enough to see more than Ben Jackson's shape in the car, but a tingle slithered through her anyway. Heat blossomed at the base of her throat. "I've heard him on the radio."

A few weeks ago she'd discovered KWBK's all-night programming. Ben Jackson deejayed the midnight-to-five music request show. A sassy boy, she had dubbed him, full of spark and vinegar, telling jokes, teasing callers and mimicking celebrities. But when he was serious he was drop-dead sexy—no, more than sexy. At times he could sound so intimate it seemed he spoke to her and her alone. More than once she'd been tempted to call, just to hear his trademark "You've got Wayback in the morning, name your pleasure."

No way could Ben Jackson live up to his radio persona. Nobody could be that sexy in person. She bid farewell to the fantasies he'd given her.

She brought out her flashlight, prepared to take her time. Once the body was moved, it was never coming back; the scene would never be fresh again. She told Billy Joe to keep the reporters out of the way.

Heather wore blue jeans and a shaggy white sweater—a frumpy look that was both fashionable and expensive. Gently moving the girl's hair away from her face, Nadine noted a single bullet hole in her left temple. Stippling on the skin said the gun had been close when it was fired.

Except for blood and dirt from the asphalt, the clothes were undisturbed and showed no sign of assault or sexual molestation. On her left hand she wore a simple silver band with a light brown stone and what looked like an engagement ring with a small diamond. A tennis bracelet, perhaps with real diamonds, glittered on her wrist. A brown patchwork-leather hobo bag lay next to the body. It was fully zipped.

Senseless, senseless... Nadine sat back on her heels. She glanced at the patrol car and prayed the disc jockey could give her a solid lead pointing at the rotter who'd done this terrible thing.

Hands behind her back, Nadine walked around the scene, absorbing details, then brought out her camera. Four rolls of film later, she felt satisfied she had pictures of every angle.

She caught a loud stage whisper: "Doesn't she ever talk? She's giving me the creeps."

Nadine glanced over her shoulder. A stranger stood with Janice Murphy. He was slender, swathed in an oversize military fatigue jacket. A camera hung from a strap around his neck, and a bulky equipment bag made him list to the side. A new reporter for the *Black Wells Bugle,* Nadine guessed.

Bob Underhill arrived lugging his evidence kit. She braced herself for his usual tasteless wisecracks, but instead his face twisted into a pained grimace. He knew Heather, too.

She helped Bob lay out a grid using wooden spindles with lead-weighted bottoms and bright white string. He began the painstaking process of collecting physical evidence, starting with the body.

The county coroner arrived. He examined Heather, officially pronounced her dead, then oversaw her removal by the emergency technicians.

It made no sense for anyone to just walk up to a young woman and shoot her. Nadine watched the departing ambulance, thinking, *I'll find him, Heather. I'll make your killer pay if it's the last thing I ever do.*

Deputy Kyle Green presented her with a bag. When she asked him what it was, he told her he'd tested their suspect for gunpowder residue.

The young reporter with Janice yelled, "Did you say you have a suspect? Who is he?"

Shooting the reporter an exasperated glare, she urged the deputy to follow her around to the other side of the van. "What the devil is going on here, Kyle? Why is Ben Jackson a suspect?"

"The sheriff said test him. I tested him." Hanging his head, he scuffed a shoe along the asphalt. He grinned sheepishly, looking more like a teenager playing dress-up than a deputy. "You know how he is."

"Well, as long as you did it, did you find anything?"

"A trace-metal test turned up negative. I did an acid swab so the lab can check for residue." He hoisted the bag.

"Did he have a gun in his possession?"

"No."

"Did he confess?"

"No."

"Did anyone see him shoot her?"

Kyle's face turned crimson. "Actually, all he did was find the body and call the police."

She peered around the van. Billy Joe was now holding court with the reporters. Since he insisted on playing Keystone Kop, she had to follow up. She said, "Give the bag to Bob, and make sure he marks it."

She caught herself hesitating, which had nothing to do with the sheriff's bumbling, and a whole lot to do with putting a face to her fantasy voice.

BEN JACKSON stiffened inside the patrol car. With her hands jammed in her coat pockets, the sheriff's investigator approached.

Show time.

She asked Ben to get out of the car. Without taking her hands out of her pockets, she said, "I'm Sergeant Nadine Shell, with the Ponce County Sheriff's Department, Mr. Jackson." Her gold shield hung clipped from her coat. "Officer Trews, be so kind as to remove those handcuffs."

"But Sheriff Horseman said—"

"Take them off. Now."

The police officer jumped to do as he was told.

Ben held out his hands, but he stared at the investigator. Her small, trim femininity amazed him—apparently all brains and no brawn. Her strong features and assured demeanor kept her from being pretty. Yet he suspected that if she ever allowed a smile to crack her hypnotic calm, she'd be beautiful.

Stunning.

She stunned him now.

Her golden, luxuriously thick ponytail and the careless bangs covering her forehead gave her appearance a certain girlishness. But there was nothing girlish about the command in her voice or about the large, dark eyes now staring into his. She reminded him of a cat perched on a windowsill, assured that soon the sun would shine and the birds would come. Infinite patience, ultimate cool, as compelling as she was unnerving.

She asked him if he had a car. He pointed to his Mustang, parked near the hotel's front entrance. She gave the police officer a stern look, then indicated Ben was to follow her to his car.

Ever since the first official arrived, he'd had cops jumping down his throat. He'd been frisked, and questioned, and had his hands sprayed with stinking, ice-cold liquid. He'd kept his head. Better, he'd kept his mouth shut. So far.

As guilty as he felt, as off kilter as she'd thrown him, he wondered how long he could keep his head around Nadine Shell.

Chapter Two

Nadine noticed the way Ben was looking at her. Despite its being the liberated nineties, female law officers were still a rarity. Her being only five feet two inches tall and weighing a mere one hundred pounds made her position even more incongruous.

"Your buddies already talked to me," Ben said. He threw a hard look toward the crime scene. "And stuff." He leaned his backside against the hood of his car and crossed one foot over the other. Red cowboy boots gleamed in the pale morning light, their hard shine a stark contrast to his faded blue jeans, flannel shirt and down vest. He toyed with an unlit cigarette, rolling it over and over between his fingers.

Smoking a cigarette could cause a false-positive result on an NAA test for gunpowder residue on his hands. She asked, "Trying to quit?"

He looked at the cigarette, as if surprised to see it. "Nasty habit."

She plucked the cigarette from his hand and flicked it far away. "Go cold turkey. Only thing that really works."

His smile deepened the twin dimples in his cheeks and lit up his eyes, and caught her completely off guard.

His radio voice had conjured an image of a model-handsome playboy with a brooding brow, sensual lips and Greek-god curls. The fantasy shriveled in comparison to the flesh-and-blood man. Despite his fatigue and tension, his smile was easy. Light brown eyes, shaded by a thick fall of dusky black hair, gleamed with lively intelligence. The narrowing of his eyes and the awareness in them brought her back to business.

"You're pretty cute," he said. "For a cop."

He'd noticed her lapse, then. Sighing inwardly, she pulled a spiral-bound notebook and a pen from her coat pocket. "You're pretty smart-mouthed. For a witness."

He chuckled. "Okay, I got it, Sarge. No cracks. What do you want to know?"

The vibes coming from him struck her as true. Strain edged his voice, and fear marked his restless hands and hunched shoulders. Murder was a scary thing; she expected fear. He looked her in the eye, and he hadn't yawned once. Why the guilty tended to yawn, she didn't know, but they did. Instinct said Ben wasn't the shooter. But Billy Joe had put her in a bad position by casting Ben in the role of villain. She needed to go through the entire routine to clear him off the suspect list.

She said, "I apologize for the inconvenience, Mr. Jackson. I hope you understand that it's difficult for all of us."

"Inconvenience." That glorious smile lit up his face again. "I guess I should count myself lucky nobody used a nightstick on me." Good humor lessened the sarcasm.

"Tell me what happened to Heather."

A faint sheen brightened his eyes. He rubbed them with a knuckle. "I don't know. I walked Heather to her van. Then I remembered some CDs I wanted to preview for the show, so I went back up to the station. I came back down and saw her van still parked. I figured she was having engine trouble, so I went over to see . . ." He fumbled in his vest pocket and brought out another cigarette.

Nadine noted the cigarette for the lab technicians, in case nitrates showed up on the NAA test.

He said, "I ran back inside and called the police from the desk. They told me to wait for them." He huffed a heavy sigh. "And that's it."

"Did you walk her all the way to her van? Wait for her to get inside?"

He ducked his head, a reaction she could interpret as guilt, embarrassment, or a cramp in his neck. He said, "I should have. I—I meant to."

"Did you touch her?"

He shook his head.

"Not even to check her pulse? See if she was breathing?"

He closed his eyes. His entire body went taut. For a moment, she thought he might leave. "It scared me, okay?"

A small alarm jangled inside her skull. "How close did you get to her?"

"Close enough," he mumbled, now studying his boots.

A shield had gone up. She dubbed him a stubborn man. Perhaps as stubborn as she was—no easy feat. "Just asking, Ben. I need to know what happened."

"I'm not a coward or anything, but... but it... I liked her."

Liked her so well that seeing her on the ground made him automatically assume she was dead? Most people, seeing someone on the ground, instinctively shake, jostle, talk or fiddle around in an attempt to rouse or comfort. Could he have known by looking that she was dead? The parking-lot lights were powerful. She supposed it was possible—but only remotely possible, considering there had been very little blood and she'd had to lift Heather's hair to see the wound.

Very strange.

"Were you dating Heather?"

He laughed, weakly. "Come on, Sarge, I'm old enough to be her... big brother."

"Are you married?"

"My wife died. Two years ago."

Something about him made her itchy. She sought clues in his eyes, and in the play of the muscles in his cheeks and jaw, and in the twitch of his hands. "You're from out of town. Got a funny accent."

His smile returned, catching her off guard again. "I got a funny accent? Ever listen to a tape of yourself, Sarge?"

His nearly perfect imitation of Billy Joe Horseman's thick good-old-boy drawl astonished her. Ben laughed, then cut it off in midnote. He murmured an apology. "I took the job at Wayback right after New Year's. I'm from Georgia. Atlanta."

"I've heard you on the radio. You're pretty good. I guess you do all those voices."

"A useless skill, offering hours of mindless entertainment." He raised the cigarette to his mouth, then lowered it and resumed twiddling it between his fingers, back and forth, under and over, like a tiny twirler baton. "I do magic tricks, too." He made the cigarette disappear, then reappear. His supple hands were quick.

He'd relaxed his guard somewhat, so she returned to the subject. "What time did you and Heather come downstairs?"

"We signed out at twenty after five."

"Did you walk downstairs or take the elevator?"

"Elevator."

Nadine guessed it would have taken them about five minutes to sign out of the station and ride down, and for Heather to reach the van. "Then you went back to the station. Anyone see you?"

He nodded. "Ralphie was picking up trash from the penthouse. He's building maintenance." His brow furrowed in concentration. "Ah, I don't know if Mark saw me or not. He's the early-morning deejay. He was in the booth."

"Anyone in the elevator? In the lobby?"

"Not too many people up and about, even in a cow town like this one." He swung his head around to face her and grinned. "You've heard me on the air?"

She ignored the question—and tried to ignore the interest crackling between them. "How long did it take you to pick up the CDs?"

"A few minutes. I'd left them on the reception desk."

"Then you came straight down."

She asked the rest of her questions. He assured her he hadn't seen anything suspicious or out of the ordinary before he went back to the station. He'd seen no one when he found the body. His matter-of-fact recounting, and the way he looked at her while he spoke, were good signs. But did she ask the right questions? He made her uneasy—a very bad sign. "How long have you known Heather?"

"Since I started working here, but she only worked weekends. She's a college student, going for an engineering degree. She keeps the machinery running, plays producer, runs errands, that sort of thing."

Nadine knew the station owner. An upright family man who prided himself on offering wholesome entertainment for his mostly college-age audience. She doubted very much he'd have placed Heather in the clutches of a disc jockey he considered morally depraved. "She ever talk to you about having problems with anyone?"

"As a matter of fact . . ." He shook his head. "She was ticked about something her boyfriend did. She didn't say much. Heather was of the school that if you can't say something nice, don't say anything." Pain rippled across his features, and his throat worked. The cigarette snapped in his fingers.

Nadine had seen Heather running around town with Reggie Hamilton, a punk with more money than sense, and parents who didn't know the difference between discipline and dillweed. Had Reggie given her the diamond ring? "Can you recall anything she said?"

He hunched into his vest, tightening his shoulders. "She was a little upset last night, and I asked about it.

She flipped off a comment and then didn't want to talk about it."

"Do you know her boyfriend?"

"His name is Reggie, but I've never met him."

Nadine couldn't wait to talk to Reggie Hamilton.

"Heather's a nice kid. This shouldn't have happened." Ben stomped his feet while casting under-the-eyebrows glances at the people working around Heather's van. "I'm freezing. Can I go now?"

She confirmed his address and phone number, then patted the hood of the cherry red '67 Mustang he leaned against. The bright color matched his ridiculous boots. "This is a nice little car."

He cocked his head and grinned. "Bet it can outrun that Chevelle of yours."

She doubted it. She looked toward the crime scene. Billy Joe was still talking to the reporters. Since he'd already called Ben a suspect, she'd have to clear Ben by the book before satisfying the sheriff. Maybe she could satisfy a little bit, too, the itch Ben gave her.

She said, "Let your car pretty up the parking lot for a few more minutes."

Ben's sudden, open annoyance eased her annoyance at herself for wanting to respond to his attractiveness. Getting all woozy about a man, especially under these circumstances, struck her as sophomoric and unprofessional. He's flesh and blood, she told herself firmly. In spite of the heated fantasies she'd created while listening to him on the radio, he was no better and no worse than any other man. She asked, "By the way, Ben... Where are those CDs? The ones you went upstairs to fetch."

He looked around, then patted his pockets. "I don't know."

The itch began to coalesce into suspicion. She asked, "What do they look like?"

He formed a rough square with his fingers. He continued looking around the car and patting his vest and jeans pockets. "There are four of them, each in a plastic case. I must have dropped them."

Nadine called Trews over and asked him to check around the parking lot for the CDs. Telling Ben to stay put for a few minutes longer, she felt his annoyance shifting into anger. She kept her expression mild and authoritative, watching Ben's eyes until he lost the break-and-run look. She went inside the hotel.

In the lobby, several people were watching the parking lot through the plate-glass windows. The rich aroma of brewing coffee made Nadine's stomach growl; she longed for a cup. Killers often hung around crime scenes to enjoy the excitement, so she studied faces. No one seemed particularly nervous because of her.

Nadine approached the desk and saw four thin plastic boxes near the guest telephone. Behind the desk, Meg Horseman, the sheriff's daughter, looked grown-up and professional in her brown blazer and white blouse.

"How long have you been on duty, Meg?"

"Hey, Mrs. Shell..." Meg shuddered delicately. "Is Heather really dead?"

"Afraid so. What time did you come on?"

"Four-thirty. That's when my shift starts. Is Dad out there? I thought I saw him." She blew a long breath and made a face. Her eyes were tear-swollen. "He hates me working at this time of the morning, anyway. Now he'll probably make me quit. This is just awful."

"Your dad is here. Did you see Mr. Jackson and Heather leave together?"

Meg patted the computerized cash register. "I was working right here. I don't think they saw me, but I saw them. Then Ben comes right back in and goes upstairs."

"Right back?"

"Uh-huh. Like he walked out, then turned right around and walked in. I said hello to him then." A light blush colored her cheeks, making Nadine think the young woman perhaps had a mild crush on the sexy deejay. "But I don't think he heard me."

"How did he act when he came in the first time?"

"Act?" Meg shrugged.

"Did you notice anything about him?"

Meg waved a hand downward. "Not really. He just walked over to the elevator."

Further questioning brought out the information that Meg had been behind the desk with a full view of the lobby since four-thirty. Meg was positive Ben had been outside with Heather for maybe thirty seconds at the most. Nadine recorded the name of every person Meg had seen this morning, then put her hand on the stack of CDs. "What are these?"

"Oh, those are Ben's. Guess he forgot them when he called the police." She reached for them. "I'll give them to him—"

Nadine picked them up. "I'll take care of it."

Meg hugged herself. "When Ben came running in, I was thinking maybe he was playing some kind of joke or something. Just fooling around, like he does on his show. Only he was too scared to be fooling." Her eyes shimmered. "Is she really dead? She was a real sweet girl, you know. Nicest person in the world."

Her poignant words caught Nadine off guard, and she stood stock-still until her control returned. Lack of sleep made her too vulnerable to emotional involvement. She couldn't afford emotion right now.

Ralphie, the janitor, also confirmed Ben's story. Like Meg, he'd seen Ben and Heather leave together, then Ben had returned alone within a few minutes. Ralphie assured Nadine that Ben had been acting normally.

She returned to the Mustang and gave the CDs to Ben. His attitude had undergone a change in the short time she was inside. Instead of fear, he displayed wariness; rather than angry, he seemed resigned.

The sheriff headed their way. Poor Ben. If he ever witnessed anything in the future, he'd probably keep his mouth shut and pretend blindness.

She patted the Mustang's white convertible roof. "Mind if I take a look inside your car?"

"I'm a suspect," he said wearily.

"Not really," she said, and meant it. Her instincts were top-notch, but facts held more weight. Itch notwithstanding, Meg, Ralphie and the CDs gave Ben a solid alibi. "Can I look in your car?"

"There's nothing in there."

Billy Joe asked, "What's the problem here?"

"No problem," she answered, "just taking care of a few little details, so Mr. Jackson can go home. He's been very cooperative and helpful. We don't want to have to bother him anymore."

Ben lifted his head. Nadine raised an eyebrow and gave him a faint smile. Comprehension dawned in his expressive eyes, and his mouth curved. For a disconcerting moment, she forgot where she was and what she was supposed to be doing. The entire world was centered in his amber brown eyes.

Ben dug a set of keys out of his jeans pocket. He tossed them with an underhand snap of his wrist. She snagged them out of the air.

She had Trews fetch a consent-to-search form from her car. Ben signed it, giving her permission to search and seize anything she felt was pertinent to her investigation. When he handed back the paper, she noticed he'd added a little happy face next to his signature. Definitely sassy.

She started to unlock the car when she noticed it was unlocked already. She mentioned it to Ben.

He shrugged. "Nothing a crook can steal is more expensive than replacing the ragtop."

With Billy Joe breathing down her neck, she searched the car's interior, trunk, wheel wells and engine compartment. In the trunk, she found a large number of cassette tapes and CDs, a tool set and a briefcase full of papers, but no gun, and nothing that looked as if it belonged to Heather Labeau.

Looking bored, Billy Joe wandered away. He loved the idea of investigating a crime, but the actual work excited him about as much as looking at library paste.

Her activity did draw the reporters, however. Janice hovered at a distance, but the new man kept inching closer.

After a thorough search, Nadine said, "Thank you for your cooperation, Ben. I really am sorry for the inconvenience. We won't bother you again." She snapped her head around and faced the reporter. The man jumped. "You want something?" she asked.

The reporter hoisted his slim notebook, keeping his hawklike stare fixed on Ben, though his words were directed at her. "Are you making an arrest, Sergeant Shell? Isn't this the suspect the sheriff claims to have in custody?" His accent sounded flat to the ear, making Nadine wonder if he'd come from the Midwest.

Janice Murphy grinned and rolled her eyes, as if to tell her, "Oh, these eager young kids." She caught the younger man's arm and dragged him away, saying, "The first thing you need to know, Daryl, is Sergeant Shell *never* talks to the press."

"Good thing he doesn't have a noose and a tree to hang me from," Ben muttered. "Thanks, Sarge." He reached for his car door, then turned to her with a dazzling smile. "Mind if I ask you a question?"

Catching herself wanting to drink in his gorgeousness, like some silly fool mooning over a movie star, she busily examined her notes. "Shoot."

He looked pointedly at her bare left hand. "Married?"

She clamped down hard on the rise of pleasure his question provoked. Bad enough he was flirting with her; wanting to respond was inexcusable. "Good day, Mr. Jackson. And thank you."

He opened the car door. "Just wondering," he said, and slid inside.

Nadine spent the rest of the morning interviewing hotel employees and guests. No one had seen or heard anything. Bob Underhill found a shell casing that told them the fatal bullet had probably come from a .22-caliber automatic handgun. Police officers and fire fighters sweeping the parking lot and surrounding area in a square-foot-by-square-foot search failed to produce the weapon.

Nadine spoke to the radio station's employees about Heather. The picture she got was of a truly innocent victim. The nicest girl in the world, Nadine heard over and over again. A hard worker with a perpetually cheerful attitude. Everyone had liked Heather; nobody had the faintest idea why anyone would want to kill her. Nadine came away from the interviews with a copy of Heather's employee record and an unhappy feeling that the solution to this murder would come neither quickly nor easily.

Late in the afternoon, Nadine returned to her office. Her temples throbbed with a fatigue headache, and depression weighted her shoulders. A cup of coffee helped a little; a hamburger helped a lot. Studying her notes, which to her tired eyes looked like chicken scratchings, she swirled a french fry idly through a puddle of ketchup. Ben Jackson's smile kept intruding on her thoughts. When was the last time a man had looked at her like that? It had been so long, it might as well have been never.

Black Wells was a small town. She might run into him someday. A nice meeting, without her badge getting in the way.

Deb Hall swished into the office. "Eating at your desk again. I swan! You look like H-E-double toothpicks." Deb, the office administrator, had been a fixture with the Ponce County Sheriff's Department for nearly forty years. White-haired, whip-thin, she conducted her business as if appointed by God. When Nadine's father was sheriff, Deb had been his right hand; under Billy Joe, Deb threatened to quit at least once a day.

"I work on it," Nadine murmured. "What's up?"

"How much sleep did you get last night?"

"I'm fine. What do you need?"

"What I need is no account. What that darned Billy Joe needs is a muzzle." She waved a sheet of paper. "Here's his press release."

Nadine scanned the statement. According to the sheriff, they had a prime suspect in Heather's murder and an arrest was imminent. Too tired to get angry, she picked up another french fry and regarded it. "Thanks, Deb. I'll handle this."

The elderly woman shook a gnarled finger at Nadine's face. "Billy Joe is your fault, you know. You and your daddy's."

"I didn't vote for him."

"You didn't run against him, either. Your daddy, God rest him, he made being sheriff look too darned easy. Had things running so smooth, no wonder the county figured any old nitwit could do the job. Now we got an old nitwit!"

Nadine conceded that there was a certain amount of truth in Deb's words. Her father, Big John Campbell, had served the county for thirty years. He'd been a good sheriff, the best. Sometimes she wondered if she was being unfair to Billy Joe by expecting him to live up to her father's standards.

"We're stuck with him," Nadine said, "so we'll have to make the best of it. Is he around?"

"He's in. Pestering folks, as usual." Deb gave Nadine a crisp, humorless smile before stalking back to her office.

Nadine took the press release to the sheriff. She laid it on his desk and said, "This won't do."

"What's wrong with it?"

"We don't have a prime suspect, and we don't have anybody to arrest," she said patiently.

"What about that deejay?"

"Ben Jackson?" A short laugh erupted huskily from her throat. "Your own daughter gives him an alibi. What I need you to do is ask anyone who might have been around the Algernon, even driving past in a car, between five and five-thirty, to come forward. Somebody may have seen the shooter without realizing it."

"I think Jackson is our man."

"Evidence says he's not. So—"

"Meggie says he's quite the ladies' man. I figure he was sniffing after Heather and she told him to go pound nails. He got mad." He cocked his hand into a gun shape and added, "Boom!"

Nadine's headache returned full force. "Please rewrite the press release. Now I'm going to go interview Reggie Hamilton—"

"Why?"

"He's Heather's boyfriend."

"That's Cooter Hamilton's boy." He looked worried, perhaps considering what the biggest cattleman in the county would think about an investigator talking to his only son. "Maybe you ought to wait until things cool down."

"I don't care if he's the president's son. I need to talk to him." She leaned both hands on his desk and met him eye-to-eye. "There are procedures, steps I have to take. It isn't comfortable for anybody, but it's necessary. So you do your part and let me do mine."

Billy Joe's eyes acquired a malicious glitter. Nadine knew they'd never be friends, but it occurred to her now that they were very close to being enemies. Her presence reminded him that almost everyone in the department compared him to Big John Campbell and found him lacking. Lecturing him in a schoolmarmish tone of voice didn't help matters any.

She pushed away from the desk. "I'll find the killer."

"You better," he said, his voice brittle with warning.

"COMING!" Ben called as he stumbled to the door. He'd slept poorly, plagued by nightmares of endless parking lots and silky blond hair matted with blood. The last thing he wanted was company, but whoever was pounding on his door refused to take the hint. The knocking continued unabated, growing louder and more insistent.

He opened the door. A skinny man with unkempt brown hair and bad posture stood on the narrow stoop. As recognition dawned, Ben snapped fully awake. His belly clenched into an icy knot. "What are you doing here?"

"The name's Daryl Wafflegate." He flashed a plastic card that could have been anything. "Reporter for the *Black Wells Bugle*. I didn't get a chance to talk to you this morning."

"No chance now, man. Beat it," Ben said, and pushed the door.

Wafflegate shoved his sneaker-clad foot in the opening.

Ben dropped his gaze to the foot. "Move it or I break it," he said softly.

"Just answer a few questions about that chick that got whacked."

Every stretched taut nerve zinged with sudden fury—and guilt, deep, hurting, sickening guilt. If not for him, Heather would still be alive and laughing.

"That chick," he said through his teeth, "has a name. And getting whacked is what happens in racquetball." The top of his head felt ready to blow off.

"Okay, how about a few questions about Atlanta?" His bug-eyed stare threatened to burn through Ben's skin. "Radio station WLBO?"

Ben almost dropped his hold on the door. This couldn't be happening. It was impossible. He was thousands of miles and a lifetime away from Atlanta.

He lunged with all his weight against the door. Wafflegate's mouth opened wide, as if in a scream, but all that emerged was a pained squeak. He jerked his foot out of the doorway. Ben slammed the door and locked it.

Sergeant Nadine Shell, with her wise, beautiful eyes and air of thoughtful intelligence—he needed to tell her about this. From that brief, almost conspiratorial look they shared before she searched his car, he'd known he could trust her. He needed her on his side. She'd understand, even if he didn't understand it himself.

But would she believe him?

Way in the back of his mind, he heard his father telling the old story about the egg-stealing dog: "Catch that old hound with egg on his face once, well, you hope yourself up an explanation. But catch him twice and there ain't nothing to do but shoot him..."

Chapter Three

Nadine stared at her interview notes regarding Reggie Hamilton. The boy was twenty-two years old, but his parents had hovered around him like hawks over a fledgling, answering Nadine's questions as if their son didn't have a mouth or the mind to speak for himself.

Reggie's alibi checked out, however. At the time of the murder, he'd been fishing on Lake Huxley, fifteen miles from the Algernon Hotel. Two of his buddies swore the three of them had gone to the lake Saturday night and been up at dawn on Sunday to fish for bass.

She leafed through the crime-scene photographs. An eight-by-ten photo of the van showed the key in the door lock. Clearly visible was the inner lock button, raised in the unlocked position. That, combined with the position of Heather's body, bothered her. It meant something, but what? She cursed the chronic fatigue muddling up her thinking.

Billy Joe strolled into her office. He said, "That darned new reporter at the *Bugle* is squealing like a pig waiting for slop. Don't you have anything for me?"

"I wish I did."

Billy Joe looked behind him, then closed the office door. He loomed over Nadine's desk. "This can't be turning up on 'Unsolved Mysteries.' Know what I'm saying? That little girl wasn't some cowboy in a bar fight."

His habit of classifying victims as either "good" or "had it coming to them" irritated the devil out of her. She said, "If I had something, I'd tell you."

"Don't you have anything on that deejay?"

Nadine lowered her eyelids. Ben was a stranger, an outsider, a big-city fella with a flashy job. The perfect villain to play against the sheriff's role as small-town hero. She wondered if Billy Joe ever took a good look in a mirror and saw what a parody he'd made of himself.

He asked, "Did you get the lab results on the gunpowder residue test?"

"Jackson was clean." Too bad her thoughts about him weren't. She'd been listening to him on the radio with even more interest than before. Meeting him hadn't dampened her fantasies a lick. If anything, they were worse. She must be losing her mind.

"Well, now, I read how the blowback on a .22 is pretty scanty. Or he could have washed his hands."

"I can't prove he did it by what isn't there," she said. "I'm not any happier about my lack of progress than you are. But we can't be arbitrary about an arrest. Facts, evidence. That's what matters."

"Best get on the stick, Nadine. I won't—"

The telephone interrupted him. "I'm expecting an important call," Nadine lied, and answered while swiveling her chair to put her shoulder to the sheriff. He took the hint and departed. "Sergeant Shell, may I help you?"

"Have you checked Atlanta yet?"

Nadine stiffened. The voice bewildered her. It sounded mechanical, and had a slight reverberation, as if echoing from within a metal barrel. She couldn't tell if it was a man or woman—or even if it was human.

Nadine demanded, "Who is this?"

"Benjamin Andrew Jackson is a killer. He put the gun right in her face and pulled the trigger. You have to stop him before he kills again."

The voice rasped her nerves like sandpaper. Short hairs lifted on the back of her neck. Calmly she said, "I take it you have information regarding my investigation into the homicide of Heather Labeau?"

"Don't let him fool you. Somebody has to stop him. He won't stop on his own. Call Detective Hoyt Boyles, Atlanta police, homicide. Ask him about Karen Bates."

The caller hung up.

Nadine wrote down the names. She'd received plenty of tips, many of them anonymous, over the years. She'd never heard anything like that. Could it have been a computer-generated voice? She'd read about the technology in magazines.

Even weirder was the comment about the gun in Heather's face. The location of the fatal wound hadn't been released to the press. It could have been a lucky guess or a figure of speech, but that strange mechanical voice had sounded very sure of itself.

She called Atlanta. What homicide detective Hoyt Boyles told her made the weirdness of the anonymous tipster pale by comparison.

Now she knew why Ben Jackson hadn't touched Heather's body. He'd played this picture-show part before.

NADINE TOOK HER TIME driving toward the south side
of town. As she passed each block, the building styles
looked more modern, and traffic grew heavier, with
compact cars outnumbering pickup trucks. Black
Wells, small as it was, seemed like two towns. The
north side was old and established, retaining its cow-
town flavor. She preferred it over the south side, with
its malls, chain restaurants, apartment buildings and
pockets of tract homes encircling Central Texas University.

She turned into the driveway of a two-story apartment complex and slowed her car to a grumbling crawl
as she studied numbers.

Ben lived at the end of the row on the ground level.
She parked at the curb, then radioed in her location to
the dispatcher. She sat, dangling the mike from her
hand. Atlanta's information was bizarre, coinciden-
tal. Nothing proved Ben Jackson was a killer—nothing proved him dangerous.

Yet the heaviness of her eyelids spoke of her vulnerability. She functioned, she did her job, but recur-
ring bouts of insomnia had taken their toll. Her inner
radar was working at less than optimal power.

Prove he's a killer, she told herself, find a single
shred of evidence, then you can let him scare you. She
got out of the car.

At the apartment door, Ben answered Nadine's
knock quickly enough for her to know he hadn't been
sleeping. Barefoot, he wore a flannel shirt hanging
open over a pair of blue jeans. His nearly hairless chest
and black hair made her wonder if he had some Native American blood in him. Not that it made any difference.

What did matter was his lack of surprise at seeing her. If she had to name his reaction, she'd call it relief.

"Good morning, Sarge. Can I hope this is a social call?"

The snap and crackle of their first encounter leapt into being now. His beautiful smile knocked at her concentration. An unhappy little voice whined in the back of her skull about the sheer unfairness of meeting this man under these circumstances. "You can hope anything you want, Ben. May I come in? I'd like to talk to you."

He stepped aside to let her enter.

The apartment consisted of a fair-size room that doubled as a living room and dining room, separated from the galley-size kitchen by a wide breakfast counter. An open door revealed a bedroom. Except for more neatness than she expected from a bachelor, and a sophisticated sound system, including a reel-to-reel tape recorder and four speakers, the apartment was unremarkable.

"Want some coffee?" he asked.

"Sure." She sat on the couch. Real-estate brochures littered a coffee table.

A faint, not unpleasant chemical odor told her the couch was new. After a few seconds, she realized she didn't smell any cigarette smoke. So what was that bit with the cigarette? Could he know enough about chemical testing for gunpowder residue to attempt to sabotage the results?

She caught herself fingering the snap holster of her side arm and made herself quit.

He moved around the kitchen counter. He paused and met her eyes. His chest raised and lowered in a heavy breath, perhaps a sigh. "I know why you're here, Sarge."

"Do you?"

He chuckled, brought out a thick white mug, and filled it with coffee. "You are the calmest woman I have ever met. Does anything shake you?"

"Not much."

"I bet in your business you've pretty much seen it all. Have you been a cop a long time?"

"Sometimes it feels like all my life. My daddy was the sheriff for near thirty years. Used to be my boss, in fact." She accepted a cup of coffee. She watched him closely as he sat on a stool and pulled a coffee mug near. She asked, "Do you smoke?"

He blinked rapidly, then grinned. "The parking lot." He shook his head. "I quit a year ago. I almost started again, but common sense prevailed. Giving up the cancer sticks is too painful to go through twice." Smile fading, he shifted uncomfortably on the stool. "You know about Atlanta."

A light prickling crawled across her scalp. "You tell me."

His laugh emerged clear and unaffected, and he shook his head. Nadine doubted he was laughing at her, but was unsure what he was laughing at.

He sobered quickly, but continued to shake his head. "This is a bad dream. I keep hoping to wake up, but it's not going to happen."

She waited patiently for him to continue.

"Last July, a woman I worked with was murdered." All good humor had fled, and his shoulders flexed under the loose shirt. "Heather was like... playing back a tape."

"So what happened, Ben? In Atlanta?"

He stared at his coffee cup. "Her name was Karen Bates. She'd come up from a station in Savannah. She was good, sharp, funny. We had a show called "Midnight Madness." A little wilder than what I'm doing here, mostly heavy rock and roll, lots of shtick and promotions. The listeners loved her."

Detective Boyles had described Karen as an exceptionally attractive young woman. Tall, slim, blond, and only twenty-four years old. "Did you love her?"

He looked up then, and a thin smile appeared. "I liked her, but we didn't have a relationship outside the station. Despite what you hear on the radio, playing macho stud is just an act."

He underestimated his appeal. "So then," she said, prodding.

"That night, we left the station around one in the morning. I walked her to her car, the way I usually did." His voice dropped to barely above a whisper. "I'd brought my new laptop computer in to work, and when I got outside, I remembered I forgot it."

Nadine held a pet theory. The number of possible incidents was limited, so coincidence was the rule, rather than the exception. Still, this story sent cat claws up and down her spine.

His voice turned rough. "When I went back to get my computer, I talked to another deejay for a while. Ten minutes, maybe fifteen. Outside, I saw Karen's car still in the lot." Blood drained from his face, and his gaze turned distant and pained.

She had to speak several times, urging him, before he continued.

"Her car was running, but the door was open, and—" He swept a hand toward the floor. "She'd fallen out. Somebody had shot her." A shudder racked his body. "You asked me why I didn't touch Heather. I freaked, Sarge. Lying there...blood. What I really wanted to do was jump in my car and drive away, as far and as fast as I could."

Either this man was hurting like the devil, or he was the finest actor in the world. "Why didn't you tell me about this?"

"Tell you what, Sarge?" He gave her a dry look over the rim of his coffee mug. "Oh, a dead woman? Yeah, by the way, this happens to me all the time?"

Weak, but understandable, she supposed.

"I started to call you a dozen times. But it sounds unbelievable. I don't believe it myself."

On one level, he made sense. If he was guilty, wouldn't he have called and tried to explain away Atlanta? Wouldn't he try to explain it now? Or had he hoped she wouldn't find out about Karen Bates? "I was gonna tell you..." were words all investigators hated to hear.

"If you want to talk, now's the time to do it," she said. "Before things get out of hand."

He jutted his chin at her coffee mug. "Too strong? Too weak?"

She looked at her untouched cup. "Got any milk?"

He hopped off the stool. She figured he weighed about 170, but he was light on his feet, making very little noise as he walked to the kitchen. He brought out a quart carton of two-percent milk and held it poised over her cup. Staring into her eyes, he said, "I don't know who killed Karen, or Heather. I just don't know."

As if a curtain had opened, her dilemma revealed itself in the light. She hated crime, but she didn't always hate the criminal. Still, she distanced herself, never getting emotionally involved with suspects. But she liked Ben.

Maybe it was exposure to his radio show. Maybe her defenses were low. Or maybe her heart and body—if not her head—were sick and tired of living only for work. Whatever the reason, she liked him.

She didn't want him as a suspect, but was that because she believed him or because she liked him? That part she couldn't figure out. She touched the carton, easing it with light pressure until he let it pour a healthy dollop of milk into the mug.

He sat beside her on the couch. "There is something else. It's in the believe-it-or-not category, too."

She could feel his body heat and smell his maleness. His skin looked as supple as finely tanned glove leather. Hair so dark it absorbed the light fell over his brow; her palms itched with the urge to ease it off his face. She forced her gaze away, focusing instead on a framed photograph atop the desk.

It showed a woman with a square face and big, dark eyes. Pale hair grew to her shoulders in an unruly but attractive mane. His late wife, she guessed.

Everything he'd said thus far matched what the Atlanta detective had told her. She understood how his confusion had made him keep silent about Karen. Witnesses at the Algernon gave him an alibi. No evidence pointed at him. "Try me," she said.

"There's a stalker after me." He emphasized the comment with a facial shrug. "It started after my wife died. At first I got packages full of dead animals. Road kill, to be exact. Then there were letters accusing me of murdering my wife and telling me to confess. I figured it was my wicked past catching up with me."

"Wicked past?"

"I used to do talk radio. The more listeners I irritated, the higher the ratings." He passed it off with a wave of a hand. "I gave the letters to the police, but I got the impression they thought my big mouth had gotten me into trouble, so it could get me out."

"I see. Did you save the letters?"

He jumped up and returned to the kitchen. "It got to the point where I didn't even open them. I threw them away. The letters stopped... then Karen was murdered."

Detective Boyles had told her he'd received several anonymous letters accusing Ben of murdering Karen. Could they have come from Ben's stalker? Her itchiness returned. A mysterious stalker was darned convenient for a man being questioned by the police. She glanced at the fancy stereo setup and the computer sitting on the desk next to the telephone. Anonymous letters and phone calls could originate from anyone— even the killer.

"Just to satisfy my curiosity, how did your wife die?"

He threw her a testy glance. "A car accident. She fell asleep at the wheel."

His wife died in a car accident, then some creep sent him road-killed animals? She shivered. "I'm sorry," she said. "So go on. What happened after Karen died?"

"I didn't get any letters, but other people did. My parents. The bigwigs who run the corporation that owns the radio station. The press. All of a sudden I had a dozen reporters shadowing me everywhere I went. It was humiliating."

"Is that why you left Atlanta?"

He leaned his forearms on the countertop. "I've had résumés out to small-town stations for a long time. I grew up on a farm. I never did like living in the city. Getting away from the nuttiness was a bonus."

Stark-naked pain gripped him, tightening his features and tensing his shoulders. Cords stood out on his forearms, and his entwined fingers turned pale at the knuckles. "But it followed me, Sarge. And Heather is dead."

Her pager loosed an imperious squeal. Nadine read the number: Billy Joe. What now? "May I use your telephone?"

She called Billy Joe, and while she waited for him to come on the line she studied the photograph on the desk. Uneasiness gripped her. Not merely three women dead—three attractive blond women. Coincidence was coincidence but this was spooky. Catching a glimpse of her reflection in the photograph's glass, she noticed light catching on the end of her blond ponytail. She brushed hair off her shoulder.

Billy Joe boomed, "Where the hell are you? I just spoke to a homicide detective in Atlanta, Georgia. He says he has clearance to send a file on one of their open cases. This has to do with Heather Labeau. What is it? You're supposed to keep me informed."

"Calm down. I'm not keeping anything from you. I'm following up some information—"

"It's Jackson! He's a suspect in Atlanta, isn't he?"

"This is not a good time."

"You're with Jackson now, aren't you?"

His occasional spurts of logic never failed to dismay her. "I am. I'll explain everything when I get back to the office."

"Bring him in. I want him properly interrogated."

The sheriff could live a thousand years and never grasp the distinction between an interview and an interrogation. Swallowing her anger, Nadine said, "I am handling this. We'll talk when I get back to the office."

"You better not show up without Jackson. I want some answers, and I want them now."

"Fine." She hung up on him.

Ben asked, "Is everything all right?"

Think, Nadine, think! Facts and evidence, evidence and facts. One of the first things her father had taught her about investigation was to keep an open mind. Beware of tunnel vision. If one track fails, try another. Never discount the power of elimination.

She asked, "Would you be willing to take a polygraph?"

He blinked once, twice. "A lie detector?"

She wished the science were that exact. Truth or lie, black or white. "Yeah. A lie detector."

"I can't read you, Sarge. I don't know if you believe me, or if you think I'm full of it."

She wished she knew. "I'm covering my bases."

He slid a hand around his neck. Slowly a grin captured his face, and his eyes sparkled with wicked light. "All right, let's cover all the bases. Get one of your papers, and I'll sign it. Then you can search my apartment and my storage shed and my car, if you want. I'll take your polygraph, then you cross me off your little list." He dropped his forearms on the counter and cocked his head. "Then, when you know I'm not a killer, you go out to dinner with me."

With Herculean effort, she managed not to show her surprise. "Thought macho man was just an act."

He laughed, this time without strain. "Looked in a mirror lately, Sarge? You are one attractive lady. So what do you say? Is it a date?"

Small alarms jangled her skull, but not loudly enough. With those amber eyes boring into hers, she felt attractive. She even, much to her surprise, felt sexy. It had been so long since she'd felt this way, the sensation was new and surprising and heady. She sipped the coffee, not tasting it, and said, "I don't make those kind of deals."

He tapped his chin. "How about you clear me, then we *talk* about dinner."

"I'll think about it." She shouldn't. She shouldn't even say she would. "Go get some shoes on."

"Want to frisk me first?"

Her biceps tightened with longing to put her hands all over his body, feel those hard muscles and long, lean lines. She grew achingly aware of how long it had been since she'd really touched a man—or allowed a man to touch her.

His smile and the subtle flex of his shoulders said he knew he had an effect on her. Heat climbed up her throat.

She turned away. "I need to use your phone again."

He made a gallant gesture toward the telephone on his desk before sauntering into the bedroom.

Keeping an eye on Ben, she called the sheriff's department first and requested a deputy. Then she called Tony Zaccaro, the county prosecutor. She explained what she needed.

"Les Libby doesn't have anything cooking," Tony said. "He can tote his machine over to the sheriff's station in twenty minutes. But I didn't know you had a suspect. What have you got on him?"

"Nothing."

Tony made a low noise thick with disapproval. "Why do I get the impression that Horseman is behind this?"

"Just get Les moving, Tony."

"I think the two of us better get together real soon and talk."

Everything inside her rebelled at the idea of going behind the sheriff's back. He might be a five-star jackass, but the position, if not the man, deserved her loyalty. She evaded Tony's suggestion by clarifying the details of what she needed done.

Ben emerged from the bedroom, buttoning a Western-style checked shirt and wearing those bright red boots. He said, "Promise not to dump everything on the floor."

"Clean and neat, Ben." She fetched a consent-to-search form from her car and filled in the blanks for his address, the make and license number of his car, and the location of his storage shed. He signed and handed over a ring of keys.

Deputy Kyle Green arrived. He looked vaguely confused, but then, he was young, and generally had an air of bemusement about him.

They began with the inside. Going through the two-room apartment, with an eye for finding a weapon, ammunition, or anything that might have belonged to Heather Labeau, didn't take long. Having conducted hundreds of searches, Nadine worked efficiently. The difficulty lay in having Ben watch her paw through his belongings.

She kept telling herself it was business; she kept feeling his eyes. Each time she glanced at him, he smiled at her. A private, for-her-eyes-only, I-think-

you're-attractive kind of smile. By the time she finished the apartment, she could barely breathe.

She told Ben to wait inside while they checked his
car and storage area.

"Are you all right?" Kyle asked her on the way to
the car.

No, she wasn't. Ben Jackson did funny things to her
head. Not to mention the rest of her body. She felt
sticky from the inside out.

They found nothing in the car. They searched the
storage shed, an eight-by-eight-foot concrete block
room filled with cartons and sports equipment.

"He doesn't even have a hunting rifle," Kyle said,
with a hint of disgust. He picked up a fishing rod and
eyed it critically before giving it an experimental cast.

"There's nothing here. Let's go."

While Nadine replaced the padlock on the door, a
woman approached. She was nearly as tall as Kyle, but
woefully thin. Her sparse hair was cut close to the
skull, emphasizing her gauntness. She wore dark sunglasses too large for her bony face.

"I know you," the woman said. "You're that po-
licewoman looking for the killer. You're much shorter
than you look in the newspaper."

Nadine exchanged a look with Kyle. He cocked back
his hat with a thumb. Nadine said, "Yes, ma'am."

"I saw you looking in Mr. Jackson's car."

"Are you his neighbor?"

The woman nodded sluggishly; Nadine wondered if
she were ill. The woman looked behind her. "He's
strange, you know. Sleeps all day, out all night. Kind
of like a vampire."

Hearing a strangled noise from Kyle, Nadine shot
him a sharp warning glance. No law officer could af-

ford to discourage a helpful citizen. She asked, "Do you know him well?"

"I see him." The woman clucked her tongue. "The streets aren't safe anymore. Criminals do what they want." She loosed a long, shuddering sigh. "And the cops never do anything. But you will. You're different. I have faith in you." Clutching her elbows, she executed an abrupt about-face and marched away, disappearing between the buildings.

Kyle snickered. Holding his forearm over his lower face, he said, "A vampire in Black Wells, aha!"

"Stop it."

The deputy gave a start, then blushed. "Sorry, ma'am."

"Fear isn't funny. Remember that."

He nodded. "So what do we do next?"

"I want you to drive Mr. Jackson to the station. I'll meet you there. Put him in the front seat, no cuffs."

Ben's neighbor made her uneasy. How many other good citizens were now locking doors they'd never locked before? How many trembled in fear over noises in the night? How many would like to see Ben, the stranger who kept strange hours, locked up so that they could feel safe again?

She headed back to the apartment. They had found no evidence connecting Ben to the murder. That, plus his alibi, was as black-and-white, cut-and-dried, as it could possibly get.

Ben would pass the polygraph. Then even Billy Joe would have to concede defeat and accept Ben's removal from the list of suspects.

Chapter Four

"Inconclusive?" Nadine exclaimed. "What the devil do you mean, inconclusive?"

Les Libby methodically fitted his polygraph machine into its case. Wires, neatly rolled and bound with twist ties, littered the tabletop. "I'm speaking English, Nadine."

Les turned a printout marked by red-and-green pen notations. The long strip of paper curled over both sides of the table. Nadine studied the black ink spikes and valleys. Seeing them all over the place, with very high highs and very low lows, dismayed her.

Les pointed out numbered sections marked in red. "Here are your key questions," he said. He shifted his finger to sections marked in green. "Here are the controls."

It couldn't be guilt. She'd talked to the man, studied him. Maybe a gifted sociopath could fool her with bald-faced lies, but Ben Jackson was no sociopath.

Les said, "He's high-strung and extremely intelligent. He thinks too much. That makes him a poor subject. We have a great big maybe here."

Nadine pictured Billy Joe jumping on the results like a fox on a mouse. Despite polygraph results being inadmissible as court evidence, despite the technology's involving more art than science, Billy Joe believed the results infallible. "Maybe he did or maybe he didn't? There's a big difference, Les. Which is it?"

Les contemplated his machine. He clucked his tongue and fingered his chin. "I hate sticking my neck out."

"I can't concentrate on finding the real killer if I have to waste my time badgering Ben. Am I wasting my time?"

He showed his palms. "He's close to the homicide. Upset about it." He pointed to a place on the print-out marked by high spikes. "I asked him if he was responsible for the death of Heather Labeau. He said no, but the response indicated a lie." He slid the paper on the table. "But when I asked him if he shot and killed Heather, he said no, and in my opinion he told the truth." He went over the printout question by question. Ben had reacted off the scale each time a question contained the word *responsible*.

Les concluded, "Apparently he feels guilt about the deaths, but I don't think he *is* guilty. That's the best answer I can give you."

His explanation relieved her. "I guess it would be odd if Ben didn't feel guilty." She watched Les for signs of confirmation. "He walked her to her car. He lapsed in his duties."

Les's nod relieved her even more. He shut the lid on the polygraph case and asked, "Do you have anything on Jackson?"

She told him about Karen Bates, the possible stalker, and the anonymous caller. She rolled the printout into a neat tube while she talked.

Les's soft whistle told her he found the similarities between the murders bizarre, too. "A stalker. Hmm… Any way to confirm it?"

"I'll find a way." She hoped. The inconclusive polygraph made her uneasy. A stalker could be Ben's version of the "bushy-haired stranger," a phantom he'd created to throw her off his trail. The anonymous call she'd received could have come from anybody, anywhere. It could have come from some concerned citizen in Atlanta who'd read a newspaper item. It could have come from Ben.

She denied the possibility as soon as she thought it. Ben was no killer.

Les patted his machine. "If you want Jackson in custody, this baby can't give him to you. Tony won't accept this as sufficient probable cause. Sorry."

Nadine didn't feel sorry in the least. She gave him a wan smile, then went to find Billy Joe.

The sheriff asked, "Well?"

"Inconclusive," she said. She unrolled the printout and showed him what Les had pointed out to her.

"False positive," Billy Joe mused, tapping his fingers on his big belly. "I bet what we got here is a psychopathic serial killer." He waggled his eyebrows.

Nadine managed to keep from braying laughter, but the effort made her throat hurt. She tapped her chest lightly with a fist. "We do not have a serial killer. Heather's death is similar to the Atlanta murder only superficially."

"Looks fishy to me. Can we arrest Jackson?"

"We don't have probable cause."

"I want you to check out the serial killer angle."

"This is not a serial killing."

"You sound pretty darned sure for somebody who keeps saying she don't know anything."

Nadine counted to ten, slowly, deliberately. Time to change the subject. "I need some help. I have a lot of checking around to do, a lot of calls and paperwork. Plus, I have other cases. Can I have Kyle?"

"He's barely got two years on the job."

"He's smart, and he knows how to follow instructions. It'd be a big help, Billy Joe." She paused, then added slowly, with emphasis, "I'd owe you one."

He lost some of his belligerence. "Yeah, I guess so. But no overtime for him. And you keep the hours down, too. I have to submit my budget in a few weeks."

How nice to know he had his priorities straight. She sighed. "I'll take Mr. Jackson home now."

She'd reached the door when Billy Joe stopped her. "You better not be wrong. Any more pretty blond ladies turn up dead, and I'll stick your hide up on my wall alongside Jackson's."

She found Ben in the deputies' break room. Sipping a soda from a can, he bounced one booted foot atop his knee while he talked to Kyle. Both men were eating leftover cookies from an office party celebrating a clerk's birthday.

Billy Joe's comment about the serial killer nagged her. Concerning the violence people committed against each other, nothing was impossible. Still, her father had always said, "Look to the obvious. Wild theories are fun, but nine times out of ten the answer is right under your nose." A stalker who killed innocent young women, then wrote letters to the police blaming Ben, definitely fitted into the wild-theory category.

Kyle noticed her, and she told him she wanted to speak to him in her office when she returned. As Kyle walked away, he told Ben, "Catfish have nothing on white bass, you dumb cracker. Not in catching, not in eating. This is bass country. Best not forget it."

Grinning, Ben arose. "Only a redneck can fail to appreciate the beauty of a cat," he said, then turned his attention on Nadine.

His welcoming smile chipped at her reserve. She allowed herself the luxury of appreciating the hard, clean lines of his face and the grace of his long-legged body. She even enjoyed the frank perusal he gave her in return. A little drama unfolded in the far reaches of her mind. Filmy, underscored by violin-thick music, seeing herself drift across the room and into his arms. She shook the image away as if she were clearing away smoke. "Have a seat," she said. "Finish your soda."

"How did I do?" He remained standing and brushed cookie crumbs off his shirt.

"You tell me." She fingered a pink carnation in the birthday bouquet. A big card read Lordy, Lordy, Julie's forty!

He studied her from the corner of his eye. "I told the truth."

"Why do you feel responsible for Heather's death?"

He flinched. "I don't." He looked away; his hand tightened on the soda can.

Quelling the urge to poke at his psyche, Nadine waited. She needed him to shred her last farfetched doubt without any help from her.

"That's a lie," he said, soft and weary. He dropped the can in the wastebasket. "I am responsible. Five minutes. That's all it would have taken to make sure she was safe." He looked at her, his expression taut and unhappy. "Same thing with Karen. But if that machine says I killed them, it's wrong."

She knew all about the kind of guilt he suffered. Her father had pulled the trigger to take his own life. But if she'd only paid more attention, she could have saved him. She lived with the guilt every day. Her heart went out to Ben. "A polygraph is never right or wrong, it just records physical reactions."

"I botched it."

She nodded. "You're a lousy test subject."

He shook his head while raking hair off his face with nervous darts of his hand. "So you don't trust me."

Criminals argued facts, logic, denial or explanations. Ben spoke of trust. "Let's put it this way. Unless you want to confess how you killed her inside of thirty seconds, without even breathing hard, you're cleared off the suspect list."

His smile appeared by fractions, cautiously.

She said, "You're cleared. Come on, I'll take you home." She walked out.

When she reached her car, Ben took her elbow in a gentle grip. "You honestly trust me?" He leaned close enough for her to catch a whiff of woodsy after-shave and to note the fine threading of crow's-feet at the corners of his eyes.

She said, "I haven't found a reason not to."

He pursed his lips, as if to whistle. "Cagey, very cagey. Did you go to school to learn how to talk like that?"

"I trust you, Ben."

"Good." He extended an arm, waved his hand in a tight circle, then produced a carnation, seemingly from thin air. "So about our dinner date," he said, offering the pink flower with a flourish.

She gawked at the carnation. "How—?"

He smiled, so relaxed and so utterly focused on her that her entire body went numb to the wind and clammy air. Drawing his face closer to hers, his eyelids lowering, he whispered, "It's magic, Sarge. Well?"

Good heavens, she thought in bewilderment, was he hypnotizing her? Her joints filled with oatmeal and her brain with mush. "Well...nothing. And it isn't magic. You swiped that from Julie's bouquet. Get in the car."

He stroked his knuckle down the side of her arm. "I've been busy trying to find a house and settling into my new job. I haven't learned much about the area. If dinner is out of the question, how about a guided tour? Think of it as public relations."

He was more than sassy, he was downright bold. How could she not like him? She took the flower and said, "I'll think about it." She backed up a hasty step and urged him into the car. His smile turned smug as he slid onto the seat.

Shaking the cobwebs out of her brain, she hurried around the car and behind the wheel. She started the engine. Unable to resist, she pressed the velvety carnation to her nose and inhaled its musky perfume before laying it on the dashboard. Maybe a little bit of magic, she conceded.

At his questioning look, she said, "I'm in the middle of a case. I can't make dates."

"You aren't allowed to eat?"

"I have kids." Wondering why she'd said that, she pulled out of the parking lot. Maybe because he was the first man since her divorce who'd been interested while she returned the interest—and that was a deep-down scary feeling. A whole lot scarier than when he'd been a suspect. "My ex-husband and I share custody. I see them whenever I have a chance."

"Boys or girls?"

Instead of turned off, he sounded genuinely interested. Why the devil did that make her feel so sexy? "Two boys. Did your wife have a job? If you don't mind me asking."

"I don't mind. She designed furniture." He pointed at a motel on the far side of the highway. "You know that heavy-duty can't-move-it-if-you-try stuff in motels? That was her specialty. She called it her revenge against traveling salesmen."

He spoke fondly, without sounding wrapped in his grief—which shot down yet another excuse for finding him unsuitable. "How long ago did you say she'd passed?" Nadine asked.

"I'm getting the distinct impression you want to control this conversation, Sarge. Is there a good reason you won't have dinner with me?"

Only an odd, disjointed fear that Ben Jackson owned the power to change her mind about some things, and she wasn't certain she was ready for that.

"Okay," he said, settling back on the seat and staring straight ahead. "How about dinner with me *and* your sons. Boys are easy. Bet I can bribe them to look the other way on occasion."

She fought a losing battle against a smile. In response, he looked far more encouraged than she wanted. Or maybe she wanted it too much.

In front of his apartment, she parked, but kept the motor running. She draped an arm over the back of the seat. "Let's try this line of talk in a few weeks," she said.

"I never argue with a lady who carries a gun." He stroked the back of her hand, his fingers warm and teasing. Tendrils of unabashed pleasure radiated up her arm. "But you keep this in mind. I'm a lot of fun, and you can't get too much of that." He gave her fingers a squeeze before he left the car.

She leaned over and rolled down the passenger window. "Hey, Ben."

He leaned over to see inside. "Yeah, Sarge."

"I do need to talk to you about that stalker."

"Come in," he said. "Have a cup of coffee. Or lunch."

Staring into his eyes, she wondered how she'd ever, for even a second, held a single doubt about his character. "I can't right now. But I'll call you."

His expression grew solemn, and he leaned on the car door. "Heather didn't deserve this. I want to help."

"You are helping. I appreciate it."

"If only I'd made sure she reached her van, this never would have happened."

She placed her hand over his. "The fault lies with her killer, not with you. Don't blame yourself."

"Easy for you to say."

She heard echoes of herself. *If only.* Heavy words to tote around. "I'll call you later, Ben."

"I'll be waiting with bated breath." He pushed away from the car and headed for his door.

BEN CALLED HER FIRST. He sounded mad enough to kill someone.

Alone in the office before 7:00 a.m., Nadine tried to make sense of Ben's nearly incoherent raving. Her thoughts fogged. Ben's yelling thudded against her ears. The only thing that made sense was his question: "Have you seen the newspaper?" He hung up with a bang. She went in search of a newspaper.

In tabloid style, unusual for the conservative *Bugle,* the headline read, Lightning-mouthed Shock Jock Struck Twice By Murder. Side-by-side photos showed Karen Bates and Heather Labeau, blond, beautiful and smiling. The lead read, "Murders in Atlanta and Black Wells share an eerie similarity, connected by the common thread of shock radio disc jockey, Benjamin Andrew Jackson..."

Incredulity growing, Nadine read the story. Very carefully, through the use of innuendo, it made Ben sound like a stone-cold killer. Nadine noticed the by-line belonged not to Janice, but to Daryl Wafflegate. An unfamiliar name.

She called the radio station and asked for Ben. The receptionist told her he'd left for the day. She tried Ben's apartment, but no one answered the telephone. She wondered if Ben was angry enough to do something stupid.

Oh, probably, she figured. She made a beeline for the *Bugle*'s office.

She intercepted Ben on the sidewalk in front of the newspaper office and stopped him before he could open the door. "Where do you think you're going?" she asked.

Hurt and confusion showed in his expression as he shook a newspaper. "Did you see this? It's slander!"

"No, it's libel. But you won't help yourself by going in there and starting a fight." She kept her hand firmly on the door and stared him down. He breathed heavily, glaring at her from under a thunderous brow. The wind whipping his hair increased his wild look.

"I'm not putting up with this, Sarge." He pulled his hand away from the door. He crossed his arms firmly over his chest. The newspaper crumpled between his clenched fingers. "Whose side are you on, anyway?"

"I'm on the side of justice."

"So where does that leave me?"

Maybe in a tar pit of trouble. Heather's murder had frightened the people of Black Wells. Violence wasn't a stranger in Ponce County, but Heather's death was different. It wasn't a crime of passion or the result of Heather's recklessness. Senseless and brutal, it could have happened to anyone. Ben's neighbor had been a fine example of public sentiment, speaking aloud of the fear many held in their hearts. Billy Joe Horseman wasn't the only person who would sacrifice Ben Jackson in order to feel safe again.

She said, "You need to trust me, Ben."

He shifted his weight from foot to foot. "This is like Atlanta all over again. Every time they printed a story about Karen, my name was in there. They never said straight out I was a killer, but it was always 'The police have no leads—ah, but Benjamin Andrew Jackson is still on the loose.' I'm not going through that again!"

"Did you talk to Wafflegate?"

"He came by my apartment, but I didn't talk to him. And he's been by the radio station, but—" he rattled the newspaper "—I notice he didn't print anything good anyone had to say. He's out to hang me, Sarge. I refuse to sit on my hands and let him do it."

She gave his forearm a squeeze. "So let's go in there, nice and calm. Maybe he has a lead on your stalker."

He gave a start, as if she'd pinched him. His jaw tightened.

"You said that in Atlanta the stalker contacted the press," she said. "Wafflegate got his information someplace, too." She led the way into the newspaper office.

She leaned her forearms on the tall wooden counter and leveled her gaze on Mary O'Connall, head editor and office manager. Nadine asked, "I see you gave the lead to Daryl Wafflegate. Where's Janice?"

Without turning her attention away from her computer, Mary said, "Her sister had an accident. Fell down a set of stairs. Janice took off for Austin yesterday."

A bad feeling swept through Nadine. "Where's Cole Duke?" The newspaper's publisher and owner considered it his civic duty to act as Ponce County's official gadfly. He did, however, run his newspaper responsibly.

"Cole's on vacation. Florida. Janice's sister broke her leg. Has two little ones to take care of. Thanks for asking."

Mary was the most contrary and uncooperative woman in Ponce County. They were traits in which she took inordinate pride. Who knew what kind of trouble she could cause without Cole or Janice to rein her in. "Very interesting story Daryl wrote. Is he around? I'd like to talk to him."

"It's news. Solid reporting." Mary put her nose nearly to her computer screen as she typed a few commands.

Nadine glanced at Ben. He had his temper under control, but dark vibes rolled off him, and he was clutching the edge of the counter as if at any moment he meant to launch himself over it. Nadine asked, "If he's not here, maybe you can answer a few questions. Where did Daryl get his information?"

"Ever hear of the First Amendment?" Mary shuffled a few papers before selecting one to hang from a clip attached to her monitor.

A slender man entered the office. He held a small box containing paper coffee cups and a waxy bag. He wore a fatigue jacket, but it hung open, showing jeans riding low on skinny hips. When he saw her and Ben, the whites showed around his eyes.

"Daryl," Nadine said. "Just the fella I want to see."

"Good morning, Sergeant Shell. Nice to see you again." His Adam's apple bobbed like a fishing float tugged by a bass. Nadine noticed his bulging eyes looked everywhere except at Ben. Interesting. She could almost have sworn the man acted guilty.

Now Mary turned and faced them. "You've got work to do, Daryl. You don't have time to waste jawing."

Daryl said, "It's all right, Mary. I'd like to find out how many women Jackson gets to kill before the sheriff's department shuts him down."

Air hissed between Ben's teeth. Nadine stepped between Ben and the reporter. "You've got a bad mouth on you, boy. You better watch it."

Daryl grinned as if he'd just scored the winning touchdown in a football game. "I just noticed something, Sergeant Shell. You're blond, reasonably young, not half-bad-looking. Will you be victim number three?''

"That does it," Ben growled, taking a threatening step toward the reporter.

Sweat popped on Daryl's forehead. "Hey, hey! You don't do your dirty work around witnesses. Remember?"

Nadine slammed a hand against Ben's chest, forcibly holding him back. His heartbeat thudded, and he breathed raggedly.

"That's enough," she said. She realized her mistake in allowing Ben to come in here. With Daryl intent on provoking him, she wouldn't blame Ben a bit if he took a swing at the man—but she would still have to arrest him.

Daryl said, "Why aren't the police investigating this angle?"

Using all her weight to hold Ben back, she said, "Let's talk about your sources."

Daryl flinched. Nadine's inner radar snapped on. Had her anonymous tipster called Daryl, as well?

Mary said, "You get nothing without a court order and there isn't a judge in this county who'd give it to you. Get out of here, Nadine. Daryl, you're needed in the back."

Daryl's tongue darted across his upper lip, and his eyes shifted. "My sources are all public. Everything is out there for anybody who wants to dig around."

He was lying. She saw it in his eyes, heard it in his voice—she smelled it. Nadine's innate curiosity roared to life, giving her a hunger so sharp it hurt.

"Public sources can be wrong," Ben said. He relaxed, a little, and jammed his hands in his pockets. "I was never a suspect in Karen Bates's murder. I'm not a suspect now." He looked to Nadine.

Nadine nodded. "You're barking up the wrong tree, Daryl. You better double-check your source."

Daryl's reaction surprised Nadine. She expected questions, or even an argument. Instead, he edged past her and Ben until he slipped around the counter. He kept grinning. Skepticism, and something else, burned in his eyes. To Nadine, it looked like hatred.

Before Daryl slipped through a doorway, he sent them a parting shot. "You better watch out, Sergeant Shell. You won't be the first woman charmed by a killer."

Ben swelled with anger, and Nadine urged him out the door. Only when he was safely on the sidewalk did she look back at Mary. "Where did Daryl come from? How long has he worked for this newspaper?"

"That's none of your business."

"I just made it my business. How did he find out about Atlanta?"

Mary rose from behind her desk. "You have no authority inside this office."

Nadine opened her mouth to inform Mary that she'd take any authority she wanted to, then decided against it. She'd catch Daryl later, when he didn't feel so safe, when he wasn't surrounded by the aroma of printer's ink and the power of the pen. When he didn't have Mary O'Connall watching his back.

In all likelihood, the reporter was merely aggressive, obnoxious, tactless and self-righteous. He carried the public's right to know as a banner and used it as an excuse for his lack of manners and common decency. He lied because his nature made him lie.

But other, darker possibilities existed. That flinch when she'd asked about his sources meant something. His lie about public sources meant something. He'd just made her list, and he'd stay there until she learned what those somethings meant.

Mulling over her thoughts, she joined Ben outside.

Hands planted on his hips, his hair ruffling in the breeze, Ben glowered at the quiet, tree-lined street. He said, "That cretin is right."

"What are you talking about?"

He touched her hair. "I'm the kiss of death, Sarge. You aren't safe with me."

Chapter Five

Ben and Nadine took a back corner booth inside a coffee shop. The waitress brought a pot of coffee. As she placed a small pitcher of milk on the table, she murmured a greeting to Nadine and eyed Ben the way she might look at a tiger in a paper cage.

Nadine waited until she was gone, then said, "Ben, listen to me. You are not the kiss of death. Don't let Wafflegate get to you."

"Don't pat me on the head and tell me not to worry, Sarge. It's finally sinking in. Those women are dead because of me. Not just because I'm forgetful. Not because of creeps in parking lots. *Me.* Somebody out there is killing women because he hates me."

"I'm not patting you on the head."

"You don't get it," Ben said. "It's not the newspaper stories. It's not my boss giving me funny looks and dropping not-so-subtle hints about my ratings."

She bit back a gasp. "Is your job in danger?"

"Probably. I won't go into a lot of explanation about ratings and advertisers, but the publicity hurts me. It hurts the station."

Her heart ached for him, but she had no answers.

"But that's not the point." His pale eyes blazed, and his fingers squeezed the coffee mug. "Jobs come, jobs go. If I get fired, it's not the end of the world. But I'm not letting another woman die because of me." He grabbed her hand with a fierceness that startled her. "I don't want you hurt." He forced a smile. "I'm growing rather fond of you."

Fond barely described how she felt about him. She entwined her fingers with his. The muscles in his jaw and the tension in his brow slowly eased, and the haunted look in his eyes faded.

She said, "For the sake of argument, let's say your stalker is a killer."

"That's easy. He's a killer." His attempt at humor fell flat, and both of them winced. He pulled his hand from hers and picked up a spoon. "Sorry."

"It all boils down to logistics. If your radio show caught his attention in the first place, then it makes sense he knew where you worked in Atlanta."

He nodded.

"But you've been working at KWBK for only a few months. How did he track you down so quickly?"

Ben sipped coffee. He fiddled with the spoon and shifted on the seat. "He could have asked one of my friends. Or called my parents and said he was a friend. He could have seen a notice in a newsletter."

"Good answer. But don't you think packing up his life in Atlanta and following you here is rather drastic?"

"Depends on how obsessed he is." He cocked a wry eyebrow. "If he killed two women, then my guess is, his obsession runs deep."

"*If* he killed them. That's a big if, Ben. I'm not convinced the cases are connected."

"They're identical."

"I haven't seen the case file from Atlanta, but from what the detective told me, the only similarities are the descriptions of the victims and you finding the bodies. That smacks of coincidence."

"Sounds identical to me."

"I know you're upset. You have every right to be. But I've been doing this a long time. Please trust me. Like my daddy always said, don't panic until it's necessary."

He slid his hands slowly across the table until they rested on either side of hers. Lightly, almost imperceptibly, he tapped her wrists with his thumbs. "I do trust you."

His long, muscular fingers and thick wrists intrigued her. Nice hands, strong hands. Her thoughts drifted, wondering if his deft and clever hands could live up to the promise of his sexy voice. She caught the waitress watching from across the small café. Lifting her cup to her lips, she took her hands out of his reach. "Then relax. The heat will die down. I'll find Heather's killer. Don't get all tangled up in blaming yourself."

His eyes narrowed. "You can look me straight in the eye and tell me I have nothing to worry about?"

She looked him straight in the eye. "You have nothing to worry about."

He leaned back and stroked his chin. "So what time are you breaking for dinner tonight?" Challenge tinged his words.

She laughed. "You are one stubborn fella."

"If that's the worst you can say about me, then I stand a pretty good chance. What time?"

"I'm taking my boys for pizza tonight."

"Your boys." He shook his head. "That's taking spitting in the face of danger too far."

She covered her eyes with a hand and laughed again. "I can't believe you're letting Wafflegate get to you like this." Along with the laughter, anger rose.

She liked Ben, and he liked her. She wanted to get to know him. She might be a cop, but nobody—and especially not small-minded, ignorant power trippers like Billy Joe and Wafflegate—had the right to dictate her feelings. She said, "I'm taking them to the new place that just opened over on College. The one with all the video games. Barkey's or Parkey's or whatever it's called."

"Barkley's."

"That's it. Around seven. I'm sure the boys will like you. That is, if you don't mind meeting them."

Her pager beeped before he could reply. She checked the readout: Deb Hall. "I need to make a call." She stood and placed three dollars on the table.

He slid out of the booth and picked up her jacket, holding it open for her arms. The intimacy of the gesture didn't escape her. Neither did the way he tugged her ponytail free of the collar. When she faced him again, he grinned crookedly.

She asked, "What?"

"Just an ironic thought."

Her eyes widened. "What?"

He looked startled. "You know, irony."

Ironic? She thought he'd said "erotic." Or maybe, hoped he'd said that. "Sorry. Misunderstood you. What's ironic?"

He indicated the narrow café with its plank-panel walls and photographs of fishermen interspersed with pieces of folksy craft work. "This town. I took the job at Wayback because Black Wells reminds me of Lawrence, Kansas. That's where I went to college and met my wife.''

She waited for him to continue, but he kept grinning at her. She figured irony was like a joke—either a person got it or didn't. ''I see,'' she said.

He tossed a pointed glance at the waitress, who apparently had nothing better to do than lean on the counter, watching them. ''I don't think you do, Sarge. Maybe I'll explain it later. In private.''

In private... The idea made her shivery.

BEN AND NADINE walked down the street toward his car. He darted glances at her, wanting to believe her. Knowing two murder victims was scary, but imagining the same person killed them both terrified him. Despite her assurances, even despite her vote of confidence in inviting him to join her and her children for dinner, Wafflegate's words gnawed at him.

Nadine didn't look much like Karen or Heather. Both of them had been model-slim, tall and leggy, and young. Karen's hair had been almost red; Heather's had been pale, nearly silvery. Nadine sported a mane of rich chestnut, shot through with bright streaks of burnished gold. She barely qualified as a blonde and had nothing to do with the radio station, either. Still...

As they passed the newspaper office, Nadine muttered, ''I just don't believe it.''

''What's that?''

''That was Deb on the phone, warning me that Billy Joe is on the warpath. Mary O'Connall called him to complain about me invading the sacred grounds of the newspaper.'' Her scowl turned into a tight smile. ''I don't know if you noticed, but Mary doesn't like me much. I busted her ex-husband for auto theft a few years back. She's still holding a grudge."

Going after the reporter had been stupid. Shame weighted his belly. "Are you in trouble?"

"Not enough that I care." She stopped beside his car and faced him. "I'm worried about you. This might turn nasty."

"You mean nastier."

"The only thing that'll pull Billy Joe off your trail is another suspect. I don't have one. Nothing solid, anyway. Bear with me, Ben, if you can."

"The sheriff considers me a suspect."

She stroked his upper arm. "Let's put it this way. It's politically expedient to cooperate with the press. Wafflegate's story fits Billy Joe's ideas." She looked back at the newspaper office, and her smile relaxed. "But don't worry. Wafflegate opened himself a big can of worms. It'll be interesting watching him trying to stuff them back in."

He touched her face, testing the softness of her cheek. Her eyes turned luminous as she leaned slightly against his fingertips. He said, "It sounds like Wafflegate is the one in trouble."

"He is if he has anything to do with the murder."

"You always get your man, huh?"

She touched his face, mirroring the path his fingers had taken. "I try. Now go home. Get some sleep." She stepped away from the Mustang.

He opened the car door, but hesitated. "You will be careful. I mean, just in case." Swathed in her coat, with the wind playing games with her ponytail, she looked tiny and delicate. With sunlight catching her hair, she looked very blond, too. Suddenly he wanted nothing more than to scoop her into his arms and haul her away someplace safe.

"I always am. See you later."

As she walked away, a current of doom dragged at him. Logic said she spoke the truth. He'd been in the wrong places, at the wrong times. The odds against it happening again were astronomical.

And his stalker was merely a legacy of his talk-radio days. Some lonely, embittered nut who blamed him for the woes of the world and got his jollies sending hate mail. Almost every disc jockey he knew had been plagued at one time or another by a weird fan. It went with the territory.

He glimpsed two young women driving past—their shining hair gleamed in the early-morning light. His real estate agent was a blonde, the receptionist at the radio station was a blonde, his favorite checkout clerk at the grocery store was a blonde. If blond hair marked a woman for death, then a lot of women were in trouble.

Finally he smiled and slid behind the wheel. He tossed a glare at the newspaper office. "To hell with you, Wafflegate. You don't scare me."

NADINE PICKED UP her sons from Fred's house. "I'm real sorry I can't have you over this weekend," she told them. "I have to work. You do understand, fellas, right?"

"Going for pizza is better, anyway," Dale said.

"'Sides," Rory said from the back seat, "Daddy's gonna take us to a hockey game up in Dallas. We're gonna spend the night with Aunt Sally."

Nadine wondered when Fred meant to inform her of that little tidbit—after she arrived to pick them up for the weekend? It amazed her that with parents who turned into the world's biggest jerks whenever they were stuck in the same room together, the boys were well behaved and well adjusted.

They arrived at Barkley's at a quarter after seven. Nadine searched the crowd of resigned-looking parents and rowdy kids for Ben's dark head. Not seeing him, she told herself it was for the best. She had no time for a relationship, anyway.

But reasoning with herself didn't ease the disappointment one little bit.

She gave Dale and Rory each a handful of quarters and turned them loose on the video games. She ordered pizza and a pitcher of soft drinks. She hoped the pizza was good enough to make up for the gaudy decor and nearly overwhelming whistles, bongs, pings and bells.

She took a booth where she could keep at least a partial eye on her boys. Elmer Fudd's voice said in her ear, "I want woast wabbit on my pizza."

Nadine turned on the plastic seat. Ben grinned at her. He looked relaxed and handsome in a brown leather bomber jacket over a dark blue shirt. Fingers of pleasure squeezed her heart.

"Mind if I join you, Sarge?"

"I do if you insist on eating rabbit on your pizza."

He slid onto the bench next to her. His well-rested appearance was an illusion. Up close she could see the lines of strain around his mouth and the weariness in his eyes. Weren't they a pair? They could start their own chapter of Insomniacs Anonymous.

"Where are your kids?"

As if summoned, Rory appeared at the side of the table. From somewhere he'd acquired a pair of oversize fluorescent green sunglasses, which were now perched on his head. Pinned to his shirt was a big yellow button that said Barkley Pizza, The Best Time in Town! He peered quizzically at Ben.

Her sons had never seen her before with a strange man. Discomfort rippled through Nadine. She said, "Ben, this is Rory. Son, this is my friend, Mr. Jackson."

Ben stuck out his hand, and in Ronald Reagan's voice said, "Well now, it does appear to me they grow everything big in Texas."

Nadine snickered behind her hand. Rory drew back a suspicious step and said, "He talks funny, Mama."

"Rory..."

Ben laughed. "He's right. No more funny stuff. Nice to meet you, Rory."

Still looking unsure, Rory slipped his small brown hand into Ben's large hand. He shook firmly, the way his father had taught him. He asked, "Are you Mama's boyfriend?"

"Rory!" She chewed her lower lip, wondering how to get out of this one.

Ben said, "We're just friends. Is that okay with you?"

Rory shrugged. "Mama, can I have another dollar? Please?"

She gave him a dollar, and he scampered away to join the noisy horde.

Ben said, "I don't think I impressed him."

"He's a tough audience." She poured him a cupful of soda from the plastic pitcher. "You really are quite the mimic. You ought to be on television."

Ben pulled a face and shook his head. "Can't go to work unshaved and wearing torn jeans on television." He gave her a sideways, searching look. "I like your hair down like that. You look nice." He stroked the end of a shoulder-length curl. "Pretty sweater, too."

Her stomach fluttered. She traced lines through the condensation on her cup. "Thanks. I—"

Dale rushed to the table and said, "It's not fair!"

You are not making a good impression, child, she thought hard at him. "What's not fair?"

"Rory got another dollar."

"He asked for it. And he said please." She lifted her eyebrows expectantly.

Dale's gaze fell on Ben. He looked between the man and his mother, then slid onto the opposite bench. He folded his hands on the tabletop. "Hello."

"Dale, this is Mr. Jackson."

"You two know each other, hmm?" He sounded so grown-up, Nadine wanted to laugh, but she didn't dare. Dale was going through a touchy stage, and didn't take teasing lightly. He looked Ben straight in the eye. "Are you marrying my mama?"

Nadine sank lower on the seat. Embarrassment encircled her throat with fire. To his credit, Ben acted as if it were a perfectly normal question. "Your mother and I only recently met. We're friends."

Dale accepted Ben's explanation with a nod. "Come Easter vacation, we're going to Colorado. Mama Crystal's gonna teach us how to ski. She says it snows a lot there. Do you know how to ski?"

"Only waterskiing. I've never been around much snow. But I hear it's fun."

"Betcha it is," Dale said. He gave no indication he meant to leave anytime soon. His big brown eyes never left Ben's face. Nadine wondered how other divorced mothers handled situations like this. Hollering at him was out of the question. Crawling under the table didn't seem too cool, either.

An announcement over the restaurant's intercom indicated her order was ready for pickup. Relieved, she told Dale to fetch his brother. Ben offered to help with the pizzas.

He said, "Nice boys."

"With big mouths. I'm sorry about that."

"No apology necessary." He nudged her arm. "You don't date much, do you?"

She looked around at the primary-colored walls and laughing, excited children. The place rated very low on the romantic-atmosphere scale. "Is this a date?"

"I guess that depends on whether or not you mean to arrest me anytime soon."

He spoke lightly, as if joking, but the dark look in his eyes said the comment was serious.

Embarrassment at how the sheriff and the press had treated Ben centered on her shoulders. Nadine concentrated on the order. The pizzas steamed, releasing a delicious aroma of hot cheese and pepperoni, making her stomach growl. She carried one, Ben carried the other. He picked up a handful of napkins on the way back to the booth.

The boys waited for them, their eyes bright with hunger. While Nadine put pizza slices on paper plates, Rory glared at Ben. "Is *he* eating with *us?*"

Dale elbowed his brother. "Shut up, stupid. He's Mama's boyfriend."

Nadine focused on her food.

Then Ben asked about the video games. To Dale's open delight and fascination, Ben knew all about Phason Fighters and Road Race 2001, and how to reach level five in Space Mutants—The Final Quest. After a while, even Rory joined the conversation. The boys devoured a whole pizza between them and drained the soft-drink pitcher. They raced off to burn their eyeballs again in the never-ending war against giant spiders and exploding bubbles from outer space.

Nadine said, "Impersonations. Magic tricks. Now video games?"

He showed his palms in a sheepish shrug. "Everyone has their little vices. So how did it go today, Sarge? Am I a suspect again?"

Nadine's smile faded. She toyed with a piece of crust. "Is that why you came tonight? To find out?" A slash of anger surprised her, and she examined it, wondering if she was angry because physically she felt lousy and her temper was on a short fuse. Or because in her heart she knew Ben wasn't a killer and she resented him presuming she thought he was.

Or worse, because her fantasy man had sprung to life even better than her imagination had dreamed— and all he saw in her was a cop.

He blew out a long breath. "I don't know why I said that. I'm sorry. I'm a little edgy, but that's no excuse for being a jerk. I am sorry."

She tore the pizza crust into tiny pills. "You wouldn't be here if you were a suspect."

Not even the bongs, whistles, bells and happy shrieks cut through the uncomfortable silence that hung over the table like a cloud.

Giving her a cautious sideways look, he finally said, "Uh, yeah, those are nice boys. They seem pretty straight. I guess your shared custody works."

Bless him for trying to reach neutral ground. "They live mostly with my ex-husband. He's remarried."

"To Mama Crystal."

Fred insisted the boys call his new wife Mama, but as much as they adored Crystal, they had only one mama. "Fred met her during our last separation. He married her the day after our divorce was final. She makes him happy, a skill that always eluded me."

"You don't like her."

She lifted a shoulder. "She's great with the kids, honest-to-God loves them like her own. She always looks great, her house is gorgeous, she's a terrific cook. Nice lady, never a harsh word about anybody."

Ben smiled. "And you hate her guts."

"Pretty much." She covered her eyes and laughed softly. "No, that's a lie. She's one of the few genuinely nice people in the world. She's everything I never could be."

"You're not so bad."

"You don't know me."

He touched his shoulder to hers in a gentle nudge. Eagerness shone in his eyes. "Not as much as I'd like to, but I like what I see so far. Smart, dedicated, cool in the most literal sense of the word. Beautiful. What's not to like?"

Don't look at his eyes, she warned herself. If she looked, she'd make a fool of herself. She'd drown. "You're some kind of smooth talker, Ben Jackson."

"Just the facts, ma'am," he said in a Sergeant Joe Friday voice. "Just the facts."

The evening passed too quickly. Ben walked the three of them to Nadine's car. She unlocked the doors and told the boys to get in and buckle up, then turned to Ben.

"I want to see you again," he said. "Tomorrow night? Dinner, dancing? Walk in the rain? Share a case of pneumonia?"

He *was* fun. "My schedule's crazy right now." In the crisp winter air, under the bright yellow glow of the parking-lot lights, his face looked as if it were chiseled from stone, all planes and angles, light and shadow. Such a beautiful man ought to be against the law.

"I'm flexible. Call me when you're free." He leaned an arm on the roof of her car. A casual gesture. Except it brought him so close his warm breath caressed her face. "I'm dying to know why you're driving this baby-I'm-so-bad car."

She laughed. He brought his hand to her face, tracing lightly the line of her jaw. That sobered her. She wanted him. She wanted his touch and she wanted to know why he laughed so easily and where he found so much resiliency and how he mustered so much good-humored energy. She wanted to know what thoughts played behind those quick, strong, kind eyes. She wanted to know what he looked like when he slept and how his skin smelled when it was hot. So much wanting all at once took her breath away. She said, "If I tell you about the car, you'll tell me about your boots?"

His fingers grew bolder, pressing gently against her cheek. "You don't like my boots?" He tenderly tucked strands of hair behind her ear. A shiver rippled through her and weakened her knees.

"They're uh . . . red."

His smile bloomed, tender and eager. "Then we definitely need to get together and share some deep, dark secrets. Come on, Sarge, say it. Say 'Yes, Ben, I'll give you a call when I have the time.' "

Oh, she wanted that, too. "When I have time."

He moved his head, having to bend down to reach her mouth with his. She had plenty of time to move away or deflect his advance. She should; encouraging him complicated her life and her job right now. But she lifted her face and he kissed her.

He tasted like pepperoni and summer; he smelled of warmth and promises. When he curled his arm around her shoulders and pulled her closer, she fitted herself against him, lost in the sheer rightness of feeling. Layers of winter clothing muffled the press of bodies, making her hungrier for the sensation of skin against skin.

A bright flash of light startled her.

Daryl Wafflegate stood by the rear bumper, his camera raised in preparation for another photograph.

Stunned, Nadine knew she was standing like a dumb, silly fool with her mouth hanging open and her shocked eyes wide. All she could do was stare.

The reporter asked, "Is this how Black Wells investigates a serial killer, Sergeant Shell? I don't think I've heard about interrogation techniques like this."

Ben lunged toward the reporter. Wafflegate loosed a high-pitched squeal, spun around, hit the car next to hers and went sprawling onto the asphalt. His camera bounced under the Chevelle. Nadine caught the back of Ben's jacket. Digging in her heels, she prevented him from touching the reporter.

"I'll kill him," Ben snarled.

"Ow— Ow!" Wafflegate scrambled to his feet. "He threatened me, Sergeant Shell! Arrest him."

"I ought to arrest you for harassment. What are you doing here?"

"I go where the stories are." Keeping a wary eye on Ben, he crouched and felt under the Chevelle.

She held up a hand as a warning for Ben to stay put. The last thing he needed was an assault charge. Arms crossed, she approached the reporter. "How did you know I'd be here, Daryl? Or are you tailing Ben?"

He scooted around the bumper, his shoes crunching gravel. His scraped hand left a streak of blood on the car. "Let me get the camera and I'll split."

In her peripheral vision, she saw Ben drop to a crouch. Gravel rattled, and he stood with the camera in his hands.

Daryl jumped to his feet and stretched out both arms, reaching for the camera. "Hey! That's the property of the *Bugle!*"

"The lens is busted," Ben said mildly, turning the camera this way and that. "Wonder if there's any internal damage?" To the accompaniment of Daryl groaning and beseeching Nadine to stop Ben, Ben opened the back of the camera and pulled out the film. He dangled it and said, "Can't see anything broken in here. You're in good shape, Wafflegate. A lens is easy to replace." He handed over the camera and the ruined film.

Nadine pressed a hand to her mouth to keep from laughing.

Wafflegate snatched the camera. "Go ahead and laugh, Sergeant Shell." Favoring his sore knees, he hobbled away. He called over his shoulder, "You won't think it's so funny when he sticks a gun in your face and pulls the trigger!"

Chuckling, Ben said, "Poor loser."

Nadine lost all urge to laugh. Only the boys, now round-eyed and wondering, with their faces pressed against the windows, kept her from running after Wafflegate.

The reporter's comment might have been merely stupid and hot-tempered. Or could it have been a slip, an exclamation of the truth? Nadine always guarded her case information carefully, allowing the press and public to know only what couldn't hurt her investigation or the county's prosecution of the criminal. So why did it seem as if Wafflegate, like the anonymous caller, knew Heather's assailant had shot her at point-blank range?

Chapter Six

Keeping one eye on traffic, Nadine looked Kyle Green up and down. A starchy collar squeezed his neck, and his tie was knotted too tight. His suit looked appropriate for a funeral. Her lips twitched. "It's a plain-clothes assignment, Kyle, not a dance."

His face reddened. She laughed softly, turning the car at an intersection.

"I don't mean to be nosy, ma'am." Kyle hefted the thick package that had arrived this morning from Atlanta. "But why are we taking this to show Ben?"

"The letters." A quick run-through of Atlanta's information had left her with a lingering case of queasiness. As much as she hated to admit Billy Joe might be right, she had to at least consider the possibility of a serial killer.

Like Heather's, Karen Bates's killer had neither robbed nor assaulted her. Atlanta's file also showed Karen had been killed by a .22-caliber automatic pistol. A .22 was a common weapon, cheap and easily obtainable. That both women were killed by a .22 might be a coincidence. Still, it left her with a chill that refused to abate.

"I don't think Ben has anything to do with it." Kyle spoke cautiously. "My money is on Reggie Hamilton." He tensed, as if expecting her to laugh at him.

No laughing matter. Reggie was her favorite suspect, too, but *only* because he'd been Heather's boyfriend. That sure wasn't evidence of anything. She asked, "Why do you say that?"

"Well, look at his alibi. Those boys are his buddies since grade school. All of them are hell-raisers. They could be lying."

"True."

"And everyone we talked to says Reggie and Heather fought a lot. Reggie wanted to get married, and she wanted to finish college. That's a motive."

"Possible." She turned into the parking lot of the apartments where Ben lived. Generic apartments, he'd called them, and she grinned to realize how apt was the description. He wanted to buy an old house with some acreage. She wondered what he'd think of the house she'd inherited from her father.

Kyle made noises with his tongue against his teeth and scowled. "And Cooter Hamilton has one of the biggest firearms collections in the county. Everybody knows it."

"Okay."

"She was shot in the face," he said firmly, then reddened. "I mean, uh, I've been studying about homicides."

Laughing, she parked the car. The young deputy's eagerness reminded her a lot of her own youth. "You're right. Lovers tend to aim for the face or head. But there's no evidence, and I can't crack Reggie's alibi. Believe me, I've tried." They got out of the car and walked to Ben's door.

Forewarned by a telephone call, Ben opened the door before she knocked. His welcoming smile enveloped her, made her feel floaty and airy inside. Her lips parted in remembrance of the feel of his kiss. Only Kyle's presence kept her from throwing herself into Ben's arms and kissing him senseless.

"'Morning," Ben said. "Come in, the coffee's ready." He looked at the packet in Kyle's hands, looked away, then looked again. His cheerfulness was a thin veneer. Nadine could almost smell his apprehension.

"Sorry I sounded so mysterious on the telephone, but I can explain better in person," she said.

"I don't mind the company." His eyes told her he didn't mind *her* company. He grinned at Kyle. "Nice suit, man."

Kyle jerked the tie loose and shoved it in his pocket.

Ben asked, "What have you got?" His hands trembled as he served the coffee.

Ben and Nadine sat on the couch, while Kyle took a chair. The deputy opened the packet and brought out a sheaf of typed papers.

"Atlanta sent most of their case file to me," Nadine said. "Ben, I have to be honest. The murders may be connected after all."

Ben swallowed convulsively.

"That's not definite. The similarities are circumstantial. There's no hard evidence."

"So what does it mean?"

Nadine shook her head. "At the moment, no telling. That's why I want you to look at these." She nodded curtly at Kyle. He handed over the letters sent anonymously to the Atlanta police.

Drinking coffee, Nadine watched Ben's face while he read. The letters were bizarre, typed single-spaced, with narrow margins and no paragraph breaks. In tone, they sounded like surveillance reports. What Ben ate, where he lived, where he shopped, what he bought, the people he talked to, his daily schedule and transcripts of, she believed, his radio-show patter. Interspersed amid the dry reporting were accusations of murder and pleas for the police to stop him before he killed again.

The crease between Ben's eyebrows deepened, and his lips tightened into a thin, puzzled line. When he lifted his head he looked shocked. "The police never told me about these. Why didn't they tell me?"

"Because as far as they were concerned, you weren't part of the investigation. They know you didn't kill Karen."

"But this guy followed me!"

Exactly what she didn't want to hear. She'd hoped Ben would call the letters nonsense, say the author didn't know what he was talking about. She asked, "Are these similar to the letters you received?"

He studied one for a moment. "They don't sound the same, but they look the same. The way they cover the page. Who are these other women I'm supposed to have killed? Charlene Wannamaker, Bonnie Jones, Eden White and Marla Oakes. Who are they?"

She took the packet from Kyle and searched for Detective Boyles's notes. She said, "Wannamaker was a victim of an accidental shooting. Jones was murdered in her bedroom by a rapist. Eden White was murdered at a convenience store. Oakes was a suicide. The only things they have in common are that all were in their twenties or early thirties, all were killed by gunfire—'' she met his eyes ''—and they were all blondes. Do any of those names mean anything to you?''

Ben shook his head. "This is too weird." He held up a sheet of paper. "This guy tracked me." A shudder gripped his entire body. "I can't believe the cops didn't at least warn me!"

Nadine found it difficult to believe, as well. "Well, a city as big as Atlanta probably has more criminals than Black Wells has residents. They're busy. And it's not a crime to send anonymous letters."

"What about following me? Making false accusations?"

"What's done is done. Let's worry about right now." She pulled out her notebook.

Kyle excused himself to go to the bathroom. As soon as he left the room, Nadine placed a hand on Ben's knee. She asked, "Are you all right?"

He shook his head. "Does anybody have any idea who this guy is?"

"Not a clue. But, Ben, understand this is a lead I have to follow up. It doesn't mean positively the murders were committed by the same person."

"What about Wafflegate? He followed us last night."

"Don't worry, I'm checking him out." A frustrated sigh escaped her. Only a court order could force a journalist to reveal a source. Ponce County judges rarely issued such orders. While Nadine cherished freedom of the press and understood the importance of restraining the law, it often made her job difficult.

Ben glanced at the bedroom doorway, then pressed a soulful kiss to her lips.

She smiled, but inside she worried. She had witnesses, no physical evidence connecting Ben to the murder, and Ben's cooperation. But Billy Joe's impatience boiled to dangerous levels. He could not or would not understand that solving a murder was far more complicated than grabbing a few clues, naming a suspect and crying, "Aha! He did it!" As soon as he laid eyes on the Atlanta file, he'd see only one thing: Ben.

NADINE PICKED UP the coffee cup, raised it to her lips, then set it down. Her stomach churned with acid sourness. More than too much coffee was giving her a bellyache. Muttering an oath, she slapped at the papers covering her kitchen table.

She'd been dead right about Billy Joe. Ever since he'd seen the Atlanta file he'd talked of nothing except a serial killer. *Ben* the serial killer.

He'd had the audacity to accuse her of being too conservative. He'd even hinted she'd lost her nerve and her faith in her finely honed instincts. He hadn't said it was because of her father's suicide, but he didn't need to say it aloud for her to know what he meant.

The sheriff had already made his daughter quit her job at the hotel. How long until he planted enough suspicion in her mind to make her waver about seeing Ben? Ralphie, the janitor, had confirmed Meg's story, but he hadn't been exact about the time Ben had taken to return to the station for the forgotten CDs. Ralphie alone couldn't clear Ben.

Would Billy Joe work on his daughter to change her story about Ben's alibi? That he *could,* Nadine didn't doubt in the slightest.

The telephone rang. At this hour, she expected a call from the office. Ben's rich voice surprised her.

"I'm sorry," he said. "I hate to wake you, but I have to talk to you." He sounded upset.

"I wasn't asleep. Where are you?"

"The station. I just taped a phone call, Sarge. You have to hear it. Can you come down?"

She looked at the clock: 3:45 a.m. "I'll be there as quick as I can."

As she dressed, excitement coursed through her. A taped telephone call. Proof of the stalker in Black Wells? She threaded a heavy belt through her jeans and attached her holster. She checked the load on her .38, fitted it into the holster, then dropped a speed loader in her coat pocket.

On the drive to the Algernon, she radioed the sheriff's dispatcher. She gave her destination and said she'd be out of radio range. If needed, she'd be on her pager.

The Algernon dominated Main Street. A driveway led to parking behind the hotel. The front parking lot was fan-shaped, landscaped with islands containing evergreens and low-growing shrubs. On one side it abutted the parking lot of the Oak Hill shopping center. The other side was an empty lot, where a sweetwater spring made it seem like a miniature Everglades swamp. Oak and cypress trees squeezed together, growing out of a profusion of hackberry and bamboo.

A battalion of killers could lie in wait there.

Hand on her gun butt, she hurried into the hotel. The desk clerk looked up, eyeing her curiously as she headed for the elevator. On the way up to the penthouse, she timed the elevator ride. It took less than thirty seconds.

The doors swished open, and Nadine stepped onto the carpet. The radio station at night was a completely different animal from the brightly lit place she'd seen during the day. The reception area was empty, all office doors were closed. A few light bulbs glowed grudgingly, illuminating a passage from the elevator to the reception area and down the short hallway to the transmission booth. Utter silence, so deep the air seemed thick, made her uneasy.

She drew a deep breath. "Hello?" No one answered. She cat-walked down the hallway.

Bright light shone through the glass door of the transmission booth. A man's shape moved. Nadine approached the door cautiously, craning her neck to peer inside. Ben was fiddling with dials and knobs on an impressive-looking control board.

She tapped on the door.

Ben beckoned her to come inside.

Nadine inched her way past stools stacked with newspapers, folders, tapes and compact discs. Electronic equipment, racks holding more tapes and compact discs, microphones and junk Nadine couldn't begin to identify crowded the narrow booth.

She whispered, "Are you alone?"

"The mike's off. You don't have to whisper." He leaned past her to see out the door. "Mark's usually in by now, but I haven't seen him yet. Hold on." He touched a finger to his lips, then turned to the control board.

Nadine watched in fascination as his hands seemed to do twenty things at once, flipping switches and twisting knobs.

He said, "Ah, the sultry Ms. Roberta Flack, the perfect way to rise and shine. Good morning, Black Wells, you're listening to KWBK, Wayback in the morning." He flicked a button, and the radio station's signature music began to play.

He grinned crookedly at her and offered her coffee. He had to squeeze past her to reach the carafe, on a shelf near the door. "Thanks for coming down, Sarge. I got freaked out."

The brush of his shoulders against her chest distracted her. He froze in the midst of searching for a clean cup and stared into her eyes.

Compelled by languorous desire, she stood on tiptoe to kiss him. He tasted fresh and moist, and deliciously of peppermint. The sudden dilation of his pupils, turning his eyes black and liquid-soft, weakened her knees.

He slid a hand under her hair, and the other around her waist. With exhilarating roughness, he had her back to the door and her breasts and belly pressed against his lean body. He kissed her, hard and hungry, his thrusting tongue as demanding as his hands. She clutched at his back, lost in the feel of him, lost in the scent and sensation turning her brain into wool. The satin sweetness of his lips intoxicated her.

He snapped back his head. His face was flushed, and his eyes were slightly glazed. She grinned dizzily, trying to pull him back.

"Sheesh, dead air." He waggled his eyebrows and turned to the microphone.

Half-afraid all of Ponce County could hear her pounding heart and ragged breathing, she listened to his banter. The way his radio persona snapped on, as if triggered by an internal switch, amused her. He introduced a series of songs, then turned to her again.

His old blue jeans did little to conceal his arousal, and his eyes gleamed with luminous excitement. Nadine's yearning knotted her up inside, sending tremors down her thighs. Struggling for at least a semblance of control, she asked, "How do you do that?"

He reached for her. "Another demonstration? If you insist—"

She fended him off. "I mean all those buttons." The booth felt stuffy and hot all of a sudden. She shrugged out of her coat. She glanced out the glass door at the empty hallway. "This is business, Ben. What about the phone call?"

He shook himself. His expressive face twisted in a struggle for control. He indicated a large reel-to-reel tape deck. "Oh, yeah, business. I tape callers while music or commercials are playing, then play back whatever is interesting. Listen to this." He punched a button.

Ben's voice said, "Wayback in the morning, name your pleasure."

A voice said, "You have to stop, Ben."

Every hair on Nadine's body jerked to attention, and her mouth went dry.

A rough, breathy noise crackled on the tape. Then the voice continued, "Don't kill her. I'm begging you. I've asked you and begged you to stop. I've tried everything, but there's too much blood on your hands. You have to stop."

"I never hurt anybody," Ben's voice said. "Who are you?"

"Put an end to the killings, or I'll have to stop you myself. I don't know what else to do. I have no other recourse. I have exhausted all my options. Do you understand me? The police won't stop you, the press won't stop you, you won't stop yourself. So I must."

"If this is a joke, it isn't funny—"

The voice cut him off. "She's too beautiful to die. All of them are too beautiful to die. I know you don't mean to do it. I know that. It's all a mistake, but it's wrong. I can't take any more death. You have to stop."

The caller hung up.

"Good Lord," Nadine breathed. She estimated the call had lasted about thirty seconds. Did the caller deliberately keep the calls short in order to prevent their being traced? She rubbed down the gooseflesh on her forearms.

Ben said, "Weird enough for you?"

"I've heard that voice before." At his surprised look, she added, "He tipped me off about Karen Bates's murder."

He pressed his arm against his stomach, as if protecting a tender spot.

Nadine fingered the panel of the tape recorder. "What time did he call?"

"About two minutes before I called you."

Nadine asked to hear the tape again. Ben rewound the tape, then gave her a set of headphones. He returned to the mike. The weird mechanical quality of the voice gave her the willies all over again. Nadine figured out how to rewind the tape and played it a third time.

She removed the headphones and waited until Ben was free. She asked, "How does he do that to his voice? A computer?"

"Probably an electronic voice changer."

"Electronic gizmos aren't my strong suit. How does it work?"

Ben squeezed past her and crouched. He pawed through a floor-level cabinet, finally bringing out a handful of catalogs. He sorted through them, selected one and searched through the pages. He showed her a picture of an innocuous-looking box.

"Sixty bucks and you can get sixteen different voices to amuse and amaze your friends. It hooks up to the phone like an answering machine." He flipped to another page and showed her a telephone. "Eighty-five bucks and you can get an entire telephone that does the same thing. Of course, someone with the know-how and a synthesizer can do special effects, too, but that's complicated and expensive."

"No way of telling if this is a local call, though. News could have traveled to Atlanta. If this guy is paying attention and read a newspaper story—"

Ben interrupted her. "This joker's in town."

"You don't know that."

He placed his hands on her shoulders and looked her in the eyes. "There's such a thing as too conservative, Sarge. You're the one he's saying is too beautiful to die. *You.*"

Chapter Seven

The glass door to the transmission booth opened, and a short man with a lion's mane of sandy hair grinned at Nadine. He said, "I knew it! Partying in the booth with a beautiful babe. Boy, get your name in the paper and you just go crazy—" His eyes widened in recognition of Nadine, and his smile dropped away. "Oh!"

"You remember Sergeant Shell, Mark," Ben said.

The deejay's face and ears turned red. "Uh, yeah. Sorry about the crack, ma'am...Officer...Sergeant... Just clowning around. Didn't mean..." He stared at her side arm. "I'm going to go make some coffee." He grabbed the carafe off the coffeemaker and backed out of the doorway.

Suspecting this would give Mark a month's worth of ladykiller jokes, Ben groaned. "Sorry. Mark is usually cool, but he has his moments."

Nadine patted his arm. "Happens all the time. Most civilians get nervous around cops."

A long, tawny curl had escaped her ponytail. He tested its heavy softness between his finger and thumb. "Is that why I break out in a sweat and forget my name whenever I'm around you?"

Her eyelids lowered, and the corners of her mouth tipped in a faint smile. He tugged her hair until she looked up at him. "This is crazy," Ben said. "Murder, lunatics, a deranged reporter. Think there's much hope for us?"

"I don't know," she said thoughtfully. "The timing could sure stand improvement. I don't think there can be an 'us' until I get this mess straightened out."

Exactly what he didn't want to hear. He turned back to the control board. He played taped commercials, then the station identification and promos, before commencing with the news. With his mouth on autopilot, his thoughts centered on Nadine. Something had happened inside him the first time he met her. Something confusing and wonderful and right.

Damn it, he was tired of being alone. Until he met Nadine Shell, with her peaceful air and beautiful smile, he hadn't known exactly how sick he was of aloneness. The idea of losing her before he really found her made him ache.

As Ben finished the news, Mark returned, bearing a pot of water and a handful of papers. He asked, "What's going on? More trouble?"

Ben sensed the deejay's willingness to protect his buddy from the bad old cop. It irritated him.

Mark said, "I don't know why y'all keep hassling Ben. He's a nice guy. He'd never hurt anybody."

"She's not hassling me, man." Ben wound the tape, then lifted it off the spindles.

"You ought to be checking out that little jerk Heather dated."

Ben could almost see Nadine's ears perk up. She stared at the deejay as Mark took over the microphone and went through his introductory routine. Ben urged her to leave the booth, but she held up a hand for him to wait.

When Mark put on music, Nadine asked, "Do you know Reggie Hamilton?"

"I don't know why the nicest girls always date the stupidest guys. Sure, his father is loaded, but Reggie's still a punk."

"When I talked to you before," Nadine said as she fished in her coat pocket and brought out a notebook, "you didn't mention this."

Mark shuffled his feet. "I didn't think about it. Hey, I'm not accusing anybody. But if I had to choose between Reggie and Ben, I'd put my money right on Reggie. He's a real scuz, know what I mean?"

"No, I don't. What do you mean?" She wrote rapidly in the notebook.

Mark acquired a trapped look, as if he were sorry he opened his mouth. Ben thought it served him right for his earlier smarting off.

Mark raked his fingers through his wild hair and shook it off his face. "Heather was a college student, carrying a megaheavy class load. She worked here because she needed the cash. She busted her tail trying to make it, but all he did was gripe because she ignored him."

"Did you witness any of this?"

"There was this time last...I don't know, November? That old pig of a van of hers was acting up. She called Reggie—I guess he was always fixing it for her. I opened it up just to see if it was a loose wire or something. Reggie showed up, and he started on her, complaining." Mark pulled a wry face, then shrugged. "But I guess she loved him."

Nadine asked, "Did you talk to her the morning she died?"

"For a little while. But she didn't say anything about Reggie."

Nadine turned to Ben. "You said you thought she'd been fighting with him."

"Mark is right. She used to make little comments. Things like she couldn't wait to get married, so she could stay barefoot and pregnant. That's as close as she ever got to sarcasm." A waste of time, he thought, even as he spoke. Reggie Hamilton hadn't killed Heather. That creep he'd caught on tape had killed her... and wanted to kill Nadine.

Mark nodded in agreement. "Sure sounds like a good motive to me. I bet Reggie did it."

"Motive doesn't cut it," she said, as if talking to herself. "Means and opportunity."

Ben exchanged a puzzled look with Mark. He didn't seem to have any more of an idea what Nadine meant than Ben did.

She said, "Thank you, Mark. If you remember anything else, please call me." She gave him a business card. "Even if it seems insignificant, call me anyway."

Mark turned back to the microphone. Ben and Nadine left the booth.

Ben asked, "What did you mean, means and opportunity?" He led her to a sound-recording room. He picked up a clipboard to log in his programming notes. "I thought you figured out who had a good motive and then..." Then what? He supposed investigating a crime was more difficult than it appeared on the surface.

"Motive," she said with a soft laugh. "Juries love motives, but it's not much help to me right now. What I have to do is put the murder weapon in the killer's hands. That's means. Then I have to place him at the scene of the crime. That's opportunity. Without at least one of those, I can't even get a warrant."

He tossed a pointed look at the tape reel. "That's the killer, Sarge. Right there."

"I can't arrest a voice on a tape, Ben. Have you ever received a phone call like this before?"

"That's the first time. How can you take this so calmly? He threatened you."

"I've been threatened before."

Dissatisfied with her off-the-cuff reply, he finished his log and his program notes. While he worked, Nadine lounged on the chair, staring distantly. He asked, "Where do you go, Sarge?"

She looked up at him. "What?"

"It's weird how you blank out sometimes."

"Just thinking."

"Deep thoughts, no doubt. Hey, how about we sneak out of here and grab some breakfast?"

She rubbed a hand over the tape reel, and a line appeared between her eyebrows. "I shouldn't..."

He hated seeing the indecision on her face. Or was that fear? Fear of being seen with him. "You're sexy when you talk mean," he said.

She released a surprised, husky laugh. "I am not mean."

Her laugh eased him, allowed him to pretend everything would be all right.

"I suppose breakfast wouldn't hurt." She looked at her watch. "But I want to reenact the crime first. Will you help me?"

Her mild request struck him like a fist slamming into his gut. Reenact? Relive finding a dead woman in the parking lot? Was she out of her mind?

"I'll level with you. Every time a major crime is committed, the nuts crawl out of the woodwork. I've received dozens of phone calls about Heather. Psychics. People telling me their neighbors are acting suspiciously. I've got people saying Heather's parents had her insured, so they killed her. Everyone wants in on the act." She held up the tape. "This caller might be your stalker. It's the same person who called me before. It could also be a nut who read the story in the newspaper and is trying to scare you."

"You can't pass this off so lightly."

She took his hand and squeezed his fingers. "I'm not. But I deal in facts, hard evidence. I don't play Sherlock Holmes. I don't use my deductive powers to come up with brilliant solutions. A murder is more like a smashed Christmas ornament. I pick up all the little teeny-weeny slivers and fit them back together. I work it one piece at a time."

She studied the tape reel front and back, as if looking at it allowed her to hear the words it contained. "This means something, but I don't know what yet. Especially since I'm still unsure whether Heather was a random victim or a target. That's why I want to do the reenactment."

Ben thrust his hands through his hair. He swallowed the nasty taste growing in his throat, but it bubbled up again, along with images of Heather lying so still on the dirty asphalt. He dug in his pocket for a peppermint and offered it to Nadine. When she shook her head, he unwrapped it and popped it in his mouth.

He shifted from foot to foot, seeking comfort in the familiar recording room, with its padded walls and its hint of locker room odor. Calm and cool, Nadine waited for his decision, her self-confidence heightened by the big revolver hanging on her slim hip.

Make a decision. Play the victim or stand up for himself. His choice. "All right, Sarge, I'll work for my breakfast. Let's go."

"Thank you," she said, her eyes searching his.

He couldn't help it; he gathered her soft, sweet body into his arms and kissed her. The womanly taste of her intoxicated him. Longing for her, all of her, gave him a pleasurable ache. Her feminine scent, her small hands inching up his neck so that her fingers could play delicately through his hair—he drowned in the feel of her.

She pulled back. Her lips glistened, fuller than before, fascinating. "We shouldn't," she whispered.

"Sorry." He wasn't sorry in the least, but he released her.

She looked away. "Don't say that. I'm not sorry. It's just..."

"You feel it, too."

She nodded and sighed; the sound held a hopeless, helpless note that made Ben's chest grow tight. "Kind of odd, isn't it?" she said. "I never thought I'd meet anybody like you. Especially under these circumstances."

"I sure never dreamed up a scenario like this one," he said. "I had in mind something more along the lines of candlelight, soft music and fine cuisine."

"After I solve the case," she said.

He didn't have any choice except to agree.

She stopped at the receptionist's desk and called Kyle. "Rise and shine, boy. We have work to do. Meet me in the parking lot of the Algernon." There was a pause. "Do you want to sleep or be an investigator?"

She grinned as she hung up the telephone. "Kyle's going to make a top-notch cop someday."

They rode the elevator down in silence. Nadine had that intense, thoughtful look on her face. Her concentration impressed Ben. Why it turned him on, he couldn't imagine, but it did that, too.

Once outside, they stopped just outside the reach of the lights spilling through the big plate-glass doors. Hunched into his coat, his hands jammed in his pockets, Ben considered—for about the thousandth time—the wisdom of purchasing gloves. Black Wells wasn't that much colder than Atlanta, but the wind blew incessantly. Add to that the pressure of a lowering cold front, and it felt like Antarctica.

Nadine inhaled deeply. "It'll rain soon. Got a good storm coming in." She cocked her head, studying his car. "Why do you park in front? Why not in back with the other employees?"

"Convenience. The hotel-staff shift changes are at ten-thirty at night and four-thirty in the morning. That's pretty close to my schedule, and I don't like fighting for space. I always try to park under a light. So what do we do?" Studying the perfect sculpting of her profile, he knew what he wanted to do. It had nothing to do with murder.

"Do you remember hearing any cars that morning? Or a car door?"

He couldn't recall anything.

She looked up at the inky sky. "Sound really travels in weather like this."

"What are you looking for?"

She pointed to the street. "It's so quiet. So empty. The street is well lit, and so is the parking lot. If anyone had been out there, just passing by, I'm sure you would have noticed."

He looked around, his gaze finally settling on the junglelike growth in the lot next door. "Not if the killer was hiding in the trees."

Nadine nodded. "That's what I'm thinking." She headed toward her car at a fast walk. Ben trotted to catch up and fell into step beside her. She had her coat tucked behind her holster, freeing the butt of her gun.

She put the tape reel in her car and brought out a small flashlight and a stopwatch on a neck cord.

A van pulled into the parking lot. Nadine raised a hand in greeting, and the van stopped beside them. Ben recognized the young deputy, Kyle Green. Hunched into a sheepskin coat, he smiled sleepily at them.

Nadine pointed. "Put your van in that slot."

Kyle's van wasn't the same model or color as Heather's, but seeing it parked in the same place where Heather had parked hers chilled Ben to the bone.

"Okay, fellas, back to the hotel." The three of them went back to the hotel entrance. Nadine said, "Ben, walk to the place where you remembered you forgot the CDs."

He walked approximately forty feet from the curb. "I think about here."

"Come back," she said. "Okay, Kyle, you play Heather, and Ben—"

"Why can't he play the girl?"

She gave the deputy a dry look. "Ben, try to approximate the timing. Can you remember if you and

Heather were talking? See if you can give me about how loud you were. Go.'' She started the timer.

Kyle said, "Spooky out here. Quiet. I bet nobody can see us from inside the hotel.''

"You can say that again." Ben stopped where he thought he'd stopped the morning of the murder. "We didn't have much to say. She kept walking." He headed back to the hotel.

Nadine stopped the watch. "Thirty-nine seconds. What do you think, Kyle?''

"It matches what Meg Horseman said.''

She gave the stopwatch to Kyle and the flashlight and notebook to Ben. "Give me your car keys, Kyle. I'll play Heather. You fellas record the times.''

Starting from the spot where Heather and Ben had separated, she strolled across the parking lot. Ben watched the sway of her hips under her coat, filling in from memory the way her blue jeans fit snugly over her derriere.

At the van, she said, "Time.''

Fifty-nine seconds. Ben recorded the time in the notebook. Then she did it again. Over and over she reenacted Heather's last walk. Ben finally figured out the pattern of her role-playing. She played a girl in a hurry to get home; a girl with her keys in her hand and ready; a girl who had to dig around in her purse and find her keys, then zipped her purse closed. The fastest time she made, at a brisk walk with her keys out, was thirty-six seconds. The longest time was one minute and thirty seconds.

Nadine looked toward the trees. The eastern sky was beginning to lighten. The trees were black, an impenetrable wall.

She said, "Kyle, this van is about the same size as Heather's, isn't it?" She raised a hand to touch the roof.

"Pretty close," the deputy replied.

Nadine held the key in the door lock. "Standing like this, she couldn't have seen the trees. Are you a runner, Ben?"

He patted his flat stomach. "Enough to keep hamburgers at bay. Why?"

She glanced at his boots. "Just to prove a point, I want you to go back to where you and Heather separated. Then I want you to run as fast as you can without making any noise. I'll turn around when I hear you."

He didn't like this part, but did it anyway. He hadn't taken three good running steps when Nadine turned around. He slowed to a jog. When he reached her, she was grinning.

"What's so funny?"

"Those darned red boots." She nudged his boot with her toe. "If you'd run up on her, she would have had her back to the van."

Kyle snickered. "I been wondering about those boots. You couldn't have bought those in Texas."

Grinning, Ben said, "They're a present from my dear old mother."

"Hush," Nadine said. "Let's say it's a creep, a stranger. He's cruising, looking for a victim. He checks out parking lots in the hopes of finding a lone woman. He's hiding in the trees. He sees Ben go back into the hotel, but once Ben gets inside, the killer has only...seventy seconds at the most to sneak up on Heather."

Kyle said, "But how does he know Ben is going to be inside for any length of time?"

"He doesn't. There was no sign of a struggle, and no sign she tried to run. One reason could be that Heather never heard her attacker. Kyle, go to the edge of the trees. When I say start, get back here as fast as you can without making any noise."

They played out the scenario. Nadine checked the time, but shook her head. "Nope, I heard you."

"It's the shoes, ma'am." He lifted a foot to show them a dark cowboy boot gleaming with polish. "A killer on the prowl wouldn't have worn these."

She thrust the stopwatch at Ben. "I'm wearing sneakers. Start when I tell you."

She jogged to the edge of the trees. Despite the pearling sky and the parking-lot lights, she melded into the brushy shadows. She called, "Start the timer."

When she reached the van, Ben said, "I heard you on the gravel."

"Me too," Kyle said.

They repeated the exercise several times. Nadine finally concluded, "Unless that sucker can float, no way could he have gotten from the trees to here in less than seventy seconds without her hearing him."

"Maybe she did hear him," Kyle said. "We really can't know, can we?"

She took his car key again. "A woman alone. A dark parking lot. She puts the key in the door, unlocks it." Her forehead wrinkled in a puzzled frown. "Unlocks it." Leaving the keys dangling, she stepped back, searched the ground, took another step. "The autopsy showed she died before she hit the ground. Instantaneous. If she'd been running, she might have taken a step or two before she actually fell, but I think . . ."

She dropped to a crouch, studied the van door a few seconds, scooted forward, then lay down.

As she imitated the position of the body, Ben thought his heart might explode. Despite Nadine's crisp, businesslike attitude, despite Kyle's jokes and complaints about the hour and the cold, despite Ben's willingness to help, her lying there so deathlike broke his nerve. His blood turned to ice; nausea churned his belly. He shouted, "Get up!" He grabbed her arm and jerked her to her feet. "Don't do that!"

Eyes wide, lips parted, she breathed raggedly through her mouth.

Ben dropped his hold and backed away. Holding up his hands, he said, "Don't . . . do . . . that. . . ."

"Oh, Ben, I am so sorry."

He thought he might vomit. Two women had died— young, healthy, laughing, decent human beings dead, when a few minutes of diligence on his part could have saved their lives. He turned on his heel and strode to his car. He leaned both hands on the hood and breathed deeply until the nausea faded.

Ashamed of herself, Nadine watched him. The only way she could function was by distancing herself emotionally from the pain and suffering of victims. But forgetting Ben was a victim, too, was inexcusable.

Kyle said, "You kind of spooked me. You looked just like Heather." His voice held accusation.

"He'll be all right." She hoped. "At least this proves something." She pointed to the rear of the van. "If he came from there, surprising her, she would have taken off running. But she was facing the van when she fell. Over here."

Kyle said, "Then he came around the front of the van?"

She went back to the door. "If she saw him and saw the gun, she'd have backed up." She glanced at the spot where the body had lain. "The night of the murder, there'd been a lodge party in the hotel. When she came to work, the parking lot was pretty full, which is why she parked here." She pointed up at the light post. "Under the light. But the following morning, the parking lot was mostly empty. There was no place between here and the hotel where the killer could have hidden. No way he could have gotten behind her."

She stepped back to where Heather had been standing when she was shot. "Why was Heather here? Facing the van?"

Ben joined them. He had his hands shoved in his pockets and his shoulders hunched. His grim expression threatened to break Nadine's heart.

She said, "I'm sorry, Ben. Lost my head."

"Just tell me this is helping."

Nadine nodded. "It helps." She looked from man to man. "I'm sure now that Heather had to know the person who shot her."

Chapter Eight

"I wonder exactly how big Lake Huxley is ..." Nadine said in a musing tone.

Nadine and Ben sat at a table inside a café in downtown Black Wells. Ben liked the café, which had its own bakery that was now releasing clouds of spice-and-yeast aromas. Nestled between a bookstore and a gift shop, the café occupied the street floor of a three-story brick building.

Assailed by the scent of fresh-baked goods, Ben ordered steak, eggs, biscuits and gravy. "You think Reggie dropped the gun in the lake?"

"If I were Reggie," Nadine said, "that's where I would drop it. And I can just hear Billy Joe if I ask him for funding to drag the lake bottom." She waved a hand. "No more talking about the case. I shouldn't be discussing it with you."

He wished she would. Thinking Reggie Hamilton had killed Heather didn't please him. But it meant no deranged stalker. It meant no string of killings in Ben's name. It meant Nadine wasn't endangered.

She filled her coffee cup to the rim with milk and stirred it idly. "I've been meaning to ask. What's a shock jock?"

Ben nearly choked on his coffee. A reputation is like a tattoo, his father liked to say. Make sure you can live with it *before* you get it. "A talk-radio host whose sole purpose is to offend listeners."

"Is that what you did in your wicked days?"

Memories made him wince. "Let's put it this way. I had a gift for running my mouth, but not the maturity to control it. I'm not very proud of my talk-radio days."

"I can't imagine you being awful."

He appreciated her vote of confidence. "I didn't start out that way. In the beginning, my motto was 'Anything for a laugh.' More comedy than controversy. Harassing callers for the fun of it. Political parodies and lampoons. Or I'd interview people who had string collections, or cats in their will. Fun stuff."

"What happened? If you don't mind my asking."

He did and didn't mind. Nadine's calm acceptance encouraged him, though. "I had personal problems, and all the anger came out on the air. I thought I was being deep and righteous. Instead I was just...mean. Snide, sarcastic, cruel." Her thoughtful silence encouraged him even more.

"When Cathy and I married, we were poor. Hand-to-mouth kind of poor. She worked in a factory at barely above minimum wage, and I wasn't doing much better. But it wasn't bad." Nostalgia for the good old bad old days made him smile. "We didn't have money, but we didn't really care, either. Life was great."

"So what changed?" Nadine asked.

"Our careers took off. She got into design, and I was making a name for myself."

"So you and Cathy had marital problems, and that was reflected in your radio show?"

"I loved my wife. Truly, deeply, and maybe that's why it was so hard. I didn't want a divorce. I don't think she did, either."

Picking apart a cinnamon roll, Nadine waited.

"Looking back, it seems stupid. I wanted kids—she didn't."

Nadine waited a beat. "That's it?"

"You know what they say about acorns and mighty oaks. It got out of hand. A constant running battle. We made stupid demands, put ultimatums on each other." He thought for a moment. "Things like, I refused to buy a house unless she agreed to have a baby. Then she said, unless I had a vasectomy, no more sex. We're talking major juvenile behavior here."

"And this anger and frustration came out while you were on the air," Nadine said.

"In spades. My diatribes against women's libbers were classics, which didn't help any. Cathy accepted a contract with a manufacturer in Augusta. She kept an apartment in Augusta and came home on the weekends. It was a great career move for her, but I played it like a declaration of war. I acted like a jackass. I'd spend all week missing her, then on the weekends all we did was fight."

Appetite sated, he pushed his plate away. "Her death almost killed me. All the compromises I could have made. All the time I could have at least tried to see her point of view. I really lost sight of her as a person. What a waste."

"I'm so sorry, Ben." She patted his hand.

"Still think I'm not awful?"

"I botched my marriage, too." Stirring her coffee, she chuckled. Sweet music, low and unaffected. Her thick eyelashes swept downward, and the corners of her mouth tipped in a faint, Madonna-mysterious smile. Her understanding and acceptance shone through.

He asked, "So what happened with you and Fred?"

She lifted a shoulder. "I'm a cop."

He waited a moment. "That's it?"

"That covers a multitude of sins." She cast him a slow, considering look. "I'm not in a position to make life easy for any man."

"Um, that sounds challenging."

"Not a challenge. A warning."

"I like challenge better." He looked around the café and listened to the faint murmuring talk coming from behind the door to the kitchen. This wasn't the intimate, candlelit romantic evening he'd envisioned, but it wasn't bad. "Besides, I get the feeling you're a lot like me. I go on the radio, and I'm a character actor. I go home, and I'm just Ben."

"Being an investigator is a little different."

"I like different. I like you." That funny flush bloomed on her throat. It tickled him. Her voice might be cool and her demeanor calm, but there wasn't a thing she could do to control the flush.

"So we're both sadder but wiser," he said.

"Let's hope so." She cocked her head and frowned. Clinking her spoon lightly against the cup, she said, "You stopped doing talk radio after Cathy died?"

"I lost my taste for annoying people." He used his fork to push crumbs around his plate. "That's not true. I was ashamed of myself. Losing her like that shocked me. It made me look at myself and see what I was doing. You might say I grew up. I quit radio altogether for a while. I was going to chuck it all and grow peaches with my father."

She nodded. "Did you return to the same station?"

"Different station. I got a job with WLBO." He straightened on the chair. "Are we back to the case again?"

Her eyes widened. Touching her fingers to her mouth, she murmured, "I'm sorry, I—"

"It's okay." He saluted her with his coffee cup. "The sooner you solve the murder, the sooner I can start raving about the stars in your eyes and plotting ways to get you alone, where I can smell your hair."

She flushed again, and he laughed.

She said, "If the stalker is involved—*if*—I'm wondering if it started because of your talk-radio show, or afterward."

A young couple entered the café. The man was skinny and serious-looking, the woman was young and fresh. Students. The young man slid into a booth. The girl stopped in midstep and stared openmouthed at Ben. She held a newspaper under her arm. She shook herself and quickly joined her companion. In a loud whisper, she said, "Oh my gosh, it's him! That disc jockey! And he's got another blond lady with him."

Tightness invaded Ben's chest. The bakery smells seemed too sweet and thick all of a sudden. As the young woman and her companion whispered and stared, Ben's face grew hot.

He dug in his pocket, pulled out a few bills and flung them on the table. Staring straight ahead, he stalked out of the café.

Nadine followed. She looked at the girl; the girl returned her perusal with an expression of mixed apprehension and awe.

Nadine found Ben standing in front of a newspaper dispenser. Hands in his pockets, shoulders slumped, he stared at the *Bugle*'s headline: Fair Maidens, Fair Game. An array of photographs illustrated the story: Karen Bates, Heather Labeau, Catherine Jackson, Bonnie Jones, Eden White and Marla Oakes—all of them blond, beautiful and smiling. Ben's photograph dominated the lineup. It depicted him in a studio setting, with a pair of headphones on.

Ben whispered, "Who do they think they are?" His voice cracked.

Nadine bought a paper and shook it open. Daryl Wafflegate had dug up the story of Cathy Jackson's death on a lonely Georgia back road. He implied Ben had escaped prosecution in his wife's death because of his semicelebrity status. It mentioned Ben and Cathy maintaining separate residences, and that Ben had collected insurance after her death. Wafflegate had listed the similarities between Karen Bates's murder and Heather's murder—including the fact that a .22-caliber semiautomatic handgun had been used. He gave short synopses of the lives and deaths of Bonnie, Eden and Marla.

Nausea made Nadine light-headed.

Moisture shone in Ben's eyes, now gone red. Head down, he walked down the sidewalk.

Nadine hurried after him and caught his elbow. He stopped, but stared beyond her.

"I'm not taking this," Ben said.

She hooked her arm with his. "Oh, Ben, I'm so sorry." Her scalp tightened with the force of her fury. Detective Hoyt Boyles in Atlanta had stated, without a doubt, that Ben had had nothing to do with any of the Atlanta murders. So where had Wafflegate gotten his information?

"Cathy died in a car accident. A stupid, senseless accident."

"What's this about insurance?"

Suspicion flashed through his eyes, and he pulled away from her.

"I don't want to ask, but as soon as Billy Joe sees me, he'll want answers."

He barked a low, mirthless laugh. "Is that what this is all about? I pour out my heart so you can take notes?"

That hurt. A lot. "That's not it. But the situation—"

"Situation?" He threw up his hands and backed away. "I lose my wife and some hotshot reporter accuses me of murder, and you call that a situation? I call it harassment. And I call it pretty damned shabby of you to pretend friendship when all you want is a way to hang me!"

If he'd punched her, the pain couldn't have been worse. He snatched the newspaper from her shock-numbed hand and shredded it, tearing and ripping it, letting the pieces drift into the gutter. *He doesn't mean it,* she told herself, *he's angry and frustrated and woefully hurt. He doesn't mean it.*

He glared at her as if she were his vilest enemy.

She said, "Ben, I'm not pretending anything. I am your friend. I—"

"Nobody's using Cathy like that! You're not using me, either!" He swiped the air in disgust and strode away.

"Ben!"

He hunched his shoulders and kept walking.

HAND RAISED, Nadine stood in front of Ben's apartment door. He'd been so hurt and angry. In a roundabout way, his anger strengthened her belief in him. Only the innocent were angered by accusations; the guilty resorted to reason.

But she hated having him angry at her.

Taking a deep breath, she knocked. Then knocked again. When he finally answered, he opened the door about three inches. His eyelids were puffy; beard stubble shadowed his jaw.

"Well, look who's here," he said, his voice raw and thick. "Come to ask if I regret killing my wife?"

She supposed she deserved that one. "May I come in?"

"Might as well." He opened the door and stepped aside. "Wouldn't want you to hurt yourself kicking in the door."

"You're in a mood."

He raked both hands through his hair, leaving it sticking up in spikes. He wore only jeans; she wished he'd put on a shirt. She'd never realized how provocatively sexy a man's bare belly could be. The sight of his, flat and hard-muscled, with the barest whisper of a vertical line of dark hair, distracted her.

He pushed the door shut with his foot. Avoiding her eyes, he headed for the kitchen. Face lowered, he slammed through the motions of starting a pot of coffee. He pulled orange juice from the refrigerator and drank from the carton.

Feeling invisible and very much unwanted, Nadine slid onto a stool. She rested her folded arms atop the counter. "I need to talk to you."

Without turning around to face her, he said, "Got a microphone in your bra? Shall I speak up?" He all but threw the juice back in the fridge.

"I'm not here to interrogate you."

He stomped around the counter. His eyes were two topazes, cold and glittering. His mouth twisted, and muscles leapt in his jaw. He loomed over her, chest heaving, his nostrils flaring with each heavy draw of breath. The smell of brewing coffee hung like fog, and the only sound was the soft chugging of the machine and the rattling drip into the pot. She leaned back, he leaned closer.

Fury seethed from his pores. Nadine's scalp prickled, and her heartbeat pulsed in her ears.

"Aren't you afraid to come here alone?" he said. "Or is the SWAT team waiting outside the door, ready to kick it in if you scream?"

"Ben..."

They nearly touched nose to nose. "You're using me! Coming on to me, pretending to be my friend! You think I'm some sort of monster. Are you scared of me? Are you? Aren't you scared I'll kill you, too?" He caught her ponytail and held the end in front of her eyes. "Pretty blond ladies don't last long around me!"

"Stop it," she said. "You don't mean any of it, so just...stop."

He flinched as if she'd tossed icy water in his face. Muttering obscenities, he sank onto a stool and slumped over the counter with his face on his hands.

For a bleak, painful moment, she hated being a cop. Shame at doing this to him washed over her.

She slid a hand over his shoulder and across the sharp jut of his shoulder blade. Rubbing a slow circle on his smooth back, she said, "I am your friend. I'd never use you like that."

"I didn't kill my wife," he said, his voice muffled. "It was a stupid, senseless accident. She was tired, she fell asleep at the wheel. I loved her. You can't come in here accusing me of killing her. I won't accept that."

Her inadequacy depressed her. Other people were good at offering sympathy and soothing wounded tempers. Other people knew how to pull out the right words and speak them in the right tone of voice. She said, "I'm sorry." Weak, pitiful words.

He lifted his head enough to see her out of one eye.

She asked, "Are you through yelling at me?" She smoothed her palm down the long length of his spine.

"I ought to throw you out. I ought to hire a lawyer with enough clout to get you people off my back."

You people. She withdrew her hand and turned on the stool, facing the door. How easy it would be if he were still her fantasy man, only a voice on the radio. A fantasy couldn't ache and bleed, wouldn't have dark, wild, wounded eyes.

Facing her, he placed both hands on her knee. "But as mad as I am, I think if I did that, I'd never see you again. I'd rather go to jail. Stupid, huh?"

Hope fluttered in her breast. "I know you didn't kill anyone, Ben."

Considering what she wanted to do, what she needed to do, she chewed her lower lip. By helping Ben, she risked her job and reputation. If she couldn't find the killer, this town—her town—would scorn her, shun her, despise her for the rest of her life.

She looked him straight in the eye and said, "Ben, the sheriff is doing his damnedest to get a warrant for your arrest. I think it's best if you leave town."

For a long time, he watched the coffeemaker work. Then he laughed, mirthlessly, low in his throat.

"I spent hours with the sheriff and the county prosecutor this morning," she said. "Now the prosecutor, Tony Zaccaro, he's a good man. A sensible fella. But the sheriff... I'm sure he's the one who leaked all that information to the press. He denies it, of course, but he wants you bad. He's convinced you're a serial killer."

"I see."

"He doesn't believe there's a stalker. He thinks you made up that tape. He thinks you wrote the letters to the Atlanta police." Pent-up emotions made her throat ache. "He thinks you're seducing me in order to get away with murder."

"Sounds like he has a pretty good case against me."

"Don't be flippant, Ben. This is serious. He made his daughter quit working at the hotel. He's scaring her with all this talk about a serial killer. He's making her think she's wrong about the time. If she changes her story, you could be arrested."

"Justice in Black Wells," he said, expressionless. "You figure a lynch mob is the next step?"

She went rigid on the stool. "I argued until I was blue in the face." She poked his chest with a stiff finger, but she wanted to grab him and scream at him. "I put my job on the line for you."

"At least you *have* a job." He glanced at her.

She gasped. "You got fired?"

"Not technically." He hopped off the stool and went around the counter to the kitchen. "The station owner called me. All the bad press has his advertisers spooked. He asked me to take an unpaid leave until this matter is straightened out." He poured two cups of coffee.

Nadine bit down on the urge to cuss.

He added milk to her coffee before he gave it to her. "Sorry I yelled at you. You're the only decent thing in my life right now, and..."

"I understand."

His chest rose and fell. "Stop being so understanding. I feel rotten enough as it is."

"Go ahead and apologize, then. I'll shut up."

He cupped her cheek in one large hand, and she leaned into it and closed her eyes. "But I'm not running away, Sarge. I can't believe you said that."

She had a tad of trouble believing it herself. Her father might applaud from the grave, but everyone else would be horrified. "Go visit your family. Take a cruise. Let the noise die down."

"Run, with my tail tucked between my legs." He rested his elbows on the counter, cradling the steaming cup in both hands. His voice was calm, but his eyes weren't. They bored into hers with a dark intensity that made her insides squirm. "You're a woman of contradictions, Sergeant Nadine Shell. Soft-spoken, but firm. Big, sweet eyes, but more guts than a grizzly bear. I still can't quite reconcile your telling me to run from the law."

"I'm not telling you to run." She brushed a piece of lint off her knee. "Exactly."

"Exactly what, then? I haven't hurt anybody, and I haven't done anything wrong. I refuse to act as if I have."

"Ben—"

"What if the killer is that creep who's stalking me? What if he hurts someone else?" He shook his head forcefully. "I'm not a bodyguard, but dark parking lots, that time of the morning . . . I should have made sure they were safe."

"You couldn't have known."

A soft, pained laugh emerged from his mouth. "But I did. Especially in Atlanta. Attacks against women are so commonplace most don't even make the news. Black Wells feels safe, but I know better. Creeps and crazies are everywhere. My stupidity got those women killed. And you want me to run?"

Focused on the pale surface of her coffee, she mulled over his argument. She finally conceded that if he did slip quietly out of town, Billy Joe would leap on that as a sure sign of guilt.

What a bogged-down, drowned-in-mud, stinking mess.

"There's another reason I won't leave," he said.

"What's that?"

"This." He took her cup from her hands, then gathered her into his arms.

She lifted her face to his. He touched her with a kiss filled with such poignant, questioning desire that she wanted to cry.

He drew back and whispered, "Will you visit me in prison, Sarge?"

"Oh, Ben. I won't let them railroad you. I won't." She slid an arm around his neck and raised off the stool to meet him. She clung to his mouth, reveling in the muscular thrust of his tongue. Desire flared with white heat, radiating throughout her body and leaving quivering weakness in its wake.

The voice of reason told her this was wrong. She was crossing the line. She was sacrificing professionalism for the damp sweetness of his mouth and the hard press of his belly against hers. When he slipped a hand under her sweater and wrought a delicious path of heat up her spine, she shut off the inner voice as if she were turning off a radio. Nothing mattered except Ben.

He pressed fervent kisses to her cheeks and eyelids. Then he froze. His entire body went taut.

He said, "I can't do things halfway." His rich voice had gone low and thick. His eyes gleamed with sultry fire.

Aching for his touch, needing the full length of his body against hers, she nodded. "I have the same problem myself."

He put his hands on either side of her face. "You are," he whispered, "the most beautiful woman I have ever known."

His smile appeared. That all-encompassing smile she'd fallen in love with. He pressed a tender kiss to her lips. A shivery little kiss that tangled her up inside and drained all the strength from her limbs.

The onrush of feelings and mind-numbing sensations frightened her. Suddenly *he* frightened her. So much feeling all at once scared her down to her toes.

"I'm, uh, not sure about this," she said. Her throat went funny on her, and she cleared it.

"I know," he said, sliding his hands down her throat to her shoulders.

She searched his eyes, and saw in them a reflection of her fears. In their golden depths, she saw uncertainty on the brink, and the vulnerability of a soul ensnared.

Reason said to stop, back away, put a stop to this. Her father's voice spoke louder: Life's too uncertain for procrastinating.

Then Ben tipped her chin and kissed her throat in the tender hollow. The erotic scent of shampoo and maleness filled her.

And she was lost.

Dancing slowly, tangled luxuriously arm in arm and legs around legs, they reached the bedroom. They shed clothing as if it were autumn leaves scattering to the winds. Gripped in shyness, she attempted to cover her breasts, but he caught her hands. An expression of pure wonder made his face glow.

"You're really built," he murmured. "For a cop." Snappy retorts failed her completely—especially when he lowered his mouth to a love-hungry breast and showed her exactly how good he could be.

His lovemaking was like his laugh, exuberant and earthy and totally unaffected. Her response embarrassed her as much as it delighted her. She wanted to devour him, possess every square inch of supple, tawny skin, kiss everything that could be kissed, drown in the dark, healthy masculinity of his scent and die fulfilled underneath the brawny press of his body.

Afterward, she lay depleted, unable to move as she curled against his side with her head against the crook of his shoulder. Her fears came creeping back like naughty children. Had he found her lacking? Had it been her making those strange, mindless, embarrassing noises? What could he really think about a woman who made love like that in the middle of the day? How could she feel this much and survive?

Would he ever want to see her again?

Had she completely lost her mind?

"Hey, Sarge?" he asked. He combed his fingers through her hair.

"Yes, Ben?"

"Does this mean you'll go out to dinner with me now?"

She raised up on her elbow and looked at his face. His smile looked so goofily satisfied, how could she not love him forever?

Her pager squealed.

He gave a start and asked, "What was that?"

"That's for me." After wrapping her now chilly body in a blanket, she found her pager. She recognized her office number. Kyle, she thought. "Can I use your phone?"

"Darlin'," he said in a Rhett Butler drawl that threatened to reduce her to a gibbering puddle, "you can have anything your sweet li'l ol' heart desires."

Chapter Nine

"We've got big troubles," Kyle told Nadine.

An arrest warrant for Ben, she thought, and slumped against the desk. Billy Joe just stuck his nose in a hornet's nest. It'd be *High Noon* in Black Wells after she got through with him....

"I just got off the phone with Detective Boyles in Atlanta." The deputy whistled. "He's spitting mad!"

She clutched the blanket tighter around her breasts. "Detective Boyles?"

"He says he got a call from Mr. Zaccaro's office. The way he hears it, the sheriff is saying the Atlanta police are too stupid to solve their own cases." Kyle paused. "He's saying he's sorry as hell he sent his case info to us."

Nadine passed a hand over her eyes. If the murders of Karen and Heather were related, then she desperately needed Atlanta's cooperation. *Billy Joe, what have you* done?

She asked, "Did he say anything about the other women mentioned in the *Bugle?*"

"And how!"

Nadine looked up and met Ben's worried eyes. He mouthed a question, asking what was wrong. She held up a hand to put him off.

Kyle said, "He's really mad about that." He whistled. "Should've heard the names he was calling the sheriff and Wafflegate. I sure can't repeat them."

"Kyle, what did he say about the women?"

"He said Catherine Jackson was closed as an accident, and there's no way they're reopening it as a homicide." Paper rattled in the background. "Marla Oakes was a suicide. He's got strong suspects in the murders of Bonnie Jones and Eden White, and he doesn't appreciate Sheriff Horseman backstabbing him like this. I tried to calm him down, ma'am, but all he did was yell."

Nadine groaned. The Atlanta homicide division was under no obligation even to talk to her, much less cooperate with her investigation. "Did he say anything about their lab sending the shell casings from Karen's homicide to our lab for comparison?"

"No, ma'am. It never came up."

"I'll call him, try to unruffle his feathers. But I have to talk to Tony first." She checked her watch. "Stand by. I'll call you back." She hung up, but kept a hand on the telephone.

"What's the matter, Sarge?" He offered her a cup of coffee, already doctored with milk. A flush of love still warmed his skin.

Looking at Ben hurt her heart. His expressive face and gentle eyes—how could people think he'd ever harm anyone? Ghostly sensations of his tender hands raised gooseflesh on her arms. A lover without guile, a man of honest emotions. That innate honesty made him refuse to run. Pure, unadulterated fear climbed from her belly and lodged in her chest.

She said, "The sheriff's out of control. He believes all that stuff Wafflegate printed, and Atlanta is madder than the devil. Wafflegate's story makes them look bad."

Ben's forehead creased.

She dialed Tony Zaccaro's number. When the prosecutor came on the line, she said, "I hear you talked to Atlanta."

Tony made a huffy noise. "I needed some confirmation."

"We need to get together for some damage control, Tony. I've got a strong possibility that Atlanta's case is related to ours. I can't afford to lose their cooperation."

"I have a meeting in twenty minutes. So let's get together tomorrow morning, my office. Eight-thirty?"

"Fine."

"Nadine, I'm sorry. I tried to be diplomatic, but as soon as I told Detective Boyles about the newspaper story, he lost it. He's taking Billy Joe's antics as a slap in the face."

"I'm not blaming you. See you in the morning."

She hung up, then called Kyle back. She told him they were meeting with the county prosecutor at his office in Tucker and asked him to bring every file they had concerning Heather's murder.

She returned to the bedroom. Seated on the bed, she smoothed her hands over the sheets. The scent of their lovemaking tied her up in knots and mingled with the fear inside her.

Ben asked, "Is there anything I can do?"

The concern in his voice threatened to undo her. When he sat beside her and wrapped an arm around her shoulders, she sagged against him.

She fingered the silky black hair on his arm. Depression dragged at her, and the prospect of getting dressed seemed like a mighty chore. What she really wanted, needed, was to lie down with him, go to sleep, and forget everything that had happened. Everything, that is, except Ben.

But she couldn't stop thinking about what *might* happen. She couldn't help thinking Ben's problems originated with her. Her inability to play politics with Billy Joe, her failure to find the killer, her failure to protect Ben from the *Bugle*'s smear campaign.

She hadn't been able to save her own father—what conceit blinded her into thinking she could save Ben?

"Sarge?"

"I have to go." She struggled out of his arms and gathered her clothing. Unable to show him her guilty face, she dressed quickly.

Ben wrapped his arms around her from behind. "It can't be that serious. Even if I'm arrested, there's no evidence. Right? I'll get a lawyer. They can't convict me of anything."

He'd walk away a free man, all right. After he spent every penny he owned for legal fees. After his name, reputation and self-esteem had been dragged through the mire. After the system had chewed him up and ripped the last iota of innocence and trust from his soul.

He tightened his hold on her. "Don't look so sad." He kissed the top of her head and nuzzled her hair.

Breaking away from his embrace, she pulled her sweater over her head. "I'm all right. Just a little tired, that's all. I'll get this mess straightened out. Some-how."

"I've never seen you like this. You look like the weight of the world is smashing you down. Is there something you're not telling me?"

She forced a smile. "All right, I'll tell you. After my daddy retired, Billy Joe ran unopposed and won. He went through law school, but he never practiced law. He never took the bar exam, but he wants to be Perry Mason. He's in way over his head."

She placed a hand on his warm, bare shoulder and looked him straight in the eye. "Billy Joe has big plans. First sheriff, then maybe the state senate, then who knows where? Catching a serial killer will look good on his résumé."

"But you said—"

"And that's not all, Ben. See, Billy Joe is scared to death I'll run against him in the next election. Hanging you is a way to get rid of me." She shied away from the bed. "I can't believe I did this! He can use me against you now."

"Use you? Not a chance." He reached for her, but she twisted out of his reach. He clamped his hands on his hips, and his brow lowered.

"I have to go. Promise me to take care. If you think anything weird is going on, call me right away." She headed for the door.

"Sarge . . ."

"I have to go."

"Don't run out on me."

She said, "I'm not running. Lay low, okay?"

"Yeah, yeah," he muttered, and helped her into her coat. Then he clamped his hand on the door, above her head, to keep her from opening it. "Let's get to-gether tonight."

"We can't." *Go,* she told herself. Every passing second made it that much harder to leave.

"Someplace private."

Don't do this, she pleaded silently. "You don't un-derstand," she said.

"Then explain it to me." Hurt roughened his voice and pulled his mouth into a frown. "The sheriff is a blowhard, but he can't have that much power."

She leaned her back against the door and sighed. "If his daughter changes her story, he'll order me to make an arrest. If I refuse, he'll pull me off the case." The bedroom drew her eye. She'd been so foolishly happy, only a few minutes ago. "Our relationship taints my investigation. If he suspects we're involved, he can use that against you."

Ben drew his head aside. "He'll say you tampered with evidence or something?"

"I wouldn't put it past him." She hugged herself. "I've messed up, gotten involved. I thought it was okay, but it's not okay."

He smiled hesitantly, suspiciously. "I'm not scared of the sheriff. The only thing that scares me is some nut making threats against you."

She stared helplessly at the bedroom door. "He's not corrupt, he's—he's stupid. He doesn't know what he's doing. He only *thinks* he knows. And that scares the devil out of me." She spun on her heel and grabbed the doorknob. "I have to go."

He moved as if to kiss her, but she turned her head away.

Barely moving his lips, he said, "I don't do one-night stands, Sarge."

"This doesn't have anything to do with how I feel about you. I'm trying to keep you out of prison."

"I'm innocent. I'm not going to prison."

He didn't understand. Maybe he couldn't understand—maybe he'd never understand. "Innocent has nothing to do with it," she said harshly. "Billy Joe wants your head. My bouncing around in bed with you could hand it to him."

He flinched, breaking her heart. Still, he reached for her, and she couldn't make herself pull away. He trailed a finger over her cheek. "I'm not scared of him, Sarge." He pulled away and jammed his hands in his back pockets. He traced a slow circle on the floor with his toe. "Go on, then."

"Take care."

He stared at the floor.

Knowing she'd handled their conversation badly, but unable to fix it, she left his apartment. She looked back once, hoping to see him in the doorway or watching her out of the window.

He wasn't there.

NADINE TURNED onto Tank River Road. It was twenty miles to Tucker, an easy drive up and down the live oak-dotted hills and cattle pastures. A building storm made her uneasy. Glowering clouds blotted out the sun. With as much rain as they had been having the past few weeks, the saturated ground wouldn't hold much more moisture and flooding was a distinct possibility.

Kyle Green put a steadying hand on his coffee cup. "Ma'am?"

"What is it?" Ben weighed on her mind. She'd never felt so incompetent in her life. She knew she'd hurt his feelings, but how could she explain the complexities and subtleties of the power plays inside the sheriff's office? Or how she'd set herself up for questions about her ethics, her morals and her dedication to her job? Making love to Ben had been the sweetest experience in her life—and her biggest mistake.

"I took the case files home with me last night."

She darted a glance at the back seat, where two sturdy cardboard boxes held all their notes, reports and photographs on Heather's murder. "Did you forget something? I don't want to be late."

"No, ma'am." He unbuckled his seat belt and twisted over the seat to reach into a box. "I was reading last night. Studying."

Don't give yourself a case of insomnia, she thought. One of them dragging around like the walking dead was too much. Of course, only one of them was falling in love with the man Billy Joe wanted to see stuffed and mounted. "Yeah? Did you find something?"

He settled back onto the seat and buckled up. He showed her a cassette tape. She guessed it was the copy of the tape Ben had made at the radio station. He also held a sheet of yellow paper.

"I don't know if I found anything," Kyle said. "But I noticed something in those letters Atlanta got. It's on the tape, too."

"What's that?"

"Don't laugh."

"Kyle, I didn't bring you in on this assignment for comic relief. What did you find?"

"It sounds weird." He scowled at the sheet of paper as he pushed the tape into the cassette player.

The mechanical voice said, "You have to stop, Ben... Don't kill her. I'm begging you. I've asked you and begged you to stop. I've tried everything, but there's too much blood on your hands."

Kyle stopped the tape. "Notice how he says, 'there's too much blood on your hands'? In one of the letters, he says—" he ran his finger down the paper "—'The blood never goes away. It stains forever. I see it every time I see his hands.' And six times where he says stop him before he kills again."

"Okay? Where are you leading?"

"Suppose you shift it from third person into first person? If you put 'me' in every place where he says 'him,' then what it says is, stop me before I kill again."

Nadine tapped her fingers on the steering wheel. Just like Lady Macbeth, with her bloodstained hands and guilty heart.

"I know this isn't a solid lead," Kyle said. "I'm not real sure what to make of it. Do you think it means anything?"

"Everything means something, but darned if I know what it is."

It began to rain, and turned dark enough for her to put on the headlights. Lightning arced from cloud to cloud. Several cars passed her, a few of them driving way too fast for the road condition. As tempting as it was to place the bubble on the dash to put the fear of God in them, she didn't have time to fool with traffic stops.

They reached the portion of the road called the roller coaster. This stretch of road drove arrow-straight over a series of hills that, taken at the right speed, could send a car airborne.

Kyle took his coffee mug off the dashboard. "Do you know Professor Packwell over at the university?" he asked. "I took some psych classes from him.

He's real interested in criminal psychology. He might be able to work up a profile for us. What if we have a serial killer who's transferred his guilt onto Ben? Is that too crazy?''

"Blood on his hands, huh? You might be on to something." She shook her head. "But we're not sure we have a serial killer. Except for Karen and Heather, all the women the letter writer claims Ben killed were killed by someone else or accidentally."

"Maybe this guy sees news stories and thinks because they all look alike that Ben killed them." He paused. "One of the women was a suicide. Say this guy was close to the victim, and he can't accept a suicide verdict. So instead he looks for a killer. Ben could have said something on the radio that set this guy off."

Playing devil's advocate, Nadine said, "Interesting, *but*. According to Detective Boyles, all the women listed in the letters died in the three years before Ben's wife died. The stalker didn't start harassing Ben until after his wife died."

Frowning, Kyle hemmed and hawed as he studied his notes. Then he snapped his fingers. "What if Mrs. Jackson's death was the trigger? What if this guy only suspected Ben, then somehow the accident proved him right?"

Behind Kyle's handsome young face lurked a tricky mind. Nadine was impressed by his reasoning, and said so.

Beaming, Kyle said, "So this guy goes after Ben. But the police don't investigate. In the nut's eyes, Ben is getting away with murder. So he kills Karen to frame Ben."

She said, "Then Ben gets away with it again. So he kills Heather."

"Exactly!"

"I still can't see how a stranger got so close to Heather. She was a healthy girl, alert. A stranger would have scared the devil out of her."

"Sure," Kyle said. "But what if he'd been hiding around the front of the van, watching her. She started to open the door, and he steps out. There's a few seconds where she's surprised, not thinking. A few seconds where he could have shot her."

"That's possible, I suppose, but wouldn't she have backed away? Toward the rear of the van?"

Kyle unbuckled his seat belt again. When he twisted, coffee sloshed from his mug onto his lap. He jumped and swiped at the paper. It fluttered to the floor. Bending over to reach it, he said, "Ben's stalker ran some impressive surveillance in Atlanta. He could have done the same thing here." Muttering, he groped for the paper and tried to balance his coffee at the same time. "He could have known Ben and Heather's schedule."

"How could he know Ben would forget the CDs?"

Twisting awkwardly, he said, "Maybe he meant to kill Ben, too—"

The passenger window exploded.

Hot needles peppered Nadine's face. She flinched, jerked and slammed on the brakes, all at the same time. Tires squealed as they lost traction on the wet road and the Chevelle went into a spin. A stand of brushy live oaks loomed like a wall. Nadine's mind went into automatic. Hit the brakes, accommodate the spin, steer with it—stop the damned car!

The brakes responded, leaving the Chevelle with the right front tire in a narrow ditch and the bumper only inches from the trees. The car now faced toward Black Wells.

Kyle grunted. He'd been thrown off the seat, and was now wedged under the dashboard. Coffee dropped off his collar and face.

Nadine slowly turned her head and stared at the burst side window. A rock? A bird? A freakishly violent change in air pressure? Under her locked fingers, the steering wheel thrummed in time to the grumbling engine. Sluggish seconds crunched by.

"What happened?" Kyle asked.

"I don't know. Sorry about that." She grasped his shoulder and helped him back onto the seat. "I never had a window blow out before." At seeing him unharmed, she loosed a long breath. "Good thing there weren't any cars around. Are you sure you're all right?"

Kyle shook himself and reached for the seat belt. He suddenly froze, staring out the windshield. "Oh, no, he's got a—"

A sharp, firecracker-like pop made Nadine jump.

"Gun!" Kyle ducked and grabbed at his side arm.

Atop the hill, almost concealed by thick, wet brush, a shape moved. Nadine threw herself across Kyle and unsnapped her holster. Her foot slipped off the clutch, and the Chevelle lurched against the trees and died. Kyle fumbled for the radio mike. She reached over him and opened the passenger door.

Several more shots fired in rapid succession. The windshield cracked in a spidery star.

Backing out of the car, Kyle said, "Code three! Code three! Officers need assistance."

The radio, always on, always full of chatter, went dead silent. The dispatcher requested details.

"Tank River Road, six miles north out of Black Wells." He lifted his head enough to see over the dashboard. "We've got a sniper!"

"Do you see him?" Nadine asked. Her heart threatened to beat its way out of her chest. She crawled across the seat, following Kyle out of the car and into the muddy ditch.

Only when both of them were out of the car, protected by the engine block, did Nadine peek up the hill again. An unseen car gunned its engine. She braced her arms in the opening between the car door and chassis, and pointed her weapon uphill.

Kyle's complexion looked dipped in flour. He steadied his arms in the empty window opening.

The rain soaked her hair and dribbled inside her collar. Waiting, listening, she barely blinked. The engine sound receded.

"He's getting away!" Kyle yelled, jumping to his feet.

She caught the back of his coat and dragged him down. She never took her gaze off the hill, but she didn't see so much as a gleam of metal before the sound of the car was gone.

She stood, thought about holstering her revolver, then decided against it. "Did you get a good look at him?"

"No, ma'am. All I saw was an outline against the trees. It's real brushy up there. Dark."

"Did you see a car as we passed?"

He tossed a guilty glance at the coffee mug and paper on the car floor. "No, ma'am."

The first car over the hill was an old rust-bucket Ford. Planting her feet in a shooter's stance, Nadine raised her weapon.

The car screeched to a halt. Nadine recognized Daryl Wafflegate's bug-eyed face. Keeping the Chevelle between her and Wafflegate, she yelled, "Pull it over! Get out of the car! Hands up! Get out of the car!"

Kyle dropped the radio and grasped his revolver in a two-handed grip. He yelled at the reporter, too. Wafflegate finally emerged, his hands held high. Nadine ordered him to bend over the hood of the car, facedown, arms extended. With his mouth opening and closing like a landed fish's, Wafflegate did as ordered.

Wafflegate stammered incoherently while Nadine cuffed his hands behind his back. She frisked him thoroughly, all the while keeping one eye on the road back to Black Wells.

A patrol car arrived, lights flashing and siren screaming. Nadine forced herself calm. The crisis was over.

Wafflegate found his voice. "Why are you doing this to me?"

"You're under arrest," she said. "Kyle, read him his rights."

"On what charge?"

Nadine glanced at her young partner. If he hadn't been bent over searching for papers, he might have taken a bullet. "The charge?" She drew a deep, shuddering breath. "Let's start with assault on a law officer and illegal discharge of a firearm. Read him his rights."

"Firearm?" Wafflegate squeaked. "I don't have a firearm." His thin shoulders worked violently as he strained against the handcuffs. "What are you talking about? I haven't assaulted anybody. This is assault! You're assaulting me! False arrest! I'll sue!''

Ignoring him, Nadine searched inside the old Ford. No gun. No ammunition. The only things she found were the registration, showing the car belonged to Mary O'Connall, a reporter's notebook filled with scribbles that might as well have been written in Chinese for all the sense they made to her, and a portable scanner. The scanner was tuned to the radio frequency used by the sheriff's department.

Her jaw tightened. Scanners weren't illegal; nor was it illegal to eavesdrop on law-enforcement activities. Acting upon the information, though, or using it for personal gain, was highly illegal. Had Wafflegate used the scanner to follow her to Barkley's pizza parlor? To follow her toward Tucker?

More deputies had arrived. By then she'd noticed that not only had she lost a side window and the windshield, but her right rear tire was completely flat, too. No wonder she'd spun out. She radioed the dispatcher and requested a tow truck.

Deputies directed traffic around the Chevelle. After ordering Wafflegate into the back of a patrol car, Nadine and Kyle hiked up the hill.

"Do you really think he's the shooter?" Kyle asked.

Between the rain and her hammering heart pulsing in her ears, she couldn't be sure the car she'd heard leaving the scene and the old Ford sounded the same. She wondered what excuse Wafflegate would have for being on Tank River Road.

Seeing her top the hill, a deputy pointed excitedly to the ground. Nadine directed deputies to sweep the surrounding hills for witnesses—anybody who might have been working in the fields, horseback riding, hiking or dog walking.

Nadine crouched. She shook rain and wet hair off her face, then used a twig to pick up a shell casing. Bits of dirt clung to its wet surface.

"I count five," a deputy said as he pointed out casings littering the ground. "Is that how many shots were fired?"

Kyle mumbled, "Sounded like a hundred to me."

She showed Kyle the casing. "Steel-jacketed .22."

Now the thin skin under his eyes picked up a distinctly green cast. Nadine imagined she looked as sick as he did. She certainly felt as sick. The casing they'd picked up at Heather's murder scene had been a steel-jacketed .22, as well.

Chapter Ten

"Did Ben Jackson know you were on Tank River Road?" the sheriff demanded.

Chin on fist, slumped on a chair, Nadine stared at a spot on the wall. It was one of the few places in Billy Joe's office not covered with an I-love-me plaque or a glad-handing photograph. She mumbled, "He might have known." She darted a glance at him. "Okay, he did know, but he didn't shoot at me."

"Two of his neighbors saw him leaving his apartment around seven o'clock this morning. One says he was carrying something that might have been a gun and he was acting suspiciously."

Ben's paranoid neighbor who felt the streets were unsafe, no doubt. "'Might have' doesn't count."

Billy Joe studied a sheet of paper. "Wafflegate says he saw you and Jackson in the parking lot of Barkley's pizza parlor. He said you were embracing. He said Jackson attempted to assault him."

"I'm not taking this from you, Billy Joe. Nobody talks to me like I'm an idiot child." She started to rise.

"Sit down!" He rose from his chair like a lion bursting from cover. "You're damned lucky I don't bring you up on charges of harassment. You were way out of line in arresting Wafflegate. Fortunately, he's willing to forget it.''

A full-scale search of both sides of Tank River Road had failed to produce a weapon. She'd had no choice except to release Wafflegate. But way out of line? She'd had plenty of sufficient cause in arresting him. She still held suspicions about the squirrelly reporter, who always seemed underfoot.

Billy Joe shook a thick finger at her face. "You're involved with Jackson. For all I know, you're sleeping with him. As of now, you're off the case. I'll handle it myself from now on."

"You can't do that!" She gripped the chair arms so tightly her fingers ached.

"Forty-eight hours' admin leave, starting now. Go home, stay there. If I see you in town, you're suspended."

"Absolutely not."

He grinned, as humorless and predatory as a shark. "That, or protective custody until Jackson is apprehended. You fit the victim profile to a T, and whether you like it or not, I'm not letting him kill you, too."

"You cannot arrest Ben Jackson. He did not shoot at me!"

"Sergeant Shell, you are dismissed."

NADINE RACED to answer the telephone. Forcing a steadying breath, she picked up the handset. "Hello?" *Please be Ben, please.*

Kyle said, "Ma'am, it's me, Deputy Green."

Her eyes ached from holding back tears. She rubbed her eyelids with the pads of her fingers. "Did you find Ben? Please tell me you found him."

"No, ma'am. I don't know where else to look. And it's gone plumb crazy here!"

"Are you at the office?"

He lowered his voice as he said, "Yes, ma'am. The sheriff's gone loco. He held a press conference, and you won't believe what he said!"

After Billy Joe's handling of the shooting on Tank River Road, Nadine could believe anything.

"Are you sitting down? He told them he has a prime suspect in Heather's murder, and he's solved the Atlanta murder and the murder of Ben's wife."

She sank to the couch. Flames crackled cheerfully in the fireplace, mocking her dismay.

"He's saying the reason we've waited so long to make an arrest is because you've gone crazy."

"What?"

"He's saying you've got mental problems because Sheriff Campbell committed suicide. He says Ben's a sociopath and a serial murderer and you're covering up evidence for him because you're having an affair with him. He's making a big deal out of how your father hired you and you're part of the old sheriff's department he means to clean up."

Only deeply ingrained manners stopped the flood of obscenities fighting for release from her mouth. She pressed her arm against the cramps in her belly.

Kyle explained how the sheriff told the reporters Ben had flunked a polygraph examination and that several witnesses in Atlanta had accused him of murder. He said Nadine had deliberately altered Meg Horseman's statement about Ben's actions on the morning of the murder. Meg now claimed he'd been outside with Heather perhaps as long as five minutes.

Ever since Billy Joe Horseman put on his badge, he'd disliked Nadine. She symbolized Sheriff Big John Campbell, and that made her his rival for the respect of the department. But never once, in spite of the tension, his interference, and his distrust of every move she made, had she dreamed he'd betray her like this.

"So what do we do, ma'am?" Kyle asked.

Over. Her career with the Ponce County Sheriff's Department was finished.

She said, "You go on home, Kyle. This is my battle. Stick with me, and the sheriff will hang you, too. So—"

"He's railroading you and Ben. No way!" he said ferociously. "What do I do?"

Deputy Kyle Green had been her father's last hire before he left office. Her daddy had made a good choice. "You'll lose your job."

"If you're out, I'm out. And hey, I'm not the only one. The guys want me to let you know that we're all behind you one hundred percent!"

The doorbell rang. Rain was pelting the windows and thunder was making the house vibrate, but she still should have heard a car or seen headlights. A clutch of fear knocked her diaphragm.

"Ma'am?" Kyle asked. "You still there?"

She whispered, "There's somebody at the door."

The ringing doorbell burred against her eardrums. She closed her fingers over the cold steel and cross-hatched grips of her revolver. She told Kyle to stay on the line.

Holding the gun next to her hip, she glided toward the front door. She stood to the side and listened to the drumming rain.

The screened door squeaked. A heavy fist plied the door. "Sarge?"

Ben? Raising the gun to shoulder level, her left hand clumsy on the knobs, she turned on the porch light, then unlocked and opened the door.

Ben's wet hair was plastered to his skull like a cap of black satin. Water stained his bomber jacket and darkened his jeans. He cradled a bouquet of daisies in the crook of one arm and held a plastic grocery bag in his other hand. Behind him, the rain came down in sheets.

"Holy smokes!" She grabbed his arm and hauled him inside. She slammed the door behind him and locked it. She hurried back to the telephone and said, "You won't believe this. Ben is here."

Ben cocked his head, and his features skewed in a puzzled grimace. Water dribbled off his hair. A puddle spread from his soaked boots.

She told the deputy, "I can't get you in trouble, Kyle. It's not worth it. Go home, get some sleep. I'll fight my own battle." Shutting out the sound of his heated argument, she hung up. She turned on Ben and demanded, "What are you doing here? Where have you been?"

Looking at her as if she were crazy, he offered the dripping flowers. "Nothing says sorry like flowers. I acted like a jerk yesterday. I apologize."

"Oh, Ben." Her heart doing flip-flops, she stared at the pretty pink-and-white bouquet. His sweet bewilderment made her want to cry. "Do you have any idea what's going on?"

His gaze darted around the room. "Nooo..." He dragged the one word out.

She wrapped her arms around his wet neck and kissed him. He dropped the grocery sack, then enfolded her in a cold, wet, passionate embrace. His smooth lips were warm against hers; the thrust of his tongue sent flares of white-hot fire through her body.

He pulled back and caught her shoulders. "No complaints, Sarge, but why are you so happy to see me?"

She absorbed the concern on his face and in his voice. How was she supposed to not fall in love with this man, when it was what she wanted with all her heart? Poor heart. Broken, tattered, and mended with flimsy tape. Ben would either make it whole again or pull it completely apart. Why take the chance?

"You are all right, aren't you?" He smiled, his dimples deepening.

That smile, she decided, made it worth taking the chance.

Water pooled around his soaking-wet boots, and his skin was pale with cold. She said, "You're ruining my floor. Get those boots off."

She hung his jacket on a hook and set his boots by the fireplace. Wet socks squishing, leaving damp footprints, he followed her to the kitchen.

She put a kettle of water on to boil. "How did you get so wet?"

"I had to park on the road. The ditch under your driveway is overflowing. I didn't know if the bridge would collapse or not." He set the bag on the kitchen table. "What's going on?"

No one had ever braved a rainstorm for her before. Or ruined a pair of red boots on her behalf, either. She handed him a clean dish towel. "You best get out of those clothes. You'll take cold. I'll get you a robe."

He caught her shoulders again, putting a halt to her bustling. "You meet me at the door with a gun, then act as if I arose from the dead. Stop playing mother hen and start talking."

She drew a deep breath. "There's a warrant out for your arrest."

He stood perfectly still, his lips parted as if he were unsure whether to laugh. She unbuttoned his damp shirt while telling him what had happened on Tank River Road. He never said a word. Not even when she told him about the sheriff's press conference, where he'd boasted about connecting Ben to three murders and one attempted murder. She peeled the shirt off his arms.

She studied his cold-blotched skin and the powerful arc of his rib cage. "You're really built. For a murder suspect."

"That's not funny, Sarge." He scrubbed his hair with the dish towel. "Are you sure you're okay?"

She nodded. "Get out of those jeans before you freeze to death."

He did as she ordered. She gave him one of her father's robes and threw his wet clothing into the dryer.

Aware of his steady smile, she asked, "What?" She looked down at her gray sweat suit and the two pairs of socks she wore. She hated imagining the condition of her face and hair. So why was he looking at her as if she were gliding down a Miss America runway?

"You're too cool for words. So how serious is this?"

She fixed two cups of instant coffee, dug out a bottle of brandy and showed it to him. He nodded. She wiped the dust off the cap and poured healthy shots into the coffee cups. She said, "Dead serious. Billy Joe's daughter changed her story. Now she's saying you were in the parking lot long enough to have killed Heather."

"That's a lie." He sounded more puzzled than upset.

"It sure is."

"But you cleared me."

"That doesn't matter." She focused on arranging the daisies in a vase. "My guess is, Billy Joe will bring me up on charges as an accessory after the fact. He's unofficially accused me of tampering with the evidence."

Ben groped for a chair and sat down hard. "You? Why?"

"He hates me, Ben. This is a way to get rid of me and make himself look good." Shame coursed through her. If only she'd kept her head—and her hands to herself—she'd never have armed Billy Joe with ammunition to use against Ben.

"He can't do that to you," Ben said.

"He'll try," she said. "The arrest warrant is for the shooting today. Where were you?" Please have an alibi, she pleaded silently, please.

"Austin."

She massaged her weary, aching temples. If she could get about twelve hours of sleep, she might be able to think. "What were you doing in Austin?"

He placed a hand on the sack. "Snooping. I went to the library to do some research, then to an office-supply store to make calls and receive faxes."

"What time did you leave your apartment?"

He frowned for a moment, then lifted his shoulders. "I got to Austin around eight-thirty, so probably...seven?'' He shifted his gaze to the flannel robe and toyed with the fabric. "I know playing amateur private eye is stupid. But I had to do something.''

"Can anyone place you in Austin around eight-thirty?''

His gaze drifted. "I don't think so. I got lost looking for the library. I ended up wasting over an hour driving around.''

"Did you stop and ask directions?''

He grinned, sheepishly.

He's a man, she told herself. Of course he didn't ask for directions. All hopes for an alibi flew out the window. She suppressed a groan.

"But," he said, "I talked to the research librarian. I even gave her my name. And the people at the office-supply store will recognize me. I tied up their fax for hours. Sarge, nobody can believe I tried to shoot you. It's the stalker. He warned—''

"What I believe isn't worth an empty sack these days. What time did you get to the library?''

"Around ten, or a little after. I don't know.''

She closed her eyes and hung her head. Billy Joe could claim Ben had had plenty of time to ambush her, then drive to Austin.

"It's my stalker," he said softly. "He's trying to kill you.''

"Don't worry about me. I can take care of myself.''

"How did he know you were going to Tucker? He's tracking you, hunting you—''

The telephone rang. Almost grateful for an excuse to end a very disturbing conversation, she invited Ben to bring his coffee and warm himself by the fire.

The caller was Deb Hall. "I quit.''

"You're always saying that," Nadine said. Ben's words nagged at her, tugged at the deep-seated places where she penned her fears. Punks and nuts had threatened her in the past. She'd been shot at, assaulted, had furious criminals try to run over her with cars. It went with the job.

Today was the first time she'd ever been ambushed.

Deb said, "Would I be out this late at the office, risking a lightning storm where I could lose an eardrum, if I wasn't serious? Lightning can travel through telephone wires, you know."

The rain had stopped at Nadine's house, so the storm must have blown over town. All she could hear was very distant thunder. "Well, don't quit yet. I need you, Deb. I'm in trouble."

"My dear," Deb said crisply, "I believe I would describe it as being in deep doo-doo. The only consolation is, that idiot Billy Joe is standing in a manure pile the size of Mount Everest! And he just keeps shoveling it on." There followed Deb's recounting of Billy Joe's press conference, to which she added that whenever a reporter asked the sheriff if Ben was the killer, the sheriff had turned coy. In essence, he'd given them tacit permission to use Ben's name in their stories.

"But," Deb said, "that's not the only reason I called. I have some information for you about Daryl Wafflegate. Turns out he's Mary O'Connall's nephew. Now why didn't I know that?"

"I can't imagine," Nadine mumbled, still boggled by the knowledge that by tomorrow Ben would be dubbed a killer in the news. Possibly even in the national news.

"He worked for newspapers all over the country. Got fired from every job. The boy's a pathological liar. His last job was in Kansas City, writing movie reviews. They caught him plagiarizing articles from other papers. Mary talked Cole Duke into giving him a fresh start."

Nadine fixed an astonished stare on Ben. He was crouched before the fireplace, rearranging burning logs with the poker. Firelight caused sparks of blue light on his midnight hair and outlined his strong shoulders in gold. He'd gone to college in Kansas. He'd met his wife there.

Except...she'd made inquiries about Daryl's whereabouts at the time of Heather's murder. Mary O'Connall had claimed Daryl was with her, at the newspaper office. Nadine doubted dynamite could budge Mary from her story.

Nadine asked, "When did he get into town?"

"Showed up around Christmastime, but didn't start working for the paper until the end of January."

"Are you sure?"

"Let's put it this way. I know about the twelve cats Mary O'Connall's landlady doesn't know about. I don't think she was lying to me this time." Deb huffed a harsh breath. "I have to clean out my desk now. Is there anything else I can do for you?"

"Have you seen Tony Zaccaro around?"

"He was in earlier. He and Billy Joe had a long talk behind closed doors. Then Tony went a-stomping out, looking like someone stuck a snake in his drawers."

"Was this before or after Billy Joe talked to the press?"

"Before."

That could only mean Tony had agreed, willingly or not, to press charges against Ben.

"Now that you have all my news, I'm leaving this madhouse. It's high time I had a little talk with Cousin Zenia."

Nadine inhaled sharply. Deb had often threatened to fill in her second cousin by marriage, Zenia Morcastle, about all the goings-on inside the sheriff's department. As senior county commissioner, Zenia determined the sheriff's budget. She could also authorize investigations.

Deb said, "When Billy Joe takes his pratfall, I think the board of commissioners ought to have the privilege of seeing it." She rang off.

As much as Nadine appreciated Deb's confidence, she held doubts about there being a pratfall. The only way to call off Billy Joe would be to deliver the true murderer into his hands. The prospects of that seemed mighty slim.

"You're looking glum," Ben said. "More bad news?"

"It sounds like the sheriff has the county prosecutor over a barrel." She rubbed her chin. Call Tony? But if he asked about Ben, she'd have to tell him the truth. She inhaled the perfumed aroma of brandy-laced coffee. She'd never been much of a drinker; funny how much getting drunk tempted her now.

She patted the couch beside her. When Ben sat down, she took both of his hands into hers. "I have to ask you something I don't want to ask."

He licked his lips.

She rubbed her thumbs over his wrists. His skin was still chilled and his hands were cold. "You first grew aware of the stalker after your wife died."

"A few months later, when I went back to work. That's right."

She needed to look at him, but couldn't do it. "Is it possible Cathy had an affair?"

His entire body stiffened, and his hands tensed, turning into rigid blocks of ice. "That's not possible."

"I'm not trying to disparage her. But somebody may have loved her enough to blame you for her death."

He jerked his hands away and clamped his arms over his chest. "We had problems, but she wasn't a cheater. She wasn't that way."

Nadine dropped the subject. If by some remote possibility Daryl and Cathy had been lovers, she realized, Ben would never cooperate in proving it. He'd loved her too much to sully her name—even if it meant staying out of prison.

At the sound of a car headed toward the house, both of them looked toward the source. Nadine's heart leapt into her throat. Ben arose and lifted his chin. His face had paled, but his gaze was fixed steadily on the door.

"They'll never take me alive, Rocky," he said in Jimmy Cagney's snarl.

BEN SHIFTED HIS ATTENTION between Nadine and Kyle Green. The deputy stood in front of the door, leaning backward to accommodate the weight of the cardboard box he carried. Hands on her hips, an eyebrow raised, Nadine glowered at the young man.

Uneasy silence filled the room. Busted, Ben thought. He wondered what kind of bail—if he could get bail in Ponce County—he'd have to pay. Where could he find a good attorney?

Kyle suddenly laughed. He glanced at Ben's bare feet and laughed harder. He set the box on the floor.

Ben asked, "What's so funny?"

Snickering and wiping his eyes, Kyle said, "That's gotta be Big John's robe."

Nadine covered her mouth with a hand. Her eyes sparkled, and her shoulders hitched.

Ben looked down at the red-and-black flannel robe. The hem brushed his ankles, and the shoulder seams drooped nearly to his elbows. "How big was this Big John, anyway?"

Kyle said, "Oh, what do you figure, ma'am? Six feet five inches? Two hundred and fifty pounds? Ground shook when he walked."

Ben cocked an eyebrow at Nadine. The top of her head barely reached his shoulder, and her father had been six feet five inches tall? She shrugged.

Kyle said, "Criminals are stupid, and boy howdy, you sure look the part, Ben. Leaving your car out on the road is pretty dumb, too."

"That's enough, Kyle." She eyed the young man in despair. "What are you doing here?"

The deputy lifted his chin and drew back his shoulders. His cheeks reddened. "I don't want the job if the only thing the badge stands for is making Sheriff Horseman look good." He toed the box. "Here's the files, ma'am."

Ben's chest tightened. The deputy had guts.

Kyle gave Nadine a cautious look. "If we go over everything again…maybe we missed something." He rubbed the back of his neck and shifted his weight from foot to foot. "I'm sure the killer wants Ben locked up. So if he's arrested, the killer will disappear. We can't let him get away."

Ben considered what he said for a moment. "Then you're sure my stalker is the killer."

"It's possible," Nadine said, in her usual conservative way.

Kyle nodded eagerly. "I think it's real possible. And I think I know why."

"As long as you're here, come sit down." Nadine beckoned both men to the couch.

Dumbfounded, Ben listened to Kyle's theory about Marla Oakes and her suicide—how someone close to Marla refused to accept her suicide and had latched on to Ben as a killer.

Nadine asked, "Where are your keys, Ben?"

"My keys?"

"Car keys. I'm going to put your car in the barn."

As the sound of water dripping off the roof and the snapping crackle of logs burning in the fireplace filled the room, Ben mulled over Kyle's theory. When he considered the anonymous letters he'd received, full of angst and accusations, it made sickening sense. Some wacko had taken potshots at Nadine—nothing theoretical about that.

Ben nodded toward the kitchen. "Can I speak to you in private, Sarge?"

In the kitchen, Nadine leaned her backside against the counter and folded her arms. Her small chin lifted stubbornly.

Ben idly rolled the too-long sleeves. "I don't know the law, but it only makes sense that if I'm a wanted man, and you don't arrest me, then you'll get in trouble."

"Let me worry about that. I'm not turning you over to Billy Joe. Now give me your keys."

"You got shot at today. It's because of me. You can't deny it."

Emotion flared in her big, dark eyes, eyes that were pained and perhaps frightened. "I can take care of myself."

"You'll be safer if I'm locked up." He pursed his lips. "I'll hire a lawyer. I'll fight this thing. Legally." He snorted. "Hey, my reputation is already shot. What have I got to lose?"

"You don't understand what is going on here."

He touched two fingers to her lips, beautiful, satin-soft lips he might never get the chance to kiss again. "I understand that I care about you very, very much. I'd rather rot in prison than have anything happen to you."

Her eyes brightened with tears. Her chin quivered. "Trust me on this," she said. "Please."

Seeing her on the brink of crying shocked him. He smoothed his thumb under her eye. "You've done everything you can. This is my fight now. You and Kyle can't help me if you're in jail, too." He pressed a gentle kiss between her eyebrows. "Besides, you'll nab the stalker."

"What if I can't? What if—"

"Sergeant Shell!" Kyle yelled from the front room.

Ben and Nadine hurried to see what had excited the deputy. He stood to the side of the front window. He held the curtain so he could see out.

Nadine asked, "What is it?"

"There's a car out there."

Nadine loosed a harsh breath through her teeth. "I bet that's a deputy."

Ben saw lights through the trees. "The jig is up," he said. "I'll get my clothes."

"Hold on a minute."

"You hold on, Sarge. I'm not getting arrested in this outfit." He returned to the kitchen.

Nadine went to her desk and found her hand radio. She turned it on. Unit 14 called in a license-plate check; the dispatcher requested a unit to respond to a woman's complaint about a prowler; a deputy reported a tree downed by lightning, now blocking a road.

"He's leaving," Kyle said. He opened the front door and stuck his head in the opening. "He's driving away."

"That doesn't make any sense." She kept listening to the radio, waiting for a deputy to report finding the Mustang.

Ben walked in, buttoning his now dry shirt. His jeans were still slightly damp. "Well?"

"He's gone," Kyle said. "Maybe it was a reporter, ma'am."

Ben said, "Or my shadow, planting a bomb in my car."

Chapter Eleven

Nadine played the flashlight beam over the ditch running parallel to the road. Normally the water was about two feet deep, home to crayfish, minnows, bullfrogs, and an occasional snapping turtle. Corrugated steel, railroad ties and packed dirt formed a bridge over the ditch. Now brown water churned, reaching the top of the banks and striking the bridge so hard that water spilled over the top.

Ben said, "I told you it was flooded."

Nadine shivered inside her coat. The rain might have ended, but icy moisture laced the air. "It does this every time we get a good rain. Don't worry, the bridge will hold."

"I drove over it with no problems," Kyle said as he flicked his flashlight at his boots. "But I don't want to walk over it. I'll go get my van."

"Give me the keys, Ben."

Grumbling, he handed her the keys. Protected from the frigid water by tall rubber boots, she sloshed through the water to the road.

Ben called, "What if it was the killer checking us out? Is there another way to get to your house?"

"The tractor path, but anyone who tries driving in this mud won't get far." She shone the light down the road, seeking signs of any vehicle other than Ben's Mustang. If a deputy had spotted Ben's car, he'd still be here, awaiting backup. "It might have been kids looking for a parking spot."

"Every kid in the county knows you live here." Kyle put the hand unit to his ear. "Still nothing on the squawk box. It couldn't have been our people."

Startled by splashing, she glanced over her shoulder at Ben. "Quit playing macho man," she said.

He stepped quickly but carefully through the water. "Who's macho? Nobody drives my car but me."

"Thank you very much for the vote of confidence."

He draped an arm over her shoulders. Leaning close enough for his warm breath to caress her face, he said, "I will trust your word that the bridge won't collapse. But, Sarge, you are not driving my car."

Even in the darkness, she knew he was smiling. "I'd let you drive my car."

"Of course you would, but you're not driving mine." He kissed her cheek.

Aware that Kyle was watching them, she tensed her shoulder, tacitly asking Ben to back off. "You're being an ass, Ben Jackson."

He gave her a tense look, then dropped his arm. "Sticks and stones."

He spoke in a teasing tone, but he was dead serious. And she suspected his desire to drive didn't have a thing to do with that cherry red classic Mustang, but had a whole lot to do with two dead women for whom he'd lapsed in his gentlemanly duties. That she and Kyle were armed and on full alert didn't matter a bit.

"Fine," she said. "But if you put it in the ditch, don't think I'll let you forget it."

She shone the flashlight on the Mustang. Ben had turned it around so that it was parked on the opposite side of the road, facing toward town. Water beaded on the glassy finish and darkened the white vinyl roof.

Ben strode toward the car, reaching for the door. Nadine ordered him to stop.

"Hold on," she said. "Let me check it out."

"I was kidding about the bomb."

"Indulge my suspicious mind." She moved past him and shone the light through the driver's-side window, studying the interior. She doubted very much that a person who favored a .22-caliber handgun as a weapon would resort to a car bomb. When dealing with a nut, however, it was safer to be sure.

Seeing nothing inside the car, she opened the door. She jerked her hand off the door handle.

Ben asked, "What is it, Sarge?"

She put the light on the handle. "Mud. A big wet glob of mud." The nasty taste of iron filled her mouth. "Kyle! Get over here."

Protesting about ruining his boots, the deputy goat-hopped through the water. He slipped on the muddy road and went down on one knee.

"If you fished for catfish," Ben said, "you'd know how to handle mud." He helped the deputy to his feet.

Nadine focused the flashlight on the door handle. "When Ben arrived, it was pouring down rain. But look at this."

Kyle studied the door. He whistled. "That should have washed off." He swiped at his muddy trouser leg. "Looks like I'm not the only one who slipped in the mud."

Through the window, she saw a dark streak on the white leather seat. Ordering the men to step back, she opened the hood. The engine compartment was as pristine and well cared-for as any she'd ever seen. She couldn't help but smile; her father had maintained his cars like this.

After closing the hood, she went back to the interior and checked the ignition, the dashboard, and under the seats. She found no wires out of place or suspicious-looking bundles. She held out her hand. "Give me the keys."

"If you think there's a bomb, there is no way in hell I'm letting you start it." Ben nudged Kyle with an elbow. "Let Kyle do it."

"There's no bomb." She shone the light on his face. "I thought you didn't argue with armed females."

"I lied," he answered, without a trace of shame. He got in and slid the key into the ignition. He hesitated. "There's no bomb."

Someone had been inside the car for some reason, but she'd seen no sign of tampering or explosives. She raised an eyebrow. "You insist on driving. Fire her up."

He drew a deep breath, then did so. The engine caught with a roar, then a purr. Ben grinned nervously as he put the transmission in gear. "You're sure about the bridge?"

"Drive slow. Kyle, you ride. I'll go open the barn."

Ben flicked on the high beams, then inched forward, swinging wide to align the tires with the center of the bridge. He continued to drive slowly on the rutted, muddy driveway. Inside the barn, an owl squeaked, as if protesting their presence, and something small and stealthy rustled in the piles of moldering hay. Dampness unlocked the aroma of long-ago cattle.

A chill that had nothing to do with the cold, rainy night crept into Nadine's bones. Someone had gotten into Ben's car. Why? A common thief would have taken the stereo.

Ben rubbed his hands over the steering wheel. He'd opened the door, but made no move to get out of the car. "This is a dumb idea, Sarge. Let's go to the sheriff's station together. I'll turn myself in. Hiding makes me look guilty."

He didn't understand how guilty he looked already. He also didn't understand how much bagging Ben for murder meant to Billy Joe.

"I say we wait until there's a reward," Kyle said. "Then we turn you in."

What were you doing in the car? she asked the unknown stalker. No bomb, no vandalism, no theft. She stiffened suddenly, scarcely daring to breathe. "Get out of the car." She flashed the light through the interior. "Both of you. Get out!"

Ben and Kyle bailed out of the Mustang as if it were on fire.

Nadine searched behind the seats, then under them, feeling with her hand wherever the light didn't reach. She reached under the dashboard and felt around cautiously. Nothing. The light picked up the button on the glove compartment. A trace of mud smeared the metal. With her mouth gone dry as dust, she licked her lips. Though she suspected what she'd find, seeing the pistol inside the compartment made her heart race.

"Sarge? What is it?"

"A gun."

"What?" Ben and Kyle said at the same time, and moved in to see.

"Kyle, give me a pen or a stick or something."

She used a ballpoint pen to fish the .22-caliber pistol out of the glove compartment, then lifted it by the trigger guard. Instructing the men to shut the barn door, she carried the gun to the house. She examined the pistol visually, then sniffed the barrel, smelled the faint, acrid scent of gunpowder, and dropped it into a paper sack.

His face gone pale, Ben asked, "Do you think that's the murder weapon?"

"A .22 automatic," Kyle said. "It's the right kind of gun, ma'am."

"Let me think." She rubbed her aching temples. Wouldn't Billy Joe just love this? "We don't have a choice. I have to call Bob Underhill."

THE SMELL of fried chicken awakened Nadine. She opened one eye, knowing she was on the couch, but not remembering falling asleep.

Ben sat on a chair, eating cold chicken and coleslaw. He grinned at her. "'Morning, Sarge."

Gray light filtered through the window curtains. The hearth was cold, the ashes dead. Nadine's eyes burned with fatigue and her entire body ached.

They had stayed up past midnight, going over the case file and the newspaper articles Ben had received from Atlanta. Ben amazed her. Who knew how much of his own money he'd spent calling newspapers, libraries and friends in Atlanta to gather information about the women mentioned in the stalker's letters. The only solid connection between the deaths was the similarity in the victims' appearances.

Unfortunately, none of the newspaper clippings gave them a ready clue about the stalker's identity.

"What time is it?"

He checked his watch. "Almost eight o'clock."

Stunned, she sat up and looked at the clock on the wall behind her. "I can't believe I slept that long."

"Shh," Ben cautioned her. "Our sentry is still snoozing."

Kyle was slumped sideways on a chair, with his long legs hanging over a chair arm and his chin on his chest. A quilt was draped over him.

"Oh, no, ma'am—" Ben mimicked in Kyle's eager tone "—I'll stick with you. Monitor the radio, yes, ma'am."

Fighting a laugh, Nadine said, "Did anyone call?"

He shook his head.

"Bob should have gotten my message by now." She'd left several messages on Bob Underhill's answering machine. "What are you doing eating chicken at this time of the morning?"

"This is evening to me. Hope you don't mind that I helped myself to leftovers. Want some coffee? I made a pot."

She pushed off the couch and stretched. She'd not only slept long, she'd slept hard. Her joints creaked. "Shower first."

"Need any help?" he asked silkily, to match the sultry invitation in his eyes.

That look was enough to drive all the strength from her knees. Shivers tingled inside her. She glanced at Kyle. "I don't think..."

Wiping his hands on a napkin, standing, he said, "Don't worry about Sleeping Beauty. I've been tossing chicken bones at him for the last hour. He hasn't budged." His smile was sweet, innocent—mind-numbing. "The boy sleeps like a babe." He tickled her cheek, then smoothed a bold hand down her throat.

She couldn't breathe.

"You're cute when you sleep," he murmured, trailing his hand downward.

Every nerve sang.

Eyelids lowering, his smile knowing, he cupped her breast and flicked his thumb over her erect nipple. Then he kissed her, his mouth so tenderly demanding, a little whimper of pleasure rose in her throat.

"How about that shower?" he whispered. "I'll wash your hair. You can wash mine."

Numb and shaky, she headed for the bathroom. Ben followed. When she reached the door, she stopped. Tactile memories embraced her—the feel of his hands, the all-encompassing power of his long body. Tightness and heat spread until her entire body ached with desire.

She felt his eyes on her back, felt him willing her to turn around. If she did, if his expressive, compelling eyes touched hers, she was lost.

Her love could destroy him.

He touched her shoulder. She flinched. Inside her head, she saw a courtroom scene, heard the prosecutor's voice. *Sergeant Shell, were you aware of the warrant for Benjamin Jackson's arrest when you made love with him? When you found the weapon inside Mr. Jackson's automobile, what was the real reason you didn't immediately arrest him? Is it because you're lovers? Isn't it true that you cleared him off your list of suspects because you're lovers?*

"I'll be out in a minute, Ben." She slipped inside the bathroom and shut the door, hating herself.

It took a long time under the pounding water before she felt reasonably sane and in control. Dressed and composed, she joined Ben and Kyle in the kitchen.

Kyle said, "Bob Underhill called, ma'am. I told him you'd call him right back."

Ben hunched over his coffee, cradling the cup in both hands. His refusal to look at her hurt. She wanted to scream at him, "I'm not rejecting you! I'm trying to keep you out of prison!"

She poured a cup of coffee and carried it into the front room. Once this was all over, once his name was cleared and the real killer was caught, Ben would understand. She hoped. As she reached for the telephone, it rang. Expecting Bob Underhill, she was surprised to hear Tony Zaccaro's husky drawl.

"Good morning, Nadine. Have you seen the *Bugle?*"

"I get the paper at the office, so I haven't seen it yet. Is it bad?"

"Billy Joe's outdone himself. He's got full-page coverage boasting how he personally ending a killing spree. I've got a Dallas newspaper, too. The story made the second page there."

"Oh, no..." she breathed, sinking to the couch. The coffee tasted like acid.

"And it gets a heap better," he said dryly. "I just got off the phone with a girl named Teresa Johnson."

The name struck a chord, but Nadine couldn't place it.

"She read the newspaper, too," Tony said, "and her conscience finally found somebody home. Your suspicions about Reggie Hamilton may have a basis."

Now Nadine recalled the name. Teresa Johnson was a young woman who'd been friends with both Heather and Reggie. One of dozens Nadine had interviewed.

Tony said, "Reggie wasn't at the lake that Saturday night. According to Teresa, he was with her until around one in the morning."

Every hair on Nadine's head raised and prickled.

"She says Reggie called her on Sunday morning and told her Heather had been killed. He asked her to not tell anyone they were together."

"Oh, he did, did he?"

"I've asked her to come in and make a formal statement. I'm also going to pick up those kids who said Reggie was at the lake. I need your—"

"I'm off the case, Tony. You know that."

Tony barked a short laugh. "So what do you want? A vacation? I need you, Nadine. You're the only one who knows what's going on."

More than you can guess, she thought, looking back toward the kitchen. Kyle and Ben were engaged in a friendly argument about something—probably fishing.

"Billy Joe is killing me!" Tony exclaimed. "Even if I thought for a minute we had sufficient evidence to take Ben Jackson to trial, the sheriff's spouting off to the press means no way could we find an impartial jury. He's got buck fever so bad he can't see straight. Plus, he has Judge Tate all excited—"

"Judge Tate?" she asked, interrupting him. Not another worry... Billy Joe and the Ponce County judge were hunting buddies from way back. "When did Judge Tate get involved?"

"Billy Joe convinced him to sign the warrant. The judge told me he thinks we have enough circumstantial evidence to build a case. He's willing to go ahead against Jackson. With that in his pocket, there's no way Billy Joe will cooperate in going after the Hamilton kid."

Nadine felt uncertainty concerning the Hamilton kid, too. Imagining Reggie killing Heather in a fit of fury was easy; imagining him laying an ambush for law officers was not. "Hold on a minute, Tony. I think I have the gun used in the shooting yesterday."

Tony's silence stretched out so far she thought they might have been disconnected. "Where did you get it?"

She straightened her spine. Tony Zaccaro was a hardworking, honest attorney who believed implicitly in justice for all. Over the years, she'd worked well with him. Trusting her feelings about him, she told him about last night.

"Good God," Tony said. "And Green is on this? Unbelievable! Do you know what Billy Joe will do to you two?"

"Yes, sir, I do. But right now I've got bigger problems. Somebody is trying to frame Ben. What do I do, Tony? I can't turn Ben in."

"Sit tight. I'll be out to your place. We'll figure something out."

After she hung up, she sipped her coffee, mulling over her dilemma.

"What did Officer Underhill have to say, ma'am?" Kyle asked.

Kyle and Ben stood side by side, looking like the best of friends.

"That was Tony Zaccaro," she said, unable to look at Ben. "I told him about the gun. He's on his way."

BEN WATCHED THE CLOCK.

Bob Underhill, the crime technician, had picked up the gun, promising Nadine to give it his all. Tony Zaccaro had grilled Ben, inspected the Mustang and questioned Nadine. After hearing her out, he'd finally said, "I'll give Bob until six o'clock to see what he can find. But that's as long as I can delay executing the warrant."

Tony had agreed, however, that if he did arrest Ben, he'd take him to the barracks in Tucker, rather than the main station in Black Wells. Doing so would protect Ben from the press. His parting words had been "Find a lawyer, Jackson."

Even Kyle's expression was grim as he left to go to Black Wells to snoop around.

Ben wasn't worried about a lawyer. He was worried about Nadine. The newspaper had crucified her. Along with a story in which the sheriff boasted about his intention to charge Ben with murder, the *Bugle* had run a side story about the suicide of Big John Campbell. It included a quote from the sheriff: *"That Sergeant Shell's father committed suicide is a direct cause of her recent behavior. I had hoped she could function, but her blatant affair with a serial killer proves otherwise."*

When Nadine saw the story, her features had tightened and naked pain had glazed her eyes. She hadn't said a word about it, though. Ben had wanted to broach the subject all day, but he didn't know how.

Nadine suddenly pushed away from her desk and threw up her hands.

Ben asked, "What's the matter?"

She turned on the chair and slumped with her elbows on her knees and her chin on her fist. "Reggie

Hamilton. I've been going through this until I'm half-blind. Even if Teresa is willing to testify Reggie lied about his whereabouts, *even* if those boys recant their stories about him being at the lake, I still don't have anything on Reggie. Nothing."

Ben said, "No physical evidence."

"You're learning the terms. I give you a star."

"But if he lied about an alibi—"

"He was out with another girl, and a lot of people knew he and Heather had problems. He could be just plain scared or stupid. Or both." She sighed, heavily, wearily. Brown smudges marred the thin skin under her eyes. Every few seconds, she darted a worried glance at the clock. "Reggie's had run-ins with the law before. He might figure we'd accept a lie better than the truth."

Moot point, anyway, Ben thought. His stalker had killed Heather, and he wouldn't stop killing until Ben was behind bars.

The telephone rang. Nadine slowly straightened. Ben tensed. The clock read twenty minutes until six. Ben caught himself crossing his fingers.

Nadine answered the telephone. She listened, nodding and murmuring in response to the caller. Suddenly she began breathing hard. She turned wide eyes on Ben.

She said, "I don't believe this. I just . . . do . . . not believe it."

Ben's mouth filled with wool. The gun was damning evidence. If Bob Underhill proved the gun had been used to shoot at Nadine, and if he couldn't prove it *didn't* belong to Ben, then Tony Zaccaro would have to issue the warrant.

She hung up. For a long moment, she merely sat, staring at nothing.

Unable to stand it, Ben demanded, "Well?"

"Oh, Ben, that was Tony," she whispered. "We've got the murder weapon."

He closed his eyes, his mouth now so dry he could barely breathe.

"The bullet we took from Heather was badly damaged, but the ejector marks on the shell casings are perfect matches. Perfect! It's also the same gun used to shoot at me."

"What about Karen? Is it the same gun used to kill her?"

She shook her head. "No telling yet. Tony said Detective Boyles isn't accepting his calls. Bob is faxing his firearms identification report to Atlanta. With any luck, it'll soothe tempers and gain us some cooperation."

"So the murder weapon was in my car. Do you know any good lawyers?" Despite his conviction that he could and would beat a murder charge, the idea of being arrested and jailed left him light-headed.

She surprised him with a merry laugh.

"Pardon my pessimism, but you said—"

"I haven't finished." She bent over him with her hands on her thighs, looking like a schoolteacher. "Whoever planted the gun took pains to wipe it clean. There wasn't a smudge on the grips or the barrel. But guess what the shooter forgot?"

"Sarge..."

She laughed again. "Bob found fingerprints on the clip."

"The thing that holds the bullets?"

"That's right. And he eliminated your prints. Without a question, unequivocally eliminated."

Ben nearly slid off the chair.

"Physical evidence, Ben. You're in the clear."

Ben hadn't realized how scared he'd been until the weight of fear lifted off his shoulders. "So I won't be arrested."

"No, Ben, no arrest." Her smile faded. "But we're not high and dry yet. Billy Joe will go off the deep end when he hears about this."

"So what do we do?"

"Right now, we sit tight. Tony dropped the warrant, but it's going to take some fancy shuffling to talk Billy Joe into putting me back on the case."

He studied her lovely face, with its clear complexion and strong features. He didn't know her nearly as well as he'd like to, but he guessed this affair hurt her deeply. The sheriff's betrayal, the blasting in the newspaper, her private matters laid wide open for the public—all of it must strike at her most vulnerable areas.

"You're going to lose your job," he said.

A fine line appeared between her eyebrows as her gaze went distant. "Probably." She sighed. "No, definitely."

"Guess you'll end up hating me."

She shook her head. "That's not going to happen."

"One day, while you're flipping hamburgers, you'll be thinking, 'This is Ben's fault.'"

She chuckled. "My daddy always used to say why you do what you do is the most important thing. I know why I'm a cop. It's not the badge or the paycheck. It's because bad guys should pay for their dirty deeds and justice should prevail. It's that simple. I can't work for Billy Joe if he doesn't care about justice."

Looking back at the newspaper folded neatly atop the coffee table, she said, "I failed my daddy."

Ben bit back the urge to interrupt.

"The autopsy showed he had cancer. He must have felt terribly alone. Deserted. I never knew he was in pain, I never knew he wanted to kill himself. He must have been suffering horrible despair, and I never knew."

He reached out to her, and she took his hand.

"That's not going to happen again," she said. "The job's not important, Ben. You're important." She lifted her head. "And no matter what happens, I'll never hate you." She squeezed his fingers. "I'll never give up on you, either."

He started to pull her down for a kiss, but the telephone rang. "Must be Tony," she said.

Ben gave her a wry grin. Getting her someplace alone and out of reach of the telephone was becoming priority number one.

Nadine answered the phone. Her smile vanished, and she staggered against the desk, catching it for balance. She said, "He's on his way?" She cupped a hand over the mouthpiece and told Ben, "It's Kyle. Billy Joe got an anonymous tip telling him you're here. He's aiming to personally arrest both of us."

Chapter Twelve

"Well," Nadine said, jerking the steering wheel to miss a big rock in the rutted tractor path, "you wanted to know why I drive this car. This is it."

Wide-eyed, jaw clenched, Ben clamped one hand on the dashboard and the other on the armrest. The Chevelle bounced and slewed on the rocky, muddy, hilly tractor path through the scrub behind Nadine's house.

"What if we get stuck?" he asked.

"I learned to drive back here. I won't get stuck." A low-hanging cypress branch slapped the windshield, then popped through the passenger side window.

Ben shouted and ducked.

Nadine winced. "Sorry. I got the windshield fixed, but the side window is on special order. You okay?"

He swiped wetness off his face and spit debris out the window. "Watch where you're going. Where are we heading, anyway?"

"Tucker. Bob Underhill and Tony Zaccaro are meeting us at Tony's office. Kyle said he was on his way there, too." She slowed the car to a grumbling, protesting crawl in order to cross a shallow ditch. The

ditch was only about a foot deep, but flooding had
turned it into a small brown river.

Ben braced himself and closed his eyes. "We should
have taken a tractor," he muttered.

"I figure I have one chance to get reinstated on the
case. Billy Joe embarrassed the devil out of himself
with that press conference. He's got his back to the
wall. I've got to cut him an escape hatch."

"How?"

"Arresting the real killer would do it."

He snorted. "Who might that be?"

She had a few ideas. While her eyes and hands focused on navigating the cross-country track, her mind
went over the case. Reggie Hamilton topped her suspect list. Heather's position when she died was easily
explained by her knowing and trusting Reggie. Reggie had lied about his alibi. Yet not so easily explained was the shooting on Tank River Road. If
Reggie had killed Heather, why hadn't he destroyed
the gun? Why go after the investigators? And how
could he have known they'd be on Tank River Road?

She reached the road. Ben loosed a long, relieved
exhale. He turned on the seat to look back the way
they'd come. In the rearview mirror, Nadine's line of
sight showed glistening wet underbrush and trees with
no discernible break. Ben plucked wet leaves and twigs
off his jacket and tossed them out the window.

The radio crackled. Unit 1 announced he'd reached
his destination and requested that all units stand by in
case of trouble. Nadine chuckled.

Ben asked, "What's so funny?"

"Didn't you hear that? The sheriff's at my house.
Hope he doesn't bust down my door."

Ben leaned close, an ear cocked at the radio. "That's what it said? Sounded like—" he imitated the static crackle and distorted voices "—to me."

"You get used to it after a while."

She drove fast on the back roads to Tank River Road, listening to Billy Joe's progress. He discovered she wasn't at home. His failure to report finding the Mustang in the barn made her shake her head in wonder. If it had been her, that would have been the first place she'd check. The sheriff issued an all points bulletin for her and Ben.

At the courthouse in Tucker, she parked in back. "Listen up, as of right now, you're in protective custody. I want you to keep your mouth shut. Talk to no one except me and Tony."

"Incognito."

"Right. There might be reporters around, so be careful. Let me do the talking." She breathed deeply and steadily, clearing her head and trying to ease the tightness in her chest. She'd never been in trouble before, never faced a situation where anyone pointed a finger and questioned her motives or methods. Knowing that if her father were alive he'd understand and even applaud her actions gave her the courage to get out of the car.

Nadine opened the trunk. Ben reached for the box of case materials, then straightened and turned to her. "Still don't think I'm the kiss of death?"

She rubbed his arm. "Oh, Ben, I explained—"

"I know how much this job means to you. You're one impressive lady. An impressive cop. You look so calm, but I know you're hurting."

She touched his face, smoothing her fingers over the strong line of his jaw. "I remember one time, I was about eight years old. Daddy had this fella in jail. He'd put his wife in the hospital. That man was screaming and yelling and saying he had the right to beat his wife. Daddy said that's what people do when other people let them get away with it." She placed a hand on his chest, imagining she could feel his strong, brave heart beneath his clothes. "I never forget that. And that's why Billy Joe isn't getting away with it."

He hugged her, pressing her head against his shoulder, and squeezed her tightly. Then he stepped back and gave her one of his endearing smiles. "I'll bake you a cake with a file in it."

She laughed while urging him to grab the box.

They entered the courthouse.

"NOTHING DOING," Bob Underhill announced.

A collective groan swept through the prosecutor's office. Seated in a corner, where for the past few hours he'd had a fly-on-the-wall perspective, Ben studied Nadine's face. The dark circles under her eyes, and her pale face, made her look small and vulnerable. Even her golden hair had lost its shine. She sagged on a chair, her cheek resting on a fist, and glowered at the crime technician. Her exhaustion made him ache with pity.

"Reggie Hamilton did not put those fingerprints on that gun," Bob said. "Sorry. And I eliminated prints from his family members. We're back to square one."

"Sorry, Nadine," Tony Zaccaro said. "Hinky as he is, we've got to turn him loose."

"Shoot," Nadine whispered.

That one soft word spoke volumes of frustration. They'd picked up Heather's boyfriend for questioning. His parents, a pair of imposing cattle ranchers who in height and white-haired ruggedness looked as if they stepped out of a novel about the Texas frontier, had accompanied their son. Ben hadn't been privy to the interrogation session, but from Nadine's expression and simmering anger, he knew it hadn't gone well.

Her usually cool voice held grudging resentment as she ordered Kyle Green to tell the Hamiltons they were free to go.

She pushed off the chair. Rubbing the back of her neck and rolling her shoulders, she faced the wall where she and Tony had pinned up crime-scene photographs, charts and diagrams.

"So we're back to the stalker. But I don't see how a stranger could have shot her."

"What if Ben's stalker made friends with Heather?" Tony looked to Ben. "We don't know who this guy is. He could have gotten a job at the hotel or taken classes at the university. Maybe he selected Heather far in advance and set her up."

Ben glanced at the array of photographs. The pictures of the parking lot, Heather's van and the hotel didn't bother him; the pictures of Heather made him sick. He said, "Excuse me, Sarge."

She turned around and picked up a cup of coffee from Tony's desk.

"If I'm out of line, I'll shut up. But, Karen's killer had been inside her car. What if Heather's was, too? Wouldn't that explain why she was facing the van?"

The coffee cup slipped in Nadine's hand. She caught it before she dropped it, but sloshed coffee on the floor. Tony Zaccaro gave a violent jerk and spun to face the photographs.

Nadine grabbed a photograph off the wall. "The key in the unlocked door." She pantomimed inserting a key in a lock. "Put the key in, turn, pull it out, open the door. *Unless* the door is opened from the inside and you step back out of the way, look up in surprise..." She turned wide, amazed eyes on Ben. "That's it! I don't believe I missed it."

"Am I right?" Ben asked.

"That explains perfectly why she was where she was. Ben, you're a genius!" She thumped her forehead with the heel of her hand. "I've only looked at that a million times, and I missed it."

Tony scratched his head, and his mouth twisted. "We still don't know who the shooter is."

"Bob!" Nadine called. "Where did he go?" She hurried out of the office.

Tony chuckled. Ben liked him. A tall, thin man with prematurely white hair, he had dark, intelligent eyes and a dry manner of speaking. Photographs of his wife and four kids covered the top of his desk.

Tony said, "Out of the mouths of babes. Good eye, Jackson." He picked up a stack of clippings from a table. "Tell me more about this stalker of yours." Heedless of the damage done to the wall, he began pinning up the faxes of newspaper clippings Ben had received from Atlanta. "Any insights? Any reasons why the stalker accuses you of killing all these women?"

"I've never even heard of those women. Atlanta is a big city." Ben raised his arms and stretched. Hands hooked behind his neck, he studied the clippings, with their nearly identical photographs. "It could be a case of more is better."

Tony gave him a questioning look.

Ben explained. "First he accused me of killing my wife. He kept telling me to clear my conscience and confess. I didn't. So then Karen was killed, and instead of telling me to confess, he wrote to my friends and family, and the police. That didn't work, either. Maybe he went through the newspaper and chose those women because they were young and blond. He only mentioned them in one letter. When that didn't work, he dropped it and tried something else."

Nadine returned. She said, "Bob's comparing the gun prints with the elimination prints we took out of Heather's van. Keep your fingers crossed."

She laid a hand on Ben's shoulder. Her weary eyes went soft as she smiled at him. "Thank you."

He patted her hand, wishing he could take her someplace so that he could hold her and love her and watch her sleep. Her ex-husband, he decided, must be the world's biggest jackass. With a woman like Nadine at his side, a man could conquer the world.

"Nadine," Tony said, "do you remember the Baker case?"

She grimaced. "How could I forget?"

Tony explained to Ben, "A woman suffered from severe postpartum depression. When the baby died of sudden infant death syndrome, the woman accused her husband of smothering it. We investigated, but the evidence proved he hadn't done it. So she shot him."

Ben winced.

"You think there's a similarity here, Tony?" Nadine asked. "Like Kyle's theory that the stalker has transferred his guilt to Ben?"

"That sure would explain the letters."

Kyle walked into the office. He said, "Excuse me, ma'am, sir, I just talked to Black Wells." His mouth worked as if he were fighting a grin, and his eyes glittered. "Some reporter out of Austin found out the warrant was dropped."

Nadine said, "And talked to Billy Joe?"

"Yes, ma'am. Word is the sheriff locked himself up in his office for about an hour, then snuck out the back door. The APB on you and Ben has been dropped."

Tony barked laughter and hoisted a coffee cup in a merry salute. Kyle laughed with him.

"Hoist on his own petard," Ben muttered, and laughed softly, too.

Nadine threw up her hands. "Hold on a minute! Kyle, hush!"

The deputy clamped his mouth shut.

"Just between you fellas and these four walls, I don't hold much fondness for Billy Joe Horseman. The man's a menace. *But*... he is the sheriff, and this kind of embarrassment reflects poorly on the entire department."

"He did it to himself, Nadine," Tony said. "We all tried to stop him."

"That doesn't matter. We have a murder to solve. How are we going to do that if we're laughingstocks? Tony, I can just see the defense team now." She cocked her weight onto one hip and assumed a snotty expression. "Oh, really, Counselor, this is the shooter? What, he's the only man left in the county after the sheriff publicly accused everyone else?" She snorted disgustedly. "This whole thing smacks of a Marx brothers movie, and don't think for a minute the defense won't use it."

Ben covered his mouth with his hand. Tony fiddled with the pens on his desk. Kyle studied his shoes.

She stabbed a finger at the newspaper clippings. "And what about Karen Bates? With our shooter being inside Heather's van, then we have another, very important similarity. Odds of them being related just went up. Do we let the perp walk for Karen's murder because our sheriff lacks credibility? We need Atlanta. We can't get their help if the press fries Billy Joe."

Tony asked, "What do you suggest we do?"

She sank to a chair and leaned forward, grasping her knees. Her ponytail slipped over her shoulder, hiding her face. "I'm so tired, I can't think. There's got to be a way out of this mess, but I don't know what it is." She looked up with a scowl. "I do know this isn't a laughing matter."

"Go home. Get some sleep," Tony said. "First thing tomorrow I'll get in touch with Billy Joe, let him know what we've got." He made a shooing gesture at Nadine. "Go on, get. You're no good this way." He glanced at the pictures on the wall. "Deputy Green, you better drive escort. We've still got a nut running loose out there."

NADINE SLAMMED on the brakes. The headlights shone on the rear end of an old, beat-up Ford. Ben lurched against the seat belt, then fell back against the seat. He stared at the car parked next to the fence around Nadine's small front yard.

Behind them, Kyle's van stopped, and the headlights filled the interior of the Chevelle.

Ben pointed at the house and said, "Look!"

Nadine glimpsed a shadow moving rapidly off the porch. The shape disappeared over the porch railing and around the house. Grabbing her gun and the door

handle, she ordered, "Get down, and don't move!"
She pushed open the door.

Crouched low behind the open door, she used hand
signals to indicate to Kyle that the prowler had gone
around the house. Wafflegate. Setting up another
ambush? She heard the passenger door of the van
open, and then Kyle's soggy footsteps on the saturated ground.

"Give me the mike, Ben. Ma'am?" he whispered.
The deputy crouched next to the Chevelle. "I'll call in
backups. That's Wafflegate, isn't it? Did you see a
gun?"

"I saw very little. You don't think that fool took off
cross-country?" Imagining having to search for a man
in the acreage behind the house, a maze of rocky hills,
scrub oak, canebrakes and miniature cypress swamps
made dangerous by the darkness, dismayed her. Fury
boiled her blood. Was an unbroken night of sleep too
much to ask? "Better request a dog, too. We might
have to track—"

Wafflegate stepped into the light. Hands high, begging them not to shoot, he sidled around the side of
the house.

Nadine ordered him to halt. He stopped. Caught in
two sets of headlights, his eyes gleamed like hard-
boiled eggs.

"Keep your hands where I can see them!" She
stood, both hands on her gun. "Do not move."

"Hey, uh, I didn't do anything. I was just... All I
want is a statement."

Nadine and Kyle converged on the reporter. Kyle
handcuffed him, and Nadine patted him down for
weapons. She demanded to know what he was doing
sneaking around her house at two o'clock in the

morning. Wafflegate stammered and stuttered about writing a story and her having no right to interfere with the freedom of the press.

Waving an all clear to Ben, Nadine hopped up on the porch. Her front door stood open, and marks on the jamb showed where the lock had been forced open. Cautiously, weapon at the ready, she felt inside for the light switch. Her foot struck something that clattered. She turned on the porch light and found a penlight on the porch. It wasn't hers.

She pushed the door open wide. The front room was empty. Muddy footprints tracked the wood floor, leading to her desk.

Ben's sudden appearance behind her gave her a start.

"Is life with you always like this?" he asked.

"No."

"Good thing."

She gave him a grim smile, then walked back to Wafflegate. Despite the temperature hovering near the freezing mark, sweat poured off the reporter's face.

"What were you doing in my house?" she asked.

"All I did was knock on your door."

She held up the penlight. "At two o'clock in the morning? Show me the bottom of your foot."

She shone the penlight on the concentric pattern on the sole of his athletic shoe. It matched the muddy tracks she'd seen. She focused the penlight on his eyes. "What were you doing in my house?"

Panting, he stared at Ben. "I don't know why you're bugging me. I'm just a reporter doing my job. There's your killer *and* my story. That's what I'm doing here. You're the one who should be answering questions. You harbored a fugitive. You're having an affair with a killer."

Turning away in disgust, she said, "You're under arrest for breaking and entering. Kyle, read him his rights. I'll call it in." She returned to the house. Ben fell into step beside her.

Wafflegate yelled, "Your door was open! I thought Jackson killed you, too. I thought you were in there lying in a pool of blood or something. I didn't break in."

"Liar," Nadine muttered. He might have found the door open, but it was her desk, not her body, that had interested him.

As she climbed the porch steps, Wafflegate said, "He's the killer! Why isn't he under arrest? He's going to kill you, too, Sergeant Shell. He already tried once."

"Shut up, Daryl. You're just making it worse."

He said, "I heard the warrant was dropped. I just wanted to know why. That's my job. The public has the right to know. Your job is taking killers off the street. You can't blame me for being concerned. He tried to kill you once, why shouldn't he try again? Then I find your door open, and nobody answers the bell. What was I supposed to think? Who wouldn't go inside? It's just normal human curiosity. I didn't mean any harm. I didn't take anything."

"Read those rights, Kyle. Daryl, I think you better shut your mouth and listen."

It took until nearly 3:30 a.m. before she was finished with Daryl and her report. Finally alone with Ben, she stood before the front door, her limbs so heavy it was too much effort to lift her arms.

"Look at that," she said. "I bet Billy Joe jimmied open the lock, then just left it open. Sheesh, and the house is full of guns."

Ben chuckled. "You sound drunk, Sarge."

"I do?"

Swinging his head slowly, he caught her around the shoulders. "Off to bed."

"Need to check the house," she mumbled.

"You need some sleep." He urged her toward the bedrooms. "Which is yours?"

He got her onto her narrow bed and ran a hand over the maple headboard carved with doves and bows. "Don't tell me, it's your childhood bed."

"Grew up in this house." Once on her back, she couldn't move. "Daddy and Mom bought it the year I was born." Ben tugged off her shoes. Her legs felt like rubber, and despite her best efforts, she couldn't help him as he pulled off her jeans. She said, "I wanted to raise my boys in this house. It's a good house, old friendly house. Lots of room outside to play and explore. There's a fishing pond out back."

"Someday, baby." He touched her belly with a playful kiss. She giggled.

The giggles died as great sadness filled her. "I'm not really a bad mother. Am I?"

"Hey, you're tired, punchy, and talking nonsense. Now close your eyes." He covered her with the blankets and tucked them around her shoulders. "Go to sleep, and dream some nice dreams."

"The boys are better off with their dad. Crystal's a good mom. She's always home when they get off school. Me, I'm just a cop."

"I've seen you with your kids. You're a good mother."

"I was a lousy wife."

"Fred's a lousy husband. He was stupid to give you up." He tugged the elastic band off her ponytail, then brushed hair off her forehead and kissed her. "I never would." He kissed the tip of her nose. "I never will. You're good and beautiful and wonderful . . ."

Her fantasy voice, soothing and sensual, caressing her ears. Try as she might, she could not open her eyes to see if he was smiling when he said that, to look into the mirrors of his soul and see if he spoke the truth.

The next thing she knew, Ben was shaking her. She fought a battle with her eyelids. As soon as she opened her eyes, she regretted it. Light burned them, and pain struck like lightning bolts inside her skull. She groaned and rolled over.

"Sarge, wake up."

"Can't."

He shook her again. "Tony Zaccaro called."

She pulled the covers over her head. She didn't care what Tony said. She craved sleep, blessed healing sleep.

Ben tugged the covers away from her face. "I didn't answer, but it's on your machine. He sounds excited."

Grumbling, she creakily sat up and swung her feet off the bed. She scrubbed her face with her hands, then looked up at him. Cocking an eyebrow, Ben gave her bare legs a long, loving look.

Let him look, she thought, and stretched luxuriously, working her sleep-stiffened muscles. She worked her toes against the braided rug next to the bed and flexed her fingers. He began stroking his jaw and making a little sound with his tongue against his teeth.

"I'm no longer a wanted man."

His silky words arrowed straight to her heart. She licked her lips. His lips parted, and desire darkened his eyes. "Not wanted for murder, anyway," she said.

Suddenly he turned away so that he faced the window. He jammed his hands into his back pockets and rocked on his heels. Sunlight streaming through the curtain picked up rich blue lights in his hair.

"The other day," he said, "that was special. Not exactly what I envisioned, but special. I...after Cathy died, I figured I'd never meet anyone again. Anyone special."

"What are you saying, Ben?" Her fingers curled into the sheets. Her heart hammered.

He turned his head enough to see her over his shoulder. A slant of bright light turned his eyes to pure gold. "As much as I lust after that gorgeous body of yours, I don't want some affair on the sly." His lips pulled into a sad smile. "I'm not good at hiding what I feel. I can't take the cold shoulder when we're in public. Or worrying if I'm going to hurt your job, or—" He shoved a hand through his hair.

She arose, reaching for him. "Oh, Ben, I'm so sorry. I didn't mean—"

"I'm not looking for an apology. But I'm an all-or-nothing kind of guy. I can't play lovey-dovey in private, then pretend I don't care in public. That's all I'm saying."

She turned her attention to her clothes. "You know I care about you."

"I figured that part out."

She pulled on her sweatpants. "I don't mean to hurt you."

"It's not a matter of hurt." His chest raised and lowered in a heavy breath.

"I'll get this mess cleared up. I promise." All the promises she'd made and broken in the past, to her former husband, to her children, to her father, rose to haunt her. "I'd better call Tony. Maybe he has good news."

"We could sure use some," he said.

Armed with a cup of coffee, she called the county prosecutor. As soon as she identified herself, he said, "Are you sitting down?"

"It's getting so every time I hear those words my teeth start to ache. What's up, Tony?"

"We've got a match on the fingerprints off the gun. None other than our favorite reporter, Daryl Wafflegate."

Chapter Thirteen

"As you are well aware," Nadine said, "we've got a small problem, Billy Joe."

Ben admired her cool, calm manner of speaking. He also admired her mastery of the art of understatement. Even so, it took all his concentration to keep from fidgeting on the hard chair near the door. The voice of reason kept telling him this was a mistake, his presence could only irritate the sheriff, he'd better walk out while he could.

People crowded the sheriff's office, turning the air close and hot. But the sweat dampening Ben's palms and trickling down his back had little to do with the temperature.

The sheriff sat rigidly behind his desk. Patchy color on his florid face and pouches under his eyes gave him a trapped expression. He looked from Nadine to Kyle to Tony to Bob Underhill, then returned his attention to Nadine. If the malevolence in his eyes held physical force, he would have shoved her through the concrete block wall. "Y'all are conspiring against me."

Me and my big mouth, Ben thought. "Hey," he had told Nadine, "let's threaten the sheriff with a lawsuit. That'll make him sit up and pay attention." He'd never dreamed Nadine and Tony would think that was a wonderful idea. Now, wanting to squirm under the seething hatred emanating from Sheriff Horseman, he considered it would be best to keep his lip buttoned.

"Daryl Wafflegate is in custody," Nadine said. "We've charged him with criminal trespass and breaking and entering. We're hoping to charge him with Heather's murder."

Billy Joe sputtered, and his big hands convulsively crumpled papers.

"As of now, he's in Tucker. His attorney has ordered him not to speak to us anymore. What do you figure, Tony? Twenty-four hours before he makes bail?"

"A reporter?" Billy Joe's eyes nearly popped from their sockets. "You can't charge a reporter with murder."

"We have the murder weapon." She gave Bob Underhill a nod.

The technician explained how matches in ejector marks on the spent bullet casings proved the casing found at the murder scene matched the gun found in Ben's car. Ballistics testing proved it was the same gun used to shoot at Nadine's car. Wafflegate's fingerprints had been on the bullet clip inside the weapon.

Billy Joe dabbed at his face with a tissue. "What are y'all saying?"

Nadine opened a manila folder. "Officer Bert Trews was the responding officer at the murder scene. According to him, the first person to show up was Daryl Wafflegate. Mary O'Connall claims Daryl was with her at the newspaper office at the time of the murder. However, no one else can corroborate the alibi." She turned a paper over.

"At first he denied ever touching the weapon. Then he insisted we made a mistake or that someone faked his prints. After repeated questioning, he said he went to my place looking for Ben. From a hiding place, he saw Ben park on the road, then walk up to my house. He then saw a person approach Ben's car. This person, who Wafflegate is unable to describe, did something inside the car. Wafflegate said he investigated and found the gun. He released the clip to see if it contained bullets. He replaced the clip and wiped his fingerprints off the gun. He then claims he drove toward town, but his car developed problems, stranding him in the thunderstorm. Which explains why he didn't report Ben's being at my home."

Kyle said, "He's lying like a sack of dirt."

Tony nodded his agreement, and added, "Wafflegate has been fired from several jobs for lying. He also refuses to take a polygraph."

Nadine continued. "When Kyle and I were shot at, Wafflegate was again the first person on the scene. He claims variously that he was on his way to Tucker because of a story, then that he heard us report the shooting, then that he received an anonymous tip that an attempt would be made on my life."

"Lying again," Kyle said.

"He possesses a radio scanner. When we confiscated it, it was tuned to the sheriff's frequency." Nadine laid a sheet of paper in front of the sheriff. "Along with the scanner, we also confiscated a Slim Jim from his automobile."

"One of those thingamabobs for breaking into cars?" Billy Joe asked.

"Exactly. We're now fairly sure that Heather's killer was waiting for her *inside* her van." She graced Ben with a quick, approving smile. "Wafflegate says the Slim Jim isn't his. Mary O'Connall says it belongs to her ex-husband, Tim O'Connall. Tim denies ownership." She shrugged. "Only Wafflegate's fingerprints were on it."

The sheriff studied the list of items confiscated during the search of Wafflegate's room in Mary O'Connall's apartment, his car, and his desk at the *Bugle* office. His double chins quivered.

Nadine said, "This is all damning evidence, but we're not willing to press the murder charge quite yet."

"Why not?" Billy Joe wiped a hand jerkily over the evidence list.

Tony answered, "Despite the fingerprints on the gun clip, what we've got is circumstantial. Wafflegate has explanations for everything. And he does have an alibi."

"Three or four explanations," Kyle muttered.

Nadine leaned over the desk and placed a finger on the paper. "Wafflegate had in his possession copies of the stalker letters sent to Atlanta homicide. He says you gave them to him."

Billy Joe started violently, and his chair squealed. "That's a lie!" His eyes darted, and he licked his lips.

"You're willing to testify to that?" Tony asked.

"That boy is lying. Besides, Nadine, you know I never had copies of those letters. I wouldn't leak case information. He's lying."

Nadine, her expression closed and unreadable, stepped back from the desk. "There are only three ways he could have gotten those letters. Either he broke in and made the copies himself, or somebody leaked them, or he wrote them himself and saved copies. I find it highly unlikely he broke into this station."

"I sure didn't leak them. I swear on a stack of Bibles! If anybody leaked anything, it sure wasn't me!"

"If he wrote them," Nadine said, "then he's the stalker. Which means he may have killed Karen Bates, as well."

"Can you prove it?"

"Wafflegate swears he's never been in Georgia."

Billy Joe swallowed hard. "Doesn't Atlanta have anything on him?"

Nadine rested a hip on the corner of the desk. Arms crossed, she studied the sheriff. "We've got a small problem. They're not communicating with us. We faxed the firearms report, but thus far no reply."

"They best get on the stick. We found their killer!"

Nadine snapped, "You embarrassed them!"

Billy Joe jumped in his seat and caught the edge of the desk in both hands.

Nadine's eyes blazed, and muscles jumped in her jaw.

Tony spoke soft, soothing words.

Ben blinked rapidly in surprise. All of a sudden Nadine's small stature didn't matter. She looked like an avenging Valkyrie swooping down from the sky. Her anger crackled dangerously; her body trembled.

Wow. Ben made a mental note never to tick her off.

"Let me put it in terms you can understand," Nadine said, each frosty word clipped. "With what we have now, if we take Wafflegate to trial, we have only a minuscule chance of convicting him. His attorney will make mincemeat out of the circumstantial evidence. That is, if it's possible to find an impartial jury."

"The gun..." Billy Joe whispered.

Nadine slapped a hand on the desk. "A gun found in Ben's car. A gun no one has seen in Wafflegate's possession. A gun we can't trace, because it's a piece of street garbage. His attorney will have a great time playing with the fingerprint evidence in court. And do you know why?" She stabbed a finger toward his face, and he flinched with her every movement. "You and your big mouth."

"Nadine, that's enough," Tony said.

"It's not enough! A sweet, innocent twenty-one-year-old girl is dead. And her killer is going to walk away a free man, because you can't keep your mouth shut!"

Tony moved in to take her arm. She shrugged him away, turning toward the door. She pressed one hand against the door and the other to her chest.

"You best watch your mouth," Billy Joe said tonelessly.

Without turning around, Nadine said, "You turned my investigation into a circus. I lost Atlanta. There are fifty reporters circling like buzzards out there. Newspapers, magazines, television shows. After they get through with turning our department into the local comedy show, we couldn't convict Charles Manson of littering!"

"I proceeded using the information available to me." Billy Joe looked from person to person. He even glared at Ben.

Ben began to believe the threat of a lawsuit might actually work.

"You proceeded on information provided by the man who might be the killer." Nadine turned around, head high and eyes flashing. "So what are you going to do about it?"

"Y'all never told me you suspected Wafflegate. This is your fault, Nadine. You're always shoving me out of the way. You were supposed to keep me informed."

Nadine rolled her eyes. She placed a hand on Ben's shoulder. "I can see this is a waste of time."

Tony placed a sheet of paper in front of the sheriff. "I think we can salvage this situation."

Billy Joe scanned the paper, then raised stunned eyes to Nadine. "It's a press release."

"That's right." She squeezed Ben's shoulder in reassurance. "If you'll read that statement without embellishment, Ben will refrain from suing you and the county."

Billy Joe's hate-filled eyes turned on Ben. He whispered, "This is blackmail."

"Call it what you want, Billy Joe."

He flung away the press release. "I'm not lying to the press!"

Kyle covered his mouth with a hand, and his eyes sparkled. Tony coughed into his fist. Bob Underhill rocked on his heels and studied the ceiling.

"Well, now," Nadine said, nodding. "Then Ben and I will hold our own press conference, I suppose."

"I'll fire you."

Nadine smiled. "Feel free."

Ben knew she was bluffing. She'd cut her own throat before harming her chance of convicting Heather's murderer. Did the sheriff know it? Vibrating from the angry tension in the room, Ben held his breath and waited for the sheriff to make his move.

BEN LEANED HIS BACK against the wall and folded his arms over his chest. He matched the posture of Nadine on his left and Tony Zaccaro on his right. On the other side of the main office in the sheriff's building, Billy Joe held court over a gathering of eager reporters. Bright lights glared on his shiny face and the shinier brass buttons on his dress uniform.

Several reporters had taken Ben's picture. As it grew apparent that neither Ben, Nadine nor Tony intended to make a statement, they had returned their attention to the sheriff.

In spite of everything, Ben had to admire Billy Joe Horseman. The man was a consummate political showman, pulling victory out of chaos. He finished reading the press release—using the word *allegedly* a lot—then indicated he was open for questions.

A reporter waved her hand. "Are you saying you deliberately fed false information to the press in order to catch Miss Labeau's killer?"

"Now, now," the sheriff said. "You misunderstood me. By enlisting your cooperation in our investigation, we were able to conduct, shall we say, a psychological campaign against our prime suspect. Lulling the alleged killer into a false sense of security, so to speak. I and the good people of Ponce County are eternally grateful for your help in this most difficult operation."

"What about Ben Jackson's role?" The reporter flipped through her notebook. "You stated he was your prime suspect and an arrest was imminent. What about the shooting attack on Sergeant Nadine Shell? You claimed you had witnesses who proved he attempted murder. What about the killings in Atlanta?"

Several reporters eyed Ben. He smiled.

Billy Joe said, "I'm afraid I may have gotten a little carried away and allowed a few too many implications to slip through the net. I never said Mr. Jackson was our suspect. I never said that once. Next question."

Nadine murmured, "He lies so beautifully."

My thoughts exactly, Ben thought. As much as he tried to ignore the troubling voice of suspicion inside his head, it increased in volume. He kept seeing Billy Joe's face when Nadine had asked if he'd leaked information to Wafflegate. If the sheriff was lying, did that mean Wafflegate was telling the truth?

A reporter called, "Who is the suspect you have in custody?"

"I am not at liberty to divulge that information at this point in time. Next question."

"What about the murders in Atlanta?"

Billy Joe glanced at his notes. "In light of the ongoing investigations, I am not at liberty to speak about that matter. I have time for one more question."

A young female reporter looked over her shoulder at Nadine and Ben.

Nadine pushed away from the wall. She touched Ben's hand.

The reporter asked, "Sheriff Horseman, didn't you publicly accuse your investigator, Sergeant Nadine Shell, of having a sexual affair with your prime suspect? You stated she was suffering from depression and psychosis caused by the suicide of her father. Are you now recanting those statements?"

Ben's jaw tightened. The atmosphere was subtly shifting from confusion to hostility.

Billy Joe said, "Rest assured, I have only the highest respect for my investigator. In light of the attempt made on her life, it was agreed by all to create the illusion of discord and confusion within the department. Illusion, that's the key. Thank you very much for your time, ladies and gentlemen. If you will excuse me." Head high, smiling a shark-like politician's smile, he strode down the hall.

Tony said, "Not all of them fell for that. I think it's time we beat it out of Dodge, pardners."

Ben wasn't exactly falling for it either. As much as he despised Wafflegate, as much as the man deserved every bit of bad luck he'd brought on himself, if he wasn't a killer, he didn't deserve to be treated like one. Having firsthand knowledge of the experience, Ben figured nobody deserved it. He followed Nadine and Tony down the hall to Nadine's office.

Once behind closed doors, Tony said, "Okay, boys and girls, we have only hours before Wafflegate gets sprung on the B and E charge. Nadine, do you figure you can sweet-talk your way back into Atlanta's good graces?"

"I haven't any choice." She nodded at Kyle. "Top priority. I want to know where Wafflegate was when Karen Bates was murdered, and I need corroborating evidence or witnesses." She smiled at Ben. "Excuse me for a few minutes, Kyle. Ben?"

She beckoned for him to follow her. In the hallway, she paused, looking and listening toward the main office. Then she headed for the back of the station.

"It's going to be another late night." She reached a steel door marked with an exit sign, leaned a shoulder against it and stared at her interlaced fingers. "Ben, thank you."

"For what?"

"For helping me. After what you've been through, I wouldn't blame you if you sued the pants off the county. You're a good man, Ben Jackson."

He eased a stray curl behind her ear. "My motives aren't pure, Sarge. I'm still hoping for a dinner date."

Chuckling, she looked up at him. "I'd like that." She reached up to straighten his collar, and her soft hands whispered across his neck.

"Tomorrow night?"

She caught her lower lip in her teeth.

"Ah, come on... You can't work twenty-four hours a day."

"It's not that. It's...my boys." She dropped her hands and scuffed a toe along the tiled floor. "I miss them. I haven't even had time to call."

He pressed a finger to her lips. "Say no more. I understand."

"Do you?"

He took her face in both hands. "I do." He kissed her lightly.

She said, "How about dinner at my place tomorrow? You don't have to say yes. I understand—"

He kissed her again. "Love it. Can I bring wine, or should I stick to soda pop?"

Her smile filled the hallway and his heart with light. "You can bring anything you want."

She lifted her face, and he kissed her properly, trying to show he didn't care if he had to meet her in the company of a battalion of Boy Scouts.

Tony called her name. She broke their embrace, trailing her hands over his shoulders and arms. "I have to go. Slip out back, and you can probably avoid the reporters. I'll call you as soon as I'm free." Her lips parted, as if she had something else to say, but she turned away.

He pushed open the heavy door.

Sighing, Nadine hurried down the hall to see what Tony wanted now. *Please be good news. Please be something we can use to tie this case up.*

Tony informed her Atlanta was on the telephone. With a healthy dose of trepidation, Nadine cleared her throat, then said, "This is Sergeant Shell."

"Boyles here." He cleared his throat, too. "I may have been too hasty in losing my head."

Nadine waved excitedly to Tony. "Maybe, maybe not. What have you got, Detective?"

"It's not what I've got, ma'am, it's what you've got. We've been looking over your firearms identification report. It's a real good chance you've got our murder weapon."

Nadine wanted to jump off the chair and scream with delight. Instead, she steadied herself with a deep breath, then said, "Is it a positive ID?"

"We'd like to run some tests on the weapon itself. The slugs we took from Karen Bates were distorted, but we think we can get matches anyway. Is it true you have a suspect?"

"In custody, yes, sir. We haven't charged him yet." She gave him Wafflegate's vital statistics, and he promised to find out if Wafflegate had been in Georgia at the time of Karen's murder. He also intended to ask his superiors for permission to travel to Texas so that he could talk to Wafflegate in person.

Only after she got off the phone did she indulge in a bit of celebratory horseplay with Tony. But she quickly sobered.

"We have a lot of work to do. Connecting Wafflegate to two murders means twice the work." She turned a pad of paper around and picked up a pen. "We need to reinterview Mary O'Connall about Wafflegate's alibi."

"And confirm the ownership of the Slim Jim," Tony said. "I'd like to find the typewriter used to create those letters, too. He may have a storage locker or something."

"Check." She tapped the pen against the paper. "Ben's late wife may be the key to all this. She's a native of Kansas. Wafflegate may have met her there."

Tony mulled over that tidbit. "You think they had an affair?"

Nadine winced. The cop part of her prayed it was so; the rest of her hoped not. "Ben says no, but I'm not so sure. They had marital problems. It could be Wafflegate's obsessive. Perhaps it didn't have to be an affair, except in his head. If we can prove a connection of any kind, I think that'll give us enough of a motive to convince a jury."

"It's a possibility, but only if we can show a history." He scribbled on a notepad. "We also need to research any old girlfriends."

"If they did meet in Kansas and carried on a long-distance affair, it might not matter if we can't prove Wafflegate lived or worked in Atlanta."

"Except the stalker letters indicate long-term surveillance. He had to have been living in Atlanta. We can't get around proving he was in Georgia. No question."

"All right, Tony, we'll see. The question right now is, should we charge him?"

They argued the point for hours. Tony's position was that as soon as Wafflegate was charged with murder, then his defense team would gain access to the prosecution's case. They'd get a head start on explaining away the circumstantial evidence. Nadine was willing to take the chance. In light of Wafflegate's history of job-hopping and lying, he made a poor bail risk. She suspected that as soon as he hit the street, he'd flee.

Around midnight, Nadine pushed away her umpteenth cup of coffee. "Look, let's compromise. See if you can get Judge Tate to order a psychiatric evaluation before he considers bail."

"Psych? On a B and E? I don't think so."

"Charge him with harassment, then. Show the judge the letters and have him listen to the tape Ben recorded. It'll buy us a few days to see if we can place Wafflegate in Atlanta."

Shaking his head, Tony made a few notes. "You should have been a lawyer, Nadine." He grinned. "Or the sheriff." He leaned back on the chair and tapped his pen against his cheek. "An election is coming up in November."

His confidence flattered her. "I'm not worried about November. It's Wafflegate I'm—"

A knock on the door preceded the appearance of a deputy. "Ma'am, sir, a report just came in on a fire."

Nadine closed her eyes. Just what she needed—an arson investigation. Messy, smelly, frustrating, time-consuming and nearly impossible to solve. She mentally crossed her fingers and hoped the deputy would tell her they had the arsonist in custody and he'd confessed.

She asked, "Where?"

"It's in Black Wells, ma'am." He blinked owlishly. "It started in Ben Jackson's apartment."

HOLDING HER BODY RIGID to keep from staggering, Nadine stared at the flames. She'd seen the orange light as soon as she crossed Main Street, over a mile away. Up close, it was an inferno. Sixteen apartments, constructed of wood and drywall, burned like paper. The Black Wells fire department fought a determined battle, but the best they could do was to keep the fire from spreading. The apartments were a total loss.

She searched the clusters of bystanders, most of them in nightclothes. Ben. Where was he?

Tony kept a firm grip on Nadine's arm. He suddenly pointed to a fireman wearing a white chief's hat and said, "There's Roger."

Garish firelight and the flashing emergency lights made it impossible for her to pick out faces. She stumbled after the prosecutor.

Roger held a walkie-talkie close to his lips. He gave Nadine and Tony a nod of recognition. Nadine stared at the black, smoke-filled hole where Ben's apartment had been.

"Any injuries?" she asked the fire chief.

"We transported six people to the hospital for smoke inhalation," Roger said. "Thank God for smoke detectors. We're fairly sure everyone got out."

"Any idea how it started?"

Roger nodded. "The woman who lived in 16 was awake, reading a book. She claims she heard breaking glass, then an explosion. The way she describes it, sounds like a gasoline bomb."

A Molotov cocktail, Nadine thought. Fill a bottle with gasoline, insert a fuse, light it and throw.

Roger pointed at Ben's apartment. "It started in there."

Nadine pressed an arm against her aching belly. "What about Ben? The man who lives there? Where is he?"

Roger said, "He's been transported to the hospital."

"Is he alive?"

"That I can't tell you," Roger said, then turned his attention back to the walkie-talkie.

Chapter Fourteen

Ben stared at the whiteness. A sensation like burning cat scratches plagued his throat. Memories slipped in like elusive beasts, popping up their heads to look around, then going back into hiding. He remembered a crazy ride and doctors and tubes and being very, very sick. Not much made sense.

"Ben, are you awake?"

He turned his head, and his stiff neck creaked. Nadine smiled at him. Her beautiful eyes were swollen and red-rimmed. Had she been crying? No, not Nadine.

"Hospital," he croaked. "In the hospital."

"Shh, don't talk. You're in the Black Wells hospital. It's not much, but as long as no one wants to cut you open, it's a fine place." She pressed a finger to his lips. "You swallowed an awful lot of smoke. Doc Halloway says your throat will be sore a few more days. Want some water?"

He nodded. She held a straw to his mouth, and he sipped the deliciously cool water. His throat cramped up while he swallowed, but he persisted. His chest ached, and he rubbed his breastbone with his fist.

"Doc Halloway will release you in the morning," she said as she adjusted pillows beneath his head. "If your lungs are clear. He's worried about pneumonia, but I promised to keep an eye on you."

Smoke? Pneumonia? "What happened?"

"You don't remember the fire?"

He raised his eyebrows.

"Somebody lobbed a Molotov cocktail through your front window."

Ben tried to sit up, but she firmly pressed him back down. "Don't worry. There's a guard on the door. You're safe." She smoothed hair off his forehead, and her hand was gentle and cool. "I'm sorry. I never should have let you go home."

"Anyone else hurt?"

"Not seriously, thank goodness. Your apartment is a total loss, though." She smiled wanly. "You'll have to find another pair of red boots."

He started to laugh, but it hurt, so he groaned instead. None of this seemed real. The last thing he remembered was going to bed. He grew aware that the funny smell, like wet, burned wood, he kept catching hints of came from him. He sniffed the palm of one hand and grimaced. "Who did it?" he asked.

"I don't know. Yet. We'll find the guy, don't worry. Try to go back to sleep."

She kept petting him, stroking his hair. Soothed by her touch and gentle murmuring, he closed his eyes.

When he awakened, it was morning. Aside from a sore throat and a dull ache in his chest, he felt fine. He wanted out of the hospital.

First he had to wait for the doctor. Dr. Halloway, whose round belly and bushy white hair reminded Ben of Santa Claus, gave him a thorough going-over. He pronounced Ben fit, but warned that at the first sign of coughing or fever, he must return to the hospital.

Nadine showed up with Kyle. The deputy handed over a gym bag, commenting that he and Ben were about the same size. His expression warned Ben not to make a big deal of his generosity.

While Nadine went to find a nurse to check him out of the hospital, Ben dressed. Kyle's jeans were a little roomy, but the shirt and shoes fit fine.

"Sure you're all right, man?" Kyle asked.

"Won't be singing for my supper for a few days." He swallowed hard against the soreness.

"You gave Sergeant Shell a good scare. I haven't seen her that tore up since her father..." His face reddened. "I mean, well, you know... She was really worried about you."

"I know." The fear snuck up on him, catching him unawares. He had to sit on the bed and steady himself by clutching the mattress. Somebody had tried to kill him.

Kyle snapped up his head. "Are you all right?"

Ben shuddered. "Do you know who did it yet?"

"My money's on Reggie Hamilton. He denies it, of course. But I bet he did it."

Ben shook his head. "Hamilton?"

"A lot of people say Reggie boasted how he was going to get you if the cops didn't." He glanced at the door, then lowered his voice. "Between you and me, man, this is exactly the kind of crap Reggie is famous for. If it weren't for his parents all the time greasing him out of tight spots, he'd be in prison. He could have killed someone this time."

"Is there any way to prove he did it?" Ben couldn't see a way. Fire destroyed everything it touched.

Kyle lifted his shoulders in a quick shrug. "We might dig up some witnesses. We might lift finger-prints off the bottle holding the gas." He suddenly looked away, and his Adam's apple bobbed. "I feel bad about this, Ben. Sorry."

"For what?"

"I should have known there'd be some backlash. A lot of folks believe everything they read in the pa-per." He cut a sheepish glance at Ben. "Vigilantes are a problem from time to time. But don't worry, it won't happen again. All the news stories are calling you a hero now. That press conference blew them away."

Accompanied by a nurse pushing a wheelchair, Na-dine entered the room. "Ready to go home, Ben?"

Home. Where was that? He was unemployed and homeless. Not much of a catch—especially if the town posse wanted his head on a platter. He forced a smile.

To his surprise, Nadine's sons were waiting in the lobby. "I'm taking the next couple of days off," she said. "Tony and Kyle are handling the legwork."

"Hey, fellas," Ben said, pushing himself out of the wheelchair.

Rory gave him a befuddled look. "You're talking funny again, Mr. Jackson."

"Rory, Mr. Jackson has a sore throat." Nadine glanced warningly at her son.

"Yeah, stupid," Dale said, elbowing his brother. Beaming, he reached into his back pocket and pulled out an envelope. Handing it over to Ben, he said, "Me and Rory made get-well cards."

Ben opened the envelope. It contained a folded sheet of notebook paper with a lopsided daisy drawn on the front. Inside it read "Dear Mr. Jackson, Hope you feel better soon. When you are out of hospital you and me and Daddy and Rory can go fishing. Signed, your friend Dale Robert Shell.''

It took some nudging and hissed orders from his brother, but Rory handed over an envelope, too. He immediately buried his face against his mother's side. She ruffled his fine brown hair.

"Thank you, Dale," Ben said. "I feel better already."

Smiling, he opened Rory's offering. The paper was folded into a very small, very neat square. He opened it, and a steel penny rolled out. Ben caught it. The message read "Dear Mr. Jackson, I am fine, how are you. My magic penny will make you feel better. XXXOOO, Rory."

Rory whispered, "Granddaddy gave me that. It's got properties." He peeked at Ben. "That's what Granddaddy said."

Ben slipped the penny in his shirt pocket, then patted it. "I'll give it back when I'm all better."

Rory smiled, then buried his face against Nadine again.

A pain formed in Ben's throat that had nothing to do with the rawness caused by smoke inhalation. Dale slipped his hand into Ben's and tugged. Ben figured if he didn't start walking he was going to make a fool of himself.

BANISHED.
Nadine sighed and turned a frown toward the kitchen. Ben and the boys had banished her from her own kitchen. Dale's laughter rang high and clear.

It had been a nice day. First they'd gone shopping for Ben. Then, at home, over her protests that Ben needed to rest, the boys had insisted on showing him the fishing pond behind the house, the creek that in the summertime turned black with millions of tadpoles, and the owl's nest in the barn.

Now the three of them had ganged up on her. They wanted to cook supper, and they refused to allow her in the kitchen.

"Mama?" Dale asked from the hallway. "Where's the key to the root cellar?"

She laid her book on her lap and said, "Forget it. It's dangerous, and if I catch you boys down there again I'll tan your hides."

"Not for me, Mama," the boy said in exasperation. "Mr. Jackson needs onions and carrots."

"Oh." She gave her son a sheepish smile. "Sorry. The key is on a nail inside the closet door, on the right-hand side. Tell him he needs the flashlight. The light isn't working." The smell of browning meat filled the house, mingling with the scent of burning hickory in the fireplace. "What are you boys cooking?"

"I'm making salad, and Rory's making biscuits. Mr. Jackson's making sumadis stew," Dale said with a grin. "Some of dis, some of dat, eat too much and it'll make you fat!" He hooted a laugh and trotted back to the kitchen.

Ben's easy rapport with the boys made her see why he'd gotten so upset when his late wife refused to bear children. It also filled her with mild regret. This was family life as she'd always imagined it. This was what she longed to come home to every day.

But why should Ben stay? He'd wanted a fresh start in Black Wells, and instead he'd nearly drowned in a caldron of troubles. He'd been unjustly accused, investigated, fired from his job, slandered, libeled, and nearly killed. Even if they caught the idiot who'd tried to take justice into his own hands by firebombing Ben's apartment, why should Ben trust the people of Black Wells to treat him fairly? Logically, Ben ought to return to Georgia, where he had friends and family.

Logically... Too bad hearts didn't break into neat, logical pieces.

The boys called her to supper.

Dale's carrot, raisin and pineapple salad was a smash hit, with both boys taking triple helpings. Rory's biscuits were a trifle tough, but the boys assured her they beat hers by a long shot.

"My cooking isn't that bad," Nadine said.

"It's real bad, but that's okay," Dale informed Ben. "Me and Rory can do the cooking. You, too, Mr. Jackson. This sumadis stew is real good."

After supper, Ben offered to clean the kitchen. Much to Nadine's astonishment, the boys chimed in that they wanted to help. Amused and bemused, Nadine returned to the front room. She tried to read a book, but listening to Ben and the boys carrying on and teasing each other was more fun.

Kyle called her on the telephone. "I checked in on Wafflegate," he said. "You know, to make sure he isn't going to kill himself or something. He says he wants to talk."

Her heart skipped a beat. "A confession?"

"I don't think so." He paused. "He says he'll only talk to you. He's dropping hints about knowing who the real killer is."

"The real killer. Uh-huh. But he won't give this phantom a name?"

Ben and the boys settled around the coffee table. Dale began shuffling a deck of cards.

Kyle said, "He'll only talk to you. He was firm about that."

"With or without his attorney present?"

"He didn't say."

"I see."

"Personally, I think it's a waste of time, ma'am. We've got him dead to rights, and he knows it."

They didn't have Wafflegate dead to rights, she thought wearily. Not yet, anyway. "I'll talk to him tomorrow."

When she hung up the phone it startled her to hear Rory say, "Hit me."

"Ben Jackson, are you teaching those boys how to play poker?"

Dale said, "Mama Crystal already showed us how." He snickered. "And I'm winning." He laid a full house with threes and queens on the table. "Read 'em and weep, suckers."

Eyes wide and innocent, Ben grinned and shrugged. His amused expression told her, *They're your kids.*

Rolling her eyes, she asked Ben to join her in the kitchen. "Want a grown-up drink?" she asked.

He yawned and covered it with a hand. "I'm fine. What's up?"

"That was Kyle on the phone. He says Wafflegate wants to talk to me."

"Now?"

"Tomorrow. He says he knows the identity of the real killer."

He grinned, folded his arms and lifted his face to stare at the ceiling. "If I tell you something screwy, promise not to laugh." His lively eyes acquired a sombre cast. "I don't think Wafflegate is the killer."

"We're not railroading him," she said. "Facts and evidence. Everything points to him."

He tapped his fingers against his biceps. "Do you think the sheriff is lying about leaking information to Wafflegate?"

Without hesitation, she said, "Yes."

Ben's mouth dropped open, and he let his arms fall to his sides.

"Those letters we found mean little by themselves. They're only a very small piece of a very large puzzle. It's like finding a rock in your breakfast cereal. You know something is wrong, but just by looking there's no telling how it got there or why."

That stubborn look came over Ben's face.

"What's really bothering you?"

"Don't get me wrong, I despise Wafflegate. What he did to us is inexcusable." He raked hair off his face and made disgruntled noises. "But, damn it, Sarge, not even Wafflegate deserves to go through what I went through."

"I feel the same way. That's why I'm going to talk to him. And I was wondering if you'd mind watching the boys. You don't have to, but I don't want to take them home early."

"You trust me with your kids?"

She'd trust him with her life and her heart. "I'll take you into town to pick up your car. Then, if you want to goof around, that's okay."

He pulled an uncertain face and shoved his hands in his jeans.

"I know what you're thinking, but it's okay. The newspaper and the television stories told the world you're not a killer. You don't have to worry about vigilantes."

"I'll pick up the car and come straight back here." His smile faded. He glanced at the doorway, then gathered her into his arms. "It means a lot, knowing you trust me."

She gave him a reassuring squeeze. "I trust this town, too, Ben. We haven't treated you all that good, but that's only a few. The folks of Ponce County are good people. I sure hope you're willing to give them a second chance."

He kissed her, softly, sweetly.

Giggles interrupted them. Nadine sprang away from Ben and caught her shirttail, tugging it down. Dale and Rory peeked around the corner, their eyes bright with laughter. Her throat warmed.

"Ooooh," Dale sang, "Mr. Jackson's kissing Mama."

"Dale . . ."

Ben said, "I'll dance with her, too." Before Nadine could react, he had her in his arms and was swirling her around the kitchen. The boys howled with laughter. When Ben dipped her, nearly bending her in two over his arm the boys all but fell on the floor.

"You're crazy, Ben Jackson," she whispered. His sparkling eyes enchanted her.

"Crazy about you," he said before setting her on her feet. He jauntily brushed hair off his face and strutted toward the door. "Okay, boys, deal those cards. I need to recoup my losses."

At eight-thirty she had the boys bathed, then got them ready for bed. The boys wanted Ben to tell them a story.

"Not tonight, fellas. His throat is still sore."

A chorus of pitiful *Aw, Mama*s made her want to laugh. Instead, she fixed a stern expression on her face. "You need your sleep. No more fooling around." She kissed them both, then left the room, shutting the door softly behind her and indulging in one moment of self-pity because she couldn't have the boys home all the time.

She joined Ben in the front room. He lounged on the couch with his long legs stretched toward the fireplace, a paperback novel hanging loosely from his hand. Chin to chest, he dozed. Poor thing, she thought fondly. He must be exhausted, but she hated making him sleep on the couch.

Letting him share her bed, small as it was, tempted her with something akin to physical pain. But if one of the boys came into her room in the night... Despite their catching her and Ben kissing, she felt far from ready to admit to her sons that she had a sex life.

She looked down the hallway. She hadn't been inside her father's room since his death. She hadn't been able to go in there—the memories hurt too much.

Or did they?

Shaking his shoulder, she said, "Ben? Come on, honey, let's put you to bed." His eyelids fluttered, and she helped him to his feet. He mumbled about not being tired, which made her grin, since he was asleep on his feet. She urged him into the bathroom, informing him that there was plenty of toothpaste in the cabinet. She gathered fresh sheets and pillowcases, and then, steeling her nerve, she opened the bedroom door.

Head down, focused on the task, Nadine made up the bed with fresh linens. Ben joined her.

Being in here didn't hurt the way she'd thought it might. In an odd way, the lingering scent of her father's after-shave and the heavy old furniture, scarred by years of use, comforted her. The memories the room conjured were pleasant. Awakening her father for early-morning fishing trips; hanging his starched uniform shirts in the closet; foraging in his desk for paper for her school art projects.

Embarrassed by all the dust, she used one of the pillowcases she'd taken off the bed to clean off the side table and dresser. "Nobody has been in here since Daddy died. Sorry it's so musty."

"No big deal," Ben said. He cocked his head, his gaze darting between her and the double bed.

Her breasts tingled with anticipation, and her belly grew heavy with heat. Maybe her having a sex life wouldn't traumatize the boys too much.

"The boys asked me if I was going to marry you," Ben said. "According to them, you really need a husband to take care of the house and make sure you eat right."

What was he saying? Nadine dared not trust her gut feeling. She chuckled. "They never have thought highly of my domestic abilities." She gave him a friendly nudge. "Best watch it. They're like stray cats. Feed them once and you can't get rid of them."

"Have you ever thought about getting married again?"

Surprised by his question, she caught herself rubbing the same spot on the dresser. Don't read too much into this, she warned herself. He's making conversation, that's all. Nothing holds him in Black Wells. "I haven't solved the problems that wrecked my first marriage."

"Maybe Fred was the wrong man."

She picked up an envelope from the floor and started to put it on the desk. Then she noticed her name on the front, written in her father's bold, looping scrawl. Air seemed to solidify in her lungs.

"Sarge? What's the matter?"

She opened the envelope and pulled out a single sheet of lined paper. Mouth dry, her own breathing deafening in her ears, she read:

Darling Nadine,
If you're reading this, then you know I'm with Mama. (Or maybe not, since I know for sure she got into Heaven, but according to her my cussing makes my chances pretty iffy.) I don't think you'll agree with my decision, but I have cancer and it's bad, can't cure it. I asked three doctors and all of them say they can slow it down some, but there's nothing they can do to stop it. Can't see me wasting like to a stick in a hospital bed, eating up all the money that can put my grandsons through college. I'd rather make my choice while I still got a mind to make it with. I'm not worried about you. You're my toughie. If you really want me winking at you from Heaven, take on that son of a bitch Horseman in an election. You'll make a damned good sheriff.

Love, Dad

P.S. Bury me in my dark gray suit. Trouser zipper is broke and the jacket lining is wore out anyway. No sense wasting my dress uniform since it's in fine shape and maybe one of your boys will grow into it someday.

P.P.S. When the boys are twelve, teach them to use my rifles. Dale can have the Winchester, give the Browning to Rory.

Ben touched a finger to her face, and she knew then she was crying. "Sarge?"

"It's his suicide note. I never knew it was in here." A faint smile tugged her lips. "It's just like him. Sloppy. Putting it someplace where it'd fall on the floor." She wiped her eyes with the back of her hand. "I buried him in his uniform."

She handed it to Ben. As he read, she could tell he was trying not to smile. She said, "Daddy wrote just like he talked."

She ran her fingers over the top of her father's desk. He hadn't been depressed, or angry at her for neglecting him. It hadn't had anything to do with her at all. He'd made one of his decisions and stuck by it, doing what he thought best. Typical Big John Campbell.

He'd sure been right about one thing, though. She didn't agree with his decision.

But, at long last, she understood why he'd made it.

Ben gathered her into his arms and held her tightly. "Are you all right?"

She nodded against his chest. "I think I am," she said. "I think I'm finally all right."

She leaned back enough to look into his gentle brown eyes. "My father would have liked you."

"Ah, but would he approve of a bigmouthed, un-employed deejay?"

"You won't be unemployed for long. Besides, I'm pretty darned close to unemployment myself."

His smile faded. Cupping her face in both hands, his long fingers smooth and warm against her cheeks, he stared into her eyes. "I feel like a jinx where you're concerned."

"If you mean Billy Joe, a showdown was inevitable." She rubbed his back. "I don't regret knowing you, or anything we've done, Ben. Except you've been hurt."

He chuckled and shook his head. "Let's not get into who's more noble." He used his thumbs to wipe the remains of tears off her cheeks. "That stuff I was saying the other day about private and public..." His forehead wrinkled. "It's a line of bull, Sarge. The bottom line is, I'm scared of losing you."

She glanced at the letter from her father. Losing hurt; she could attest to that. Especially when, along with the hurt, came guilt and wondering and self-recrimination. Unpleasant emotions, sorrowful emotions. Emotions any sane person avoided.

And yet, if she hadn't married Fred, she wouldn't have her sons. If she hadn't loved her father whole-heartedly, she'd have missed his wisdom, humor and high-minded character.

Ben placed a soft kiss between her eyebrows.

Something broke loose inside Nadine's chest. The sensation made her light-headed.

It also made her feel curiously free.

The telephone rang. She backed away from his embrace. "I better answer that."

He held her elbows and darted a glance at the freshly made up bed. Then, slowly, beautifully, warmly, his smile appeared, deepening his dimples and lighting his eyes. "Dinner, tomorrow night, you and me. Say yes, Sarge."

He was asking for more than dinner. He was asking for a fresh start and a chance to put their relationship on the right track—a normal track that had nothing to do with cops, crooks or suspects.

"Yes," she said, then hurried to answer the telephone.

It was Tony. "I've got fifteen witnesses willing to testify Reggie Hamilton threatened to get Ben Jackson."

"Have you picked him up?"

"Can't. His mama and daddy shipped him out of town. They say he's visiting a sick relative."

"Isn't that typical?" She kicked a chair. "But at least the little devil's out of our hair for now. Got a warrant for him?"

"Not yet. I want to question him first. *Without* his daddy breathing down my neck."

Nadine chuckled. "And talking for him like he's a ventriloquist's dummy." She told him about Wafflegate's request to see her. Tony asked if she thought he'd have anything of interest to say. "Nah. But you never know. We have to get lucky sometime."

Chapter Fifteen

"Oo-whee!" Dale exclaimed. "It stinks!"

"Pee-yew!" Rory said in agreement.

"Hush, fellas." Nadine stopped the car next to a yellow tape reading Do Not Cross—Crime Scene.

Glumly Ben studied what remained of his apartment building. If not for the supports jutting into the air like pieces of charred bone, it would have been hard to tell it had been a building at all. Rain glistened on lumpy burned wood. Black soot spread from the building's remains across the churned-up lawn and the parking lot.

"I hope you had renter's insurance," Nadine said.

"As a matter of fact, I did." Small consolation, though, for losing irreplaceable photo albums and his music collection. He pointed at the separate building containing the tenants' storage sheds. "At least those are still standing. I have some clothes and things in there." Sudden anger clenched his jaw. "I hope you catch the creep who did this."

"Yeah," Dale said. "The creep."

Rory echoed, "Yeah. Get 'em, Mama. Put 'em in handcuffs and send 'em up the river." He tapped Ben's shoulder. "Mama always gets the bad guys."

Ben patted the boy's hand.

"Hold on a minute." She left the car and approached a police officer guarding the scene.

Dale said, "Mama's got medals, Mr. Jackson. 'Cause she's brave." He patted his chest. "She puts them on her dress uniform. They're gold."

"Real gold?"

Dale frowned in puzzlement. "I think so."

Nadine returned to the car. "You've got clearance to get your car, Ben. You can go into your storage shed, too." She pulled the seat forward so that the boys could get out. "You fellas mind Mr. Jackson. Don't be giving him a hard time."

"They'll be fine," Ben said, feeling thankful he had responsibility for the boys. They wouldn't give him time to brood or get depressed over the destruction. "We'll stop for ice cream on the way home."

She glanced at the sky. The clouds hung low enough to touch, so dark they mirrored the burned-out hulk of the building. Every so often the clouds glowed yellow with lightning. "Don't fiddle around too much. A good storm is coming in."

Ben gave her a sassy salute. "Roger, Sarge."

The boys mimicked him and giggled. She kissed them goodbye and slid behind the wheel.

"You boys want to help me get some clothes?" He ducked under the tape and headed for the storage building. The boys bounced after him like a pair of puppies. Inside his shed, the kids latched on to his fishing gear, oohing and aahing over his Fassler reel and carbide pole.

The boys seemed equally impressed by his Mustang. He placed his belongings in the trunk, then flipped a nickel to decide who got to ride up front. Rory called heads and won. Dale raced to the door and piled into the back, yelling that he won because he got in first.

Ben opened the driver's door, then stopped. Rory stood on the opposite side of the car, staring at the interior as if it were filled with snakes.

"I'm a good driver," Ben said. "Trust me. Not a scratch on this baby—"

Dale squealed.

Ben peered into the rear seat. The gloomy day and the shadow of the covered carport made the interior dark. But he had no trouble seeing the gun. His heart lodged in his throat.

"Get in."

Dumbfounded, Ben gaped at the neighbor he'd dubbed the Stick. He'd never spoken to her. As far as he knew, she never spoke to anyone. Thin and ill-looking, she drifted as if wearing a sign that read Don't Touch!

Now she had one wiry arm wrapped around Dale's throat and a big black revolver pointed at his head. "I said, get in the car right now."

Ben knew there was a cop not fifty feet away, on the other side of the storage shed. A cop with a gun, and a radio for backup. He opened his mouth to tell Rory to run when the little boy suddenly scrambled into the car and shut the door. Tearful and shaky, he fumbled with the seat belt, then turned wide eyes on Ben, as if asking what to do next.

Ben slid behind the wheel. "Be cool. Ease up on the kid. You don't want to hurt him."

"I knew you'd be back," she said. "You can't love a woman, but you can love a car. You escaped my fire, but you won't escape this. I should have known the fire wouldn't get you. I should have known."

Dale squirmed violently, then gasped.

"Leave him alone!" Ben shouted.

Oh, Sarge, I'm so sorry, he thought miserably. I won't let her hurt your kids. I promise, I promise, I promise.

"Do exactly what I say," she said. "I can't take any more blood on your hands."

YOU WANTED TO TALK TO ME, so talk," Nadine said.

Garbed in an orange jumpsuit, his hands and feet shackled, Wafflegate slumped on a metal folding chair. His eyes had lost their buggy look, and now were sunk in the sockets. Beard stubble and gauntness made him look ill.

Elbows on the table, her expression blank, she studied Wafflegate. "Do you know who the killer is?"

"Not by name." He looked directly at her. "But you've got the wrong person."

"This is a waste of time." She started to rise.

"All I heard when I started at the *Bugle* was how good you are, Sergeant Shell. Fair, open-minded, a real plugger who always gets her man. So is it true your father's suicide made you crazy?" Chains rattled as he tried to gesture with his hands.

"I'm thinking the only thing you're doing is ruining my day off."

"Look, I admit I touched the gun. What would you do? It was there. I saw a person plant it in Jackson's car. That's your killer."

He shifted on the seat, wincing as if his body ached. Maybe it did. The Tucker jail wasn't famous for comfort.

"All right, I lied to you before. The sheriff didn't give me those letters. He gave me some inside stuff, but only on the phone. He never gave me those letters."

"Who did?"

"There was this . . . person who called me."

The way he hesitated alerted her. "Person? Man, woman, child?"

He shook his head. "I don't know for sure, but I think it's a woman, using something to disguise her voice. I thought it was Jackson. You know, he does that on the radio, mimicking people, doing sound effects." Color suffused his cheeks—he actually blushed. "I thought I had some kind of weird psycho on my hands." The blush deepened, and his voice dropped to a mumble. "Thought I could solve the murder."

"What did this voice sound like?" She gritted her teeth against her impatience.

"Mechanical. I got the first call right after the murder. She told me Jackson killed Karen Bates in Atlanta. That there were other dead women, too, but Jackson was too slick for the cops to catch him. I figured it was Jackson boasting, egging me on. One of those catch-me-if-you-can games."

"How often did this person call?"

"Several times. I started taping all my calls. I have her on tape."

She sagged. They hadn't found any tapes during their searches of Wafflegate's property.

"You don't believe me."

"Where are the tapes?"

"In Mr. Duke's office. My cassette recorder broke. I was using the stereo in his office."

"Why didn't you tell me about this?"

"I didn't think you'd believe me." He buried his face in his hands. "I'm just trying to do my job. Get the story. All right, all right, it was dumb handling the gun. Dumb not reporting it." He looked up. "I thought Jackson was the killer."

"So what changed your mind?"

He sighed. "Yesterday one of the deputies said I'd gotten a call from a fan."

Nadine lifted her eyebrow. "Which deputy?"

"The short one. Clay, I think his name is. He said some woman called. When he wouldn't let her talk, she told him to tell me not to worry, because I wasn't the one with blood staining my hands."

Every nerve in her body leapt to attention. "Definitely a woman?"

"That's what the deputy said. He thought it was funny, but Sergeant Shell, if you'd listen to those tapes you'd know why it hit me. That's all my caller talked about. The blood on Jackson's hands."

"And you think this woman is the killer?"

"I'm sure of it. During one of the first calls, before I started taping, I wanted proof. So she tells me she witnessed the murders. She said Jackson didn't leave the radio station with Karen Bates, he left *before* her. He broke into her car and hid in the back seat. Karen had just put her car in reverse when he sat up and fired a shot into the back of her head."

Nadine fought to maintain an impassive air.

"The first shot didn't kill her. She got the door open and started to run, so Jackson shot her again."

"Did you ask this so-called witness why she didn't come forward?" Nadine asked.

"I thought I was talking to Jackson! Especially after I went through Atlanta newspaper files with a fine-tooth comb and not a single story said Karen Bates had been shot twice. I didn't even believe it myself, until the sheriff confirmed how Karen died."

"The sheriff told you."

"He did." His cheek twitched, making him appear to wink. "We had a deal going. I do the legwork and get the story, he catches Jackson and makes a big name for himself. Same thing with Heather. How Jackson supposedly waited inside the van, then opened the door and shot Heather in the face." He held out his shackled hands. "Honest to God, I thought it was Jackson playing a sick game. I thought..."

"You thought I was covering for him." Her heart raced.

"I did. But the person I saw putting the gun in the car wasn't Jackson. The light was bad, but I can definitely say it wasn't Jackson."

"And the shooting on Tank River Road?"

"I got a tip. That call is taped, too. You can hear for yourself." He rubbed his temples so hard he left red marks on his skin.

"What about the letters?"

"Hand-delivered to Mary's house. I found them on the doorstep."

Nadine dredged through her memory. "That story you wrote about the serial killing. You left one of the names off. Um..."

"Wannamaker. Charlene Wannamaker. I did my research. Bonnie Jones and Eden White are still unsolved murders. Marla Oakes was a suicide, but her family doesn't believe the suicide verdict, because she used a gun. Women rarely use guns to kill themselves."

"Why didn't you use Charlene Wannamaker's name?"

He lifted a shoulder. "That wasn't a murder. She was a college student, involved in some kind of prank. She was looking for lawn ornaments to swipe. She crawled into the wrong yard. She scared the hell out of the woman who lived there and got herself whacked.''

Nadine sat back hard on the chair. Guilt, Kyle had said. Blood on her hands.

"I screwed up, okay? But I didn't kill anybody. And if that call I got was for real, you've got a real wacko out there."

She stood. "Okay, Wafflegate, you get your shot. But if I find a single lie..." She let the implication dangle.

"The only reason I went in your house was because the caller said you were working with Jackson. I thought you were covering for him."

"I'll let you know." She turned to the door.

"Sergeant Shell?"

"What?"

"When you find out I'm on the level, can I have an exclusive?"

Squirrelly didn't begin to describe Daryl Wafflegate. Not even her honed instincts could tell if he was lying or telling the truth. Maybe he was insane and honestly didn't know the difference. Maybe in some twisted way he'd just confessed to her.

She still couldn't help but smile.

"YOU GUYS aren't afraid of the dark, right?" Ben couldn't face the terror in Dale's and Rory's eyes. Itching with awareness of the gun pointed at his back, he settled the boys atop burlap sacks. "You'll be safe. Trust me." With any luck at all, he could make this nutty woman forget all about the boys. He slipped the magic penny into Rory's pocket and whispered, "It's got properties, kids. You'll be safe."

He straightened, his heart aching at how small and helpless the boys looked, bound up with silvery duct tape, their eyes enormous and glazed in the harsh flashlight beam.

"Move," she said in her dry, toneless voice. "Back upstairs." She gestured with the flashlight. Light bounced around the root cellar, reflecting on the rivulets of rainwater running against the one tiny window.

Ben turned slowly, unwilling to do anything to make her start shooting. He kept his hands raised. She backed up the wooden stairs, urging him to follow.

Once she reached the kitchen, Ben almost lunged at the door. It had a sturdy lock. He could slam it, shut her out. But reason prevailed. She could easily shoot off the lock. And once she started shooting . . .

As casually as he could, he caught the doorknob and turned the lock, coughing to cover the sound. He pulled it shut behind him and heard the lock click. At least he hoped it was the lock. With him out of the way, the woman had no reason to go after the boys.

He hoped.

He prayed.

She backed into the front room, then gestured toward the desk chair. He sat down.

She said, "I believe in justice. The guilty should pay. The United States has the finest justice system in the world."

He nodded agreement.

"I'm not a vigilante, but nothing is perfect. You're proof of that."

Lightning illuminated the windows, and the storm broke with a vengeance. Rain rat-tat-tatted against the roof like bucketloads of pebbles.

"But I've tried everything else. I even tried to burn you out, but you're not human." She sat on the arm of the couch. "But yes, you are human. Your mistake was killing your wife. Until then, I only suspected. The things you told me, the little hints you dropped... But when you killed her, that's when I knew for sure."

"I didn't kill my wife."

She raised the gun. His rib cage contracted, squeezing his lungs. She said, "I can put two and two together. Now pick up a pen. I want you to write your confession. I want the whole world to know just what you've done."

"Okay, be cool." He picked up a pen, but when he tried to turn on the chair to face the desk, she leapt to her feet and ordered him to freeze. "I'm just—"

"None of your tricks. You might fool everyone else, but you don't fool me."

His lips pulled into an incredulous grin. "Are you going to shoot me?"

She shook her head. Her large, sunken eyes were blanks. "I'm not the killer, you are. As soon as you write your confession, as soon as everyone knows exactly what kind of man you are, you're going to do the right thing."

Around her lean waist, she wore a small black pack. The rasp of the zipper made Ben flinch.

He wondered if she'd shoot him cleanly or make him suffer. After all the dead-animal packages, letters and phone calls, he guessed suffering.

From the pack, she withdrew pill bottles. Brown with white caps, they were of various sizes. She set the bottles on the desk. She said, "For once in your life, you're going to do the right, decent thing. There will be no more deaths. Do you understand me?"

He stared at a bottle. The prescription label read Stelazine. The name of the patient was Angel Partineu. He remembered that name from his research.

She'd accidentally shot and killed a college student named Charlene Wannamaker.

Her feet shuffled restlessly on the floor. The gun in her hand remained rock steady, aimed directly at his head. "Start writing."

"I don't have anything to confess," he said.

"Liar!" She thrust her open left hand nearly in his face. "Look at the blood on your hands! See that? The stains never come out. Never! I've tried everything. Bleach, pumice stones. I even asked the doctor to do dermabrasion, but he says it's impossible. The stains will never come out. Once the blood is there, it's there for good. *And it's all your fault!*"

Her bony hand was so white it seemed made of bread dough.

She settled back onto the chair arm. "Night after night I listened to you, trying to figure out what you were up to. All your hate, all your lies. You're an evil creature, wicked and heartless. You've got to stop. Now start writing."

Unable to take his eyes off the pill bottles, Ben groped for a pen. His thoughts churned. She wasn't that big; he could tackle her. But if he failed, and she retaliated against the boys... if she shot him and really went nuts and went after the boys...

He held the pen poised over the paper and said, "Okay, Angel, be cool. What do you want me to say?"

NADINE'S HEAD REELED. Having Wafflegate tell the truth for once boggled her almost as much as the contents of the tapes he'd made. That deadpan, mechanical voice conversing with Wafflegate—a firsthand account of Heather's murder!—gave her the creeps.

Kyle burst into her office. "Your hunch was dead on, ma'am. I reached Angel Partineu's mother." He glanced at his notes. "She has a long history of psychotic episodes. After killing Charlene Wannamaker, Partineu had a total breakdown. She was institutionalized for six months. Mrs. Partineu said she tried to keep her daughter locked up, because she's bad about taking her medications, but the doctors kept discharging her. Now there's a missing-person report on her filed in Atlanta. No one has seen her since January fifteenth. When I mentioned Ben, Mrs. Partineu said her daughter had listened to Ben's radio show. She was obsessive-compulsive about it—her words." He looked up, and worry shone in his eyes. "You know Ben's weird neighbor? The one who said he was a vampire and then told the sheriff she'd seen him with a gun? She matches the description."

The telephone rang, making both of them jump. Nadine answered.

Fred exclaimed, "What the hell is going on?"

Nadine flinched. "Fred. Hello."

"Do you know what time it is? It's after five o'clock. You were supposed to have the boys home by four. I've been calling and calling, no one answers the phone. I can't reach you on the pager. So why does it surprise me to find you at work?"

She heard Crystal in the background, telling Fred to stop shouting.

No one answered the phone? It was raining fit to drown ducks, so the boys and Ben couldn't be outside.

"I'll bring them straight home," she said, then hung up on him.

"Ma'am? Is everything okay?"

"Sure, Kyle." She grabbed her coat. "I have to run home. Look, let's pick this up tomorrow. Go ahead and issue an APB on Angel Partineu."

"Should I call Mr. Zaccaro?"

She shook her head. "Let him enjoy Sunday dinner in peace." She headed out the door.

"Are you sure everything is okay?" he called to her back.

Of course it was. Ben didn't feel comfortable answering her telephone, that was all. Or he and the boys were rooting around in the barn. Or the storm had knocked out her telephone service.

Still, a bad feeling nagged at her. A bad, bad feeling.

"WHERE IS SHE?" Angel asked.

Ben rested his chin on the back of the chair. Angel had found a pair of handcuffs in Nadine's desk, so now he sat backward on the chair, with one arm through the ladder back and his wrists cuffed together. Simple and effective.

Up until she asked that question, he'd been congratulating himself on making Angel forget about the boys. Now he knew what she was waiting for. Nadine.

The telephone rang again. Her answering machine clicked on, and the caller hung up.

"Is that her calling?" Angel demanded.

"If you'd let me answer, I could tell you."

"She betrayed me. I put all my faith in her, but she joined forces with you. What am I supposed to think? She's as bad as those policemen in Atlanta." She barked a short, toneless laugh. "I even gave her the murder weapon you used. What more does she want from me?"

A car pulled into the driveway. Ben gave a violent start, but barely felt the cuffs biting into his wrists. "Angel, look, I'm sorry. I—I fooled her, too! Sweet-talked, charmed her, played around with the evidence. She did her job, but she's a victim, too. An innocent victim."

Headlights flashed against the windows. Angel moved to the door and opened it a crack.

"She's a conspirator. There's blood on her hands, too." She gave him a bland look. "There is no excuse for aiding and abetting a murderer."

Angel suddenly threw the door open wide, kicked the screen door open, and fired.

Ben screamed, "Nadine!" He lurched, tangled in the chair and fell, hitting the floor with stunning force.

Angel fired again.

She slammed the door and locked it. Her eyes were wide with shock. "She's just like you. Like a cat, or something. Never mind, it doesn't matter." She gestured with the gun. "Get up. Sit up."

Ben untangled himself and righted himself and the chair. Nadine was alive. She had to be.

"Open those bottles. You're going to take your medicine now."

He drew a deep breath and awkwardly reached for a bottle of Seconal. A tranquilizer, if he wasn't mistaken. The other bottles contained various medications. How much constituted a lethal dosage? "This is what you want? I take these and you go away?"

"Take your medicine. All of it. Then everybody will feel better."

NADINE PRESSED against the house and made a futile gesture at wiping rain out of her eyes. Her heart pounded so hard her chest hurt.

The driver's door of the Chevelle stood open, and the dome light illuminated the interior. She imagined she could hear the radio over the rain.

But reaching the radio meant crossing the open driveway.

Above her head, light gleamed from a window. She cursed her shortness. The only way to peek inside would be to use both hands to haul herself up on the sill, leaving her vulnerable to the shooter inside. The rain battered her, stinging her face and soaking her clothes. Lightning flared, and thunder made the house vibrate against her back.

The storm gave her an idea. She hurried around to the back of the house and the small window leading to the root cellar. She picked up a chunk of wood and watched the sky. There was one advantage to being small; she prayed she was small enough.

Lightning lit the sky. Nadine drew back the wood. At the crack of thunder, she hit the window. Too numb to know if she'd cut herself, she cleaned shards of glass off the frame. She peeled out of her coat and removed her holster. Holding the .38 in a tight grip, she sat on the muddy ground, then slid her feet through the opening. With her knees through, she turned onto her belly.

She slithered inside, pushing with her elbows. Her hips stuck against the sharp ridge of the frame. Spurred by visions of the killer inside coming down to the root cellar to investigate the noise, she writhed and twisted, finally getting herself positioned to squeeze diagonally through the opening.

You'll laugh about this someday, she told herself, but that reassuring thought did nothing to slow her racing heart. Groping with her feet for a wooden vegetable bin, she worked her shoulders through the opening. Mud acted as a lubricant, and she went through almost too fast, catching her balance at the last moment.

A muffled noise nearly made her scream.

The root cellar, with its sixty-year-old stone walls and dirt floor, stank of mud and mold. It was pitch-dark. She listened, willing her breathing to slow.

Rustling and noises like a dog whining made her crouch. "Ben?" she whispered. "Dale? Rory?"

Excited whines—two distinct sounds—rose in volume. She groped and found a small, sneaker-clad foot. "Hush, fellas, hush. Not a sound. Be quiet." She stuck her weapon in the back waistband of her wet jeans. The boys were trussed like turkeys, but safe. She dug and tore at the tape, freeing first Rory, then Dale. She kept telling them not a word, not a sound.

She caught the boys to her in a tight hug. She whispered, "Dale, where is Mr. Jackson?"

"The bad lady has him." His voice choked with tears. Sour fear mingled with his precious boy-scent. "She has a gun. She was hiding in Mr. Jackson's car."

"Is there just one bad lady?"

"Uh-huh." He hugged her around the neck so tightly she choked.

"You boys are okay, though. Are you hurt?"

They assured they were unhurt. Oh, but they were scared, so very scared. The fear gripped her, too. At any moment that woman could enter the root cellar—and she could come in shooting.

"Okay, fellas, I have a plan. Are you with me?" Both of them nodded against her. "I want you to go out the window. But don't go down the driveway. Do you understand? Take the path to the Hawks' house. You can do that in the dark, right? You know the way." She prayed her neighbors were home. "I want you to hold hands. Stay together. Tell Mr. Hawk to call the police. Tell them everything that's going on here. Can you do this?"

Dale snuffled, then asked, "You're gonna save Mr. Jackson?"

"You bet. But you have to do your part. Are you with me?"

"We can do it, Mama," Rory said. "We're brave, like you and Granddaddy." He handed her a coin. "Better take my magic penny. You're gonna need it."

She shoved it in her pocket. "Up we go." She turned toward the window.

She helped Dale wiggle out the window first. Then Rory. She cautioned them again to stay out of the driveway and stick together. Clinging to the icy window frame, she watched until they were out of sight.

Then she made her way by feel to the steep wooden stairs. At the top of the stairs, she pressed her ear to the door. She couldn't hear anything, and she prayed that meant no one was in the kitchen.

Her gun ready, she turned the knob. The lock clicked. To her ears, it sounded as loud as a gunshot. Heart in her throat, she waited.

Another burst of lightning flared, followed immediately by the crack of thunder. Nadine turned the doorknob a millimeter at a time, then pushed open the door. The kitchen was dark. Light came from the front room. She heard a woman's voice, but couldn't make out the words.

On the wall to her right was the circuit-breaker box. Keeping an eye on the hallway to the front room, she opened the metal cover. It squeaked like a surprised mouse, and gooseflesh broke anew on her arms. Grasping the main breaker handle, she waited for the next bolt of lightning.

The flash brightened the kitchen, making the kitchen table and chairs stand out in stark black and white. Nadine pulled the breaker. All the lights went out.

The woman let out a harsh, wavering, terror-filled cry that cut through Nadine's eardrums and made her teeth ache.

She crouched low and went through the doorway.

The woman screamed, "Where are you? I'll shoot! Where are you?"

Nadine dropped to the floor and wriggled on her elbows and pushed with her knees. A beam of light cut through the darkness. Nadine froze.

The woman said, "Take the rest of your medicine." She aimed the flashlight toward the desk; she aimed a gun, too. "Do it."

"Dry swallowing is killing my throat. I need some water."

"Do it now. Or should I go downstairs and get one of those little boys to help you?"

"Okay, okay. Look, last ones," Ben said.

Nadine's mouth went dry. Was that woman making Ben swallow pills?

"You missed her," Ben said, his voice furry and slow. "You know what Nadine will do. She'll go to a neighbor, call the cops. They'll be here any minute. You better get out while you can."

A new kind of fear chilled Nadine far more than the wet denim clasping her legs. Ben sounded drunk. She crept forward another inch. Each gritty swish from her clothing made her clench her teeth. She needed a clear shot, but the woman was shielded by the heavy table lamp. And if Nadine missed...

The telephone rang. The woman gave a ferocious start, turning this way and that, leading with the gun.

Ben said, "Want me to get that?" He laughed.

"Shut up!"

The telephone burred, seemed to grow louder. The answering machine clicked on, only to be cut off by a tremendous crash.

Ben kept laughing. Then, in Sheriff Billy Joe Horseman's voice, he drawled, "Well, now... Seems to me, what we got here is a failure to communicate."

"Shut up or I'll shoot you!"

Ben *tsk*ed. "And let all these wonder drugs go to waste? Ah, ah, I'm the cold-blooded killer, Angel, not you. Remember? Want my blood staining your hands? Huh?" His voice turned high-pitched and womanish. "'Out, out, damned spot!'" The words trailed off into chuckles. "You're a bad angel, Angel. Angel of death, angel of doom. Very naughty to follow me around. I think you should leave. Take my car keys, take my car. Just don't put it in the ditch. I don't think my insurance covers drowning."

"Please be quiet. I don't want to listen to you anymore. Be quiet."

Ben said, "It's Benjamin Andrew Jackson, presenting Angel Partineu—did I pronounce your name right, sweetheart? It's twelve o'clock, do you know where your crazy person is?"

"Please," Angel begged. "Shut up."

"Tell me, Angel, why did you break the telephone? Do you hear ringing even when there's no phone? Yes, indeed, you better get out while you can. Run, Angel, run!"

The flashlight beam wavered crazily around the room.

Nadine reached the doorway. All Angel had to do was flick the beam in her direction...

Ben coughed. "Cause and effect, action, reaction. Person can go nuts trying to figure it all out."

"Please shut up," Angel whimpered.

"Gotta stop beating yourself up." He sounded as if he were speaking from the bottom of a wool-lined well. "I know about guilt. It's a killer. Makes you crazy if you let it. Guilt's a funny thing. It's not your fault you shot that girl...shouldn't been in your yard...accident..."

Panic tried to claw its way free inside Nadine's chest. Whatever was wrong with Ben, it was getting worse. He was dying.

The woman said, "You've done your duty. It's all over." In the sudden silence, Nadine could hear her own heartbeat.

A soft clunk made Nadine tense. Had Angel put the gun down? Nadine waited for the count of ten. Angel took a step forward, raising the flashlight. Her other hand was empty.

Nadine stood and shouted, "Freeze!"

In a split second, she absorbed the scene. Ben slumped on the desk chair, his head hanging. Angel shone the flashlight on his black hair. Light gleamed dully on open pill bottles and white bottle caps.

"Do not move," Nadine ordered. "Keep your hands where I can see them."

"I caught him. I made him pay for what he did. He won't hurt anybody else." Her lips pulled back in a thin smile. "Justice has prevailed."

Where was the gun? Nadine advanced slowly, darting her gaze between Angel's eyes and her hands. More than anything, she wanted to see if Ben was breathing, but she dared not take her eyes off Angel.

A siren wailed in the distance.

Angel threw the flashlight.

Nadine ducked and dropped to a crouch. The flashlight struck the wall, bounced to the floor and spun, shooting strobes of dancing light. Tensed for return fire, knowing without doubt that Angel was going for her weapon, Nadine raised her revolver.

Ben burst into life. He jerked the chair from beneath him and swung it at Angel. The chair caught her squarely across the back. Angel fell against the wall. Nadine dived to the side, grabbing up the flashlight.

"Ben! Move out of the way!"

Angel clawed at the door, tore it open and scrambled outside.

Shocked by the woman's speed, Nadine shone the light on Ben. Handcuffs glittered. She whispered, "You're alive. I thought... The pills... She made you..."

He gave her a strained smile and shook his arm. Pills tumbled out of his shirtsleeve and clattered to the floor. "It's magic, Sarge. Maybe not such a useless skill. Man, am I glad to see you."

Staring at the pills, realizing now that Ben's crazy talk had been a ploy to drive Angel out of the house, she dug in her pocket for her keys. She shoved them into Ben's hands. "Handcuff key is on there. Circuit breaker is by the cellar door."

"Where are the boys?"

"Safe. Oh, Ben, my babies are safe. Hear those sirens? It means they're safe."

She raced after Angel.

She caught up to the woman at the culvert. Water overflowed the ditch, churning over the driveway bridge. Flashing emergency lights bounced off trees and lit the air as sirens grew louder. Angel stood poised at the water's edge, her arms spread wide.

"Stop right there, Angel. It's all over. Nobody is going to hurt you."

Angel slowly lowered her arms. Nadine focused the flashlight on Angel's collarbone. One false step, and Angel would be in the ditch, with water six feet deep running at flood speed. Freezing cold, debris-filled water that could kill a person in minutes.

The first sheriff's vehicle roared into view.

"Come on, Angel, step away from the water." She glanced at the deputy emerging from the car. "She's unarmed!" she yelled. "Don't shoot!" A powerful spotlight broke the darkness.

Angel's descent happened quickly. One second she was standing, the next she was sliding on her belly into the water. Dropping the revolver and flashlight, Nadine lunged forward, grabbing, grasping, praying she could catch the woman before the brown water swept her away. She caught an icy hand.

Angel never made a sound as the muddy bank disintegrated under her body, as the water beat and battered her, striving to rip her from Nadine's hold. On her belly, digging in her toes for purchase, Nadine agonized and strained, gritting her teeth, knowing the water was winning, but refusing to relinquish her hold. An engine gunned. Water splashed. Nadine slid slowly on the slippery mud and grass toward the water.

"Come on, Angel! Help me! Give me your other hand!"

Dead weight, dragging them both deeper into the raging flood.

"Angel, nobody is going to hurt you. Help me," Nadine pleaded.

Then Ben was there.

Angel suddenly came to life, twisting and squirming, fighting. Nadine fought to maintain her grip, but Angel kept slipping, sliding.

"The blood on his hands! Let me go! The blood!"

"Not yours, Angel," Ben said. "Not yours." He hauled her out of the water.

NOT AGAIN. No, this can't be happening.

Ben froze with his fork halfway to his mouth. He stared at the purse lying next to Nadine's plate. She stared at it, too. The echo of her pager's imperious summons hung over the table.

Nadine slowly lifted her gaze to his.

Ben's heart caught in his throat. A dark blue silk dress, cut low in the bosom, showed off her delicate neck and the soft swell of her breasts. Her golden hair was piled high on her head, with a riot of curls framing her face. She was stunning, and each glance at her stunned him anew.

The past few weeks had been nutty. Georgia and Texas had engaged in a battle over who got custody of Angel Partineu. Whoever won, Ben hoped they would live up to their responsibilities and care for her properly, instead of filling her pockets with pills and turning her loose. Then the media had dubbed Ben and Nadine national heroes. Magazine and television reporters wanted their story. A few Hollywood types had dropped hints about a made-for-television movie—a prospect Ben found both hilarious and distasteful.

The best thing to come out of the attention was getting his job back. In light of Ben's popularity, the station owner was making noises about a daytime programming slot.

Even better, he finally had Nadine to himself. Or so he'd thought. He sighed. "Guess you have to make a phone call."

Her fingers twitched on the purse clasp. "Might be the office."

He lowered his fork. "I'm actually getting used to you being on call twenty-four hours a day. This way we don't have time to grow bored with each other."

"I'm sorry." She slipped off her chair and hurried away to find a pay telephone.

Ben grinned, amusing himself watching her legs. When she disappeared from view, he picked up his wineglass and silently saluted her.

Nadine returned within minutes. She shook out her napkin and replaced it on her lap.

Ben said, "I meant to save this for dessert." He reached into his jacket pocket. "But I am swiftly learning how to manage my time around you." He presented her with the small velvet-covered box.

Her lips parted, and she exhaled a breathy "Oh."

"I'm not scared of losing you, Sarge, but I'd sure like to have more of you to myself." Her silence made him nervous. In his best Humphrey Bogart voice, he said, "This could be the beginning of a beautiful friendship."

Her eyes shimmered like dark jewels in the candle-light. As she opened the box to reveal the diamond engagement ring, her chin quivered. "Are you sure you can stand being married to the sheriff?"

He tilted his head. "Was that Deb Hall?"

She nodded. "The county commissioners voted unanimously to hold a recall election. Billy Joe didn't bother waiting for the vote. He resigned in lieu of an investigation. They want to see me tomorrow morning at nine o'clock." She reached into her purse and brought out the pager. With an emphatic gesture, she turned it off.

Ben reached across the table and picked up her hand. He kissed the back of it. "I love you, Sarge. With all my heart and soul. So could you stand being married to a loudmouthed deejay?"

"Facts and evidence, Ben Jackson, and that's a fact."

"Do you love me?"

"That's a fact, too."

"Then say it, Sarge. Say, 'Yes, Ben, I'll marry you.'"

She slipped the ring on her finger. Evidence. "Yes, Ben, I will marry you."

On the most romantic day of the year, capture the thrill of falling in love all over again—with

Harlequin's

Valentine

Bachelors

They're three sexy and *very single* men who run very special personal ads to find the women of their fantasies by Valentine's Day. These exciting, passion-filled stories are written by bestselling Harlequin authors.

Your Heart's Desire by Elise Title
Mr. Romance by Pamela Bauer
Sleepless in St. Louis by Tiffany White

Be sure not to miss Harlequin's Valentine Bachelors, available in February wherever Harlequin books are sold.

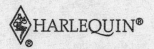

HARLEQUIN®

VB

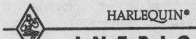

HARLEQUIN®

Don't miss these Harlequin favorites by some of our most
distinguished authors!
And now, you can receive a discount by ordering two or more titles!

HT#25577	WILD LIKE THE WIND by Janice Kaiser	$2.99	☐
HT#25589	THE RETURN OF CAINE O'HALLORAN by JoAnn Ross	$2.99	☐
HP#11626	THE SEDUCTION STAKES by Lindsay Armstrong	$2.99	☐
HP#11647	GIVE A MAN A BAD NAME by Roberta Leigh	$2.99	☐
HR#03293	THE MAN WHO CAME FOR CHRISTMAS by Bethany Campbell	$2.89	☐
HR#03308	RELATIVE VALUES by Jessica Steele	$2.89	☐
SR#70589	CANDY KISSES by Muriel Jensen	$3.50	☐
SR#70598	WEDDING INVITATION by Marisa Carroll	$3.50 U.S. $3.99 CAN.	☐
HI#22230	CACHE POOR by Margaret St. George	$2.99	☐
HAR#16515	NO ROOM AT THE INN by Linda Randall Wisdom	$3.50	☐
HAR#16520	THE ADVENTURESS by M.J. Rodgers	$3.50	☐
HS#28795	PIECES OF SKY by Marianne Willman	$3.99	☐
HS#28824	A WARRIOR'S WAY by Margaret Moore	$3.99 U.S. $4.50 CAN.	☐

(limited quantities available on certain titles)

	AMOUNT	$
DEDUCT:	10% DISCOUNT FOR 2+ BOOKS	$
ADD:	POSTAGE & HANDLING	$
	($1.00 for one book, 50¢ for each additional)	
	APPLICABLE TAXES*	$_____
	TOTAL PAYABLE	$_____
	(check or money order—please do not send cash)	

To order, complete this form and send it, along with a check or money order for the
total above, payable to Harlequin Books, to: **In the U.S.:** 3010 Walden Avenue,
P.O. Box 9047, Buffalo, NY 14269-9047; **In Canada:** P.O. Box 613, Fort Erie, Ontario,
L2A 5X3.

Name:_____

Address: _____ City:_____

State/Prov.:_____ Zip/Postal Code:_____

*New York residents remit applicable sales taxes.
 Canadian residents remit applicable GST and provincial taxes.

HBACK-JM2